I0544607

— Within Without —

Five books in THE GOD'S CYCLE

God's House:

Return to God's House
Within Without
In Winter

God's Wilderness:

Mystery Gottheim
Balder's Wilderness

Plus

Gott'im's Monster

THE GOD'S CYCLE

Within Without

S. Dorman

~ ~

S. Dorman
P.O. Box 172
Greenwood, ME 04255
USA

(Second book of *The God's Cycle*)

Within Without
Copyright © 1994, 2014 by Susan C. Dorman.
ISBN: 978-0-578-07346-0

Cover illustrations by S. Dorman

Dedication

To Ev, with love

What life it is, and how that all these lives do gather—

With outward maker's force, or like an inward father.

—from *Within and Without*

George MacDonald, 1855

Contents

Burning Down the House

The pond on her right yet reflects sunlight as Gloria signals a turn to point her Caprice up the mountain road. The radio beats out frenetic heavy metal but, gripping the wheel, she scarcely hears its screaming. This music enflames her subconscious, tightening muscles along her neck and back. Gloria Fay's brother James would be happy to say it's music to set fires by— if you are interested in burning down your own house.

The hill road leading to *Simons Ledge* is steep. Her tires spitting gravel, Gloria presses the pedal to the floor. I hope Balder is done bonding with Chrischana's boys. *Don't really want to run into them again just now.*

Wonder what he'll be wearing?—not the flannel and jeans. She tugs on the rearview, glances into it, scrutinizing her eye shadow. Is it the best shade for a summer evening, casual?—or too dark?

Eveledore lent her the makeup late this afternoon as they sat in the other's condo, sipping Diet Sprite, laughing and plotting strategy for the campaign to energize Gottheim.

If only Balder would show some interest in the focus groups. Surely he's read about her activities in *The Village Voter*. He might even collaborate with Theodora Prescott at the Gottheim Chair Factory by encouraging production and maintenance people to take part. This has been Gloria Fay's advice to mill owners and business people.

"Reach down and tap into the vast potential of your associates," is how she put it. Some were enthusiastic, but others seemed uncomfortable at the suggestion. One looked very dubious, and another actually smirked. That staring, standoffish Lyman Bearce never even bothers with the sessions. The second most powerful man in town, if you count ski magnates Harry and Julius Golding as one. And you can't expect them to come. At least Mrs. Bearce was there, a sensible, articulate woman, older.

The brainstorming session at Eveledore's turned into a giggle fest with Gloria's comic description of their faces. What! —involve the employees?!

Sometimes Gloria feels like knocking their cold or grinning muttonheads together. They just can't stand to democratize the process. Probably think it would be like inviting shop class to a meeting of the honor society—but it's absurd to compare the business community's sheep-headed mediocrity with aspiring intelligence.

Evela said this reaction was typical. She's been facilitating IICE seminars in Gottheim for three years and is familiar with all the lumps, people smugly satisfied with the town as is.

"But these are the 80's! Things are changing, they have to! The sod's been cracked, Gloria. We've broken them in for you. It's so much better than it used to be. When I first came, people here were a bit less inclined to involve themselves in things we proposed. And I've heard horror stories from the mature members of hostile resistance. So maybe your seeds will slip right into the broken soil and germinate. You know that they really do take to you. They are impressed by your graduate study, flattered by the attention of your happy personality. The town's come a long way, but I think you could be instrumental in helping it go further."

The kind words were balm after the childish snub of Chrischana's kids.... And Balder's hurtful failure to smooth things over when it happened early this afternoon. If he will just give a little nod over her committee work. Nothing big—just a sign that he is even aware of it.

Of course, I haven't tried to get in touch since the letter I sent him... hoping he would make the first move.—But it works both ways! If only that missile from Phoenix had never penetrated the woods of Gottheim!

The curve in the steep road distracts her. She has come up this way before—once—just idly and apprehensively trying to spot out the place where he lives. But the house was not visible from the road. That day she went past his lane, way up the hill, past a few more lanes, all the way to the mysterious dead-end at a logging track. The woody hills below great Jasper Mountain are woven with them... intriguing places... With a start she realizes that *this* is Jasper Mountain. The very backside of her deity! Balder lives on Jasper Mountain, too! He always has.

She may now engage herself at night thinking of his being just over the mountain from her. Just over this great monolith. Asleep and tenderly godlike, just beyond her great God, Jasper Mountain.

Switching off the commercial break and the rude rock-and-roll, Gloria smiles. Great to believe in what I love! And not be a Baptist anymore, have to sit in church and be oppressed by its mores, its superior insularity.

There's his lane. Secret, tangled, beckoning. Oh, please let the Twitchell kids be gone. Please let it be enough for today. (Where's

Chrischana's man, the father of the other two?)

Having released the Caprice from the madness of music and pressure on the gas, she wants to calm down now. Be leisurely on this green lane... Tree bordered and dusky, with gleams of light pouring through... The lane is glorified with amber and emerald green. Silent, she rides slowly, the car gently dipping in and out of ruts, deep in the sensation of trolling through gemlight. The woodlight is mysterious with penetrating shafts. It could be a haven for fairies. Something out of Tolkien. Still slowly driving, she turns her head more toward the source of golden light.

Then, on a sharp intake she holds her breath, slows, stops the Caprice. Among the shaftlight stands strange beauty. Delicate beauty, small. A... china white fawn, gleaming like some fragile being from another world. Is it real? Should she blink just to prove it imaginary? But she can't. Gloria cannot look away from the quiet gentle sight. It will never come again. She must imprint the image, fix the fawn in her feeble mind. For all is fragile, feeble. She sees it now. Everyone, everything... tender and bruiseable as this deer.

A white etching in hazy green, the fawn is backlit with hushed light. It stands as though hallowed, transfixed.

Now Gloria understands that her presence, watching from the car, has entranced it. As though its miniature beauty is poised for her sake... Its helpless innocence transforming her. She will never be careless with anyone again, never give harm. She will not vaunt herself, scheme or grasp. Oh, that this moment might last forever.

Suddenly comes a blast, echoing. Gloria drops out of her dream, awakening to see the fawn flinch. It pivots, springing away into the dusty shafts of light. And a reddish deer leaps up out of nowhere, herding after it. Stunned Gloria sees the tawny rump vanish among the trees, its white tail flying.

Peripheral movement takes her gaze to the head of the lane. On the foliaged corner of the dingy house stands a small figure in T-shirt and jeans, wearing a red bandanna. Cradling a gun. Outraged, Gloria presses the accelerator, speeds thumping toward the figure.

Elda Simon has long since changed her tactics. She will cease desiring to see Sugarloaf: She must prevent Posey bringing her white fawn to the house. And Posey herself must not come. To do so would only encourage the fawn's presence. So Elda Simon lives in a dither, waiting, watching lest they come in her absence. She stays home and does not make rounds in search of ill or wounded wild animals. Instead she tends those she has, cleans out the barn, shyly speaks to Chrischana's children when they visit.

And she tries to prepare for Balder to do his worst to the house.

She continues to be baffled at Chrischana's status here in Gottheim. Apparently the young woman has returned to town only as Balder's friend. And Elda fears that, except for his attention to the children, he is going against the best in all: his application was accepted at Adirondack Paper; he has plans to refurbish *Simons Ledge*, and he rejects the mother of his only child at a time when she needs his help.

None of this is right. And the last is not like him at all. But it is Elda's way rudely to shove off these concerns as often as they show their faces. It is none of her business to speak of these things, only—apparently—to obsess over them in her mind.

But she does feel safe in understanding that no one knows Balder as well as she does. Even so, she scarcely knows him at all, she guesses. Don't I know his heart anymore? Well, she knows the contours of his serious face, and how it puts on a grin in the presence of others. She knows his inner gentleness, his outward mocking grimness born mostly of Vietnam.

She knew him from a babe on the breast... but he knew her from the womb. Embla had cleaned off the blood and placed him on her chest, and when Elda said thank you, he arched his live back and looked into her eyes. The eyes of newborns, she knew, were not fully focused, but he looked right into her eyes. She pondered every so often over this scrutiny of the newborn. What did it mean? She could not pass it off as signifying nothing. He *did* attend, evidence of a pre-birth bond. And puzzling it out she came to understand that it was her *voice* Balder recognized. He knew the voices he heard in the womb from the moment his cochlea were fully formed. Probably the aural sense provided his only stimulus from outside the womb. And donning human experience, he hadn't much else to work with.

Stopping at home, resting, he speaks little. Sometimes she thinks she resents this, but mostly only that she *should*. She's never been much of a talker herself. Someday she will finally grasp that it is nature to her to receive almost nothing from him. All she really needs is to see him at peace, even happy. (Hopefully, in a house of his own somewhere, now that all this is happening.) Will he be at peace now...with Daniel?—After the terrible fires of Vietnam? His life must be whole—occupied, at least. *I'll be at peace when he doesn't need me.*

In her heart, Elda would be needed by no one. That way she can give herself wholly to animals. (... While diminishing sight allows, this twilight that seems to be coming to her.) The littleness of creatures, their cunning simplicity flightiness agility grace, their unconscious verve. The squatting toad, self-assured fox, sleeping dove. Only this. Everything else will take care of itself.—Even blindness? How then will she experience...?

Stop.

Now she stands at the corner of the overgrown house, gaping as a red convertible halts in the boiling gravel, a young person flying from its door. Elda steps back in consternation. She turns, hops stiffly toward the back door, still lugging that heavy gun.

But Gloria is too fast for her. Flying after, she grabs the older woman's bony shoulder, steps angrily into her path. "What's the idea—shooting at that helpless fawn?!"

Each is furiously breathing, their overwrought features inches apart. Elda sputters but brings up no answer. Trying to wrench free, she turns her bemused face away.

Then, beyond Elda's head Gloria sees Balder pop from his '55 Chevy, as out of nowhere, hollering. "It's only Mutha, Gloria! Wait a bit!"

She is distracted enough to note that he wears jeans and a corduroy jacket, a striped tie against the dark shirt. He lays a hand on them, saying, "L'me explain y'each to the other. Mutha, this is Gloria Fay. We been dating since spring. Gloria, this is Mutha. She's not the dangerous hand she looks. She was only scaring off Sugarloaf. Hunters likely'd kill him, if she didn't. He durst not be used to people."

At this Gloria sags, her face crumpled in sympathy. "Oh, Mrs. Simon, I am *so sorry*! Please, I completely misunderstood! I should have known—Balder's told me of your interest in wild animals. I should've known. I should've!" She pants and ceases, her features still absurdly contorted.

"S'all right, deah," says Elda. "Cuss you'd think I was harming him; cuss you would. S'all right." Looking shyly at Balder, she starts toward the house, saying, "Well, I expect you waunt get away now. Nice t'meet you, deah."

Chuckling, Balder stops her. "Hold on, Mutha. Caunt brush us off that easy. We all got get acquainted!" He grins at Gloria. "Got time fah tea, ain't we?"

"Yes! Sure! Tea's great!" Gloria smiles on the fallen old face. "We've hardly spoken. I can't let my rude treatment be all you know of me." She gives Elda an imploring look.

"But—house's a mess... kids'n all, whatnot—theya gone now," she hastens to add.

"Be easy, Mutha. Got to meet folks proper like'n all." He gives her a grin.

Unaccustomed as she is to its warmth, Elda loosens a bit. Still, her look is dubious. His grin grows.

"Well... I guess I can stand the mess if you can."

15

—

"She really is sweet," said Gloria, as they coasted out the lane toward the roadway in her little Caprice. "Terribly shy.... There is *no* mess in that house!"

Preoccupied, Balder grunted his agreement. He was off the subject of mother. His darkly bearded face, beneath a blond head with sugar bowl haircut, was turned toward her. She felt his gaze taken with her and, when the road permitted, sneaked a peek. He grinned.

Out on the highway, lightly she said, "How was the bonding today?"

For a moment he said nothing. Then, "Glad you asked, Glory. I can warm to that subject. Have any idea how *real* kids ah? Theya's no telling how they'll be. Chain reaction from the moment they explode out of bed. Doaw, take that back: Nathan explodes out, Benaiah slouches. Daniel comes yawning'n scratching his head. But when they rev up, it's something to behold."

"Oh kids are real, all right. Have you had to clean up after them yet?" She couldn't resist a little innocent needling.

"Well, you saw the house. Didn't looks'bad, did it? We got caught up before driving'em home." The grin again: "Have to admit—Chrischana whipped 'em into action some."

"Uh haw," came the knowing response. She smiled, but there was an inward sting. Chrischana had been there.

He said stoutly, "Don't really believe I couldn't'o got them to do it myself. Couldn't very well shut her up, could I? We worked on it together." He was irritated to find himself explaining so much. "What's the big deal? If I have to clean up after 'em, I will. Mutha taught me." At another twitch of her mouth, he said, "All right, so she made me. Been wiping my bottom since before I was a toddler!"

"Well, good for her!"

Softly, he replied, "S'pose I get no credit—won't pin no rose on me?" He reached out to smooth a stray strand of her sleek pageboy. Gently he curved the strands around her ear, letting his finger linger. "I could kiss that sweet ear, I could, Glory." His voice was soft and low.

"Please. Do."

He leaned close, softly wetly tickling her ear with the tip of his tongue. A faint acrid taste made him withdraw a bit. "Sweet," he murmured, now moving still nearer.

They were on the highway, wind-buffeted and zooming down country toward Farmington. "Why won't you love me, Glory?"

"But I do. You know it."

"Do I?"

"Balder Simon, I *said* I did!"

"Uh huh."

"Balder, you're making me mad."

"Guess so."

(Pleading) "Why can't you be nice?" Her eyes in the rearview gleamed irritation at him. "I'll wreck!"

"Guess y'betta pull over. Up theya's the roadside park."

Evening shadow was beginning to settle over the Meguntics, the sky still light with summer dusk. She parked a bit above a small group of willows rustling gently down by the river. Balder said, "I waunt your love, Gloria."

"Balder, I *do* love you. *You* are the one who will not make love." She turned and put her arm on his corduroy shoulder. Gently she rubbed his bearded cheek with the back of her thumb. He said nothing, made no move, and hardening up, she pulled back. "What is this, a new twist on the old argument?—If you love me you'd have my child?"

He looked at her now, her face knotted and stricken. He grinned that maddening grin. "Maybe."

She sat back, staring out the windshield. The breeze reached them, the leaves of the willows, gently lifting, falling. Bitterly she said, "I suppose you'd like to pull down under those willows and get all cozy in the shadows. You know I'm for the lovemaking. You've always known this. But— instead—it's, I take down my panties, you'd unzip and we get right to making babies."

But, seriously, low he said, "We could be married down in those willows." His finger moved gently down her arm. A soft slow movement, barely touching. He had time, eternity, to treat her so. She felt herself pooling beneath his touch. "We can be married in church first," he finished.

She wanted to stiffen, but she heard herself saying, a syllable at a time as though mesmerized, "well... you... can... for... get... it." She was clear, but not loud for she did not want him to stop. And, slowly and low, word by word: "Balder, where is your love for me?" (*Aren't my dreams and goals anything to you? I showed interest in your newly found fathering. Can't you encourage me in my Gottheim work?*)

But his voice was beside her, intent in her ear. "My love for you's in my dive into home life. Get married, and we'll plunge in theya together. Do all the dirty work of raising kids together. Just pour ourselves into it. Glory 'n Balda. Do it together."

Her voice, still mesmerized by his touch, answered soft and low. "... Not possible...."

Very gently he withdrew. "Maybe y'betta start the car."

—

In her bed during the small dark starry hours, she thought about it. The movie, the conversation, the meal. Outside the window loomed Jasper Mountain, blotting out a large part of heaven. If she were back in her women's studies class, she would have mentors, peers, to hash this over with. She should get together with Eveledore tomorrow. But then again... maybe not. Gloria thought of the seething women, angry, railing against millenniums of oppression, abuse. She remembered another course: Dr. Velma Arlington's harsh manner toward the young males in class—small town boys who didn't have a clue. If they'd known what their course in Communications was going to be like....—But the professor's style was _meant_ to be confrontational, challenging, and taken impersonally... Yet Gloria was sure they felt personal rancor. But the girls in Dr. Arlington's class were inflamed by her vision. Gloria felt its fire even now and, under that influence, how could you help but see the white house of male domination burning? Sometimes I long to see it burn. (What is this Balder's pulling? It fits—and doesn't fit—the pattern. Be careful. Paternalism can be very slippery.) Grimacing, she remembered Ithiel Whitman's wife found only this morning—buried in concrete, the victim of murder, abuse. It's not just rhetoric. Men *are* out to get you!

Get a grip! Balder? It's nothing to do with him. Get a grip! She punched up her pillow. If she could not find the word she nonetheless recognized that it was his spirit that was different.

She glanced up at the mountain, good Jasper, and grew quieter, calmer. His grandmother did right, naming Balder after some old god. With that old beard he looks like one. How can his beard grow in black with his hair so white blonde? What a contrast. She grinned: facial hair, professionals call it—on purpose to denigrate beards. Balder would probably grow one for that reason alone, then make some crack about Egyptians shaving their slaves.

She had dropped him off at the end of the lane near the tree-tangled house... strange house. The kitchen in back beneath the ledge, Simons Ledge. A house drowning in trees. Front room and kitchen back-to-back, sharing a wall and the chimney. And the whole of it swimming in the overgrowth of green light. But she had not been comfortable there. The house was decaying, its furnishings dilapidated, the atmosphere musty and dim. Alien to me. I need a fresh, bright, shiny habitation, full of new, bright things.... It has a deep history, *Simons Ledge*, but that's *all* it has.

Her reverence was dutiful, certainly, but no matter how she...—that house was better burned! Respectfully, ceremoniously *burned*. Build a new one. An exact replica if you must. But *please*—purify the ground of that rotten old structure.

She rolled over, entangling herself in the bedsheets still fresh smelling from tumbling in the dryer. He had told her about starting at Adirondack Paper, lampooning the orientation sessions of Human Resources. The marshmallow toss, balloon blowing, role-playing, etc.... She had had to laugh, his take was so on the mark. But Gloria understood the importance of such testing, such play. It was crucial to get a handle on the employees in order to develop a harmonious atmosphere on the job. He should take it in token of the corporation's wanting to get it right. It took the 1980s to really evolve the world of work toward a more compassionate sense of community. A corporation is really a community of people. If the place stank and had an abominable exterior, at least Adirondack had a decent managerial *soul*.

That stench!! Balder will have to shower till he's blue. But his clothes will be clean when we meet. He'll probably have two sets of clothes—*never* get the smell out completely.

When we next meet.... She paused. Or?... will we ever? Where does this doubt come from?

He had stood outside the car, looking down on her... the soft sighs of night about them in the dark. What was it he had said? Goodnight... you know where to find me... Simons Ledge... What was he saying there?

That she had to call him?

(Or, is this hyper-imagining?)

Then she had turned the car around, nosing slowly back on the lane toward the road where stars awaited, not thinking of what he had or had not said, but of the white fawn. In fact, she had stopped to look for it in the dark. Would it gleam out, a living delicate icon? Staring through the darkness, such darkness all about the tree-tunnel... with that faint starlit gleam at its end. Except for that it was an empty dark; silent, the fawn long gone.

Gloria lay in bed, unseeing, thinking about the little deer. Is it true? All those things revealed upon seeing Sugarloaf? Could I really become like the fawn? She sighed, turned this way and that. Now on her back again, staring out at Jasper.

No. She would never be like the fawn. She had only seen him. Seeing doesn't translate into being. It can only set up a longing inside. Probably I will forget. Forget all the virtue seen in its little bit of being.

Fair weather this morning in the Meguntics. Descending from Gottheim into Guildford, Balder looks toward the vast cauldron in the river valley where Adirondack Paper sends up smoke and steam. Vapor, pouring densely off the paper dryers within, piles up over the valley, drizzling. Looks like Guildford has its own weather breeder, hunkering like a hurricane at sea, circling; gaining moisture, momentum, force. Maybe one hundred years it sat there, swirling out its own smell and weather.

Get used to it, Balda boy. Your hands and tools are used to help keep the place running. Go down into the maw and do what they tell you. Help cook those forests, keep madly spinning out the paper. Take your part in turning spruce and birch woods into envelopes and office paper so folks down in Washington and Harvard can make work grinding out studies. You've been looking all your life for a way to help 'em keep occupied, out of trouble. Go down Balda. Go down into Egypt and lend those poor boys and girls a hand. How many bricks can you help make today for old Pharaoh's monument? He'll be sure to stop by, when you're up in the chip loft or down in the digester basement, and give you his personal thanks.

He was down in the basement, sweating it out under a five-story pulp digester. He had thought it impossible to sweat more than he did in the Kraft mill, where it often reached 120°. Wrong. Nineteen tons of woodpulp, liquor and steam were cooking above him. It would be his job to change a blow valve. As the digester heats, the blow valve releases pressure from the load. Reaching maximum pressure, the great digester begins quaking. The first time he felt this he was just entering the area under the pink glare of the sodium vapor lamps, the sharp caustic smell of white liquor in his nostrils already quickening his senses. When the quaking started he thought the monster was getting ready to blast off. It's not war exactly—but you return there.

He had read of that happening once, somewhere in a community down South: a digester ejected onto a block of stores during business hours. Balder backed up, ready to flee, until he noticed his mate continuing onto the platform as though this quaking happened every two hours. During what should have been a normal blow, its seals giving way, the valve had come apart choking on an errant eight-inch rock from the wood yard. Digested pulp stock 180°F flooded out. That was the day of his on-the-job baptism into the life of Adirondack Paper.

Working, beginning to feel the telltale slippery film of white liquor sticking to your skin, comes a point when you begin to wonder whether humor has enough thrust to carry you through these conditions. You begin to notice if OSHA's safety requirements are being enforced. Are there eyewash stations near your next job? Can you get a shower before white liquor starts breaking down your skin cells the way it takes apart the lignin of cellulose? Digesters, lines and valves, wood and skin cells can only stand so much heat, pressure, chemical burning. The nerve endings of the millwrights' skin (sooner or later) will tell: you've been burned by white liquor.

Even so, driving down into Guildford, Balder is sorry to understand that probably you *can* get used to working in a paper mill; that exposure and familiarity can inure you to just about anything. Even a place that is an exact spiritual replica of hell. Paper is made in hell.

Chrischana and her son, Benaiah, were hiking up through tired greenness, greenness spotted here and there with the light of late summer. Goldenrod and asters were already showing in the warmth of the July day. In absolute stillness, they rounded a thicket of beech and yellow birch. No movement of creatures, whether raven or squirrel, broke the heavy hush about them.

Benaiah, older son of Peter Prince, was quiet, tired, but just now uncomplaining over the steep ascent of Buck Hill, a spur of Blackwell Mountain. Perking up, he spied something of interest and hurried along the track ahead of his mother. Chrischana approached the scorched thickets, their leaves curled and brown. Silent, hushed, she saw first the pile of corrugated iron, twisted sheets of roofing washed in rust. Once the crown and protection of the house where she was raised, the roofing had been heaped up in ruins by the hands of firemen in the wake of what vandals had done. She came closer, stepping gingerly, peering into the pit of the great cellar where blackened timbers had fallen every which way. The beams glistened with hardened black bubbles, as though having effervesced out of a charred interior. If sawn through, would a cross-section of white be revealed? Idly she wondered it.

She was weary from her climb but did not think of resting. Chrischana was hungry to look over the fire cleansed remnants of a former existence. One that had been very dear to her. More dear in memory than in actual experience? She would have to muse over that. Memory was so often accused of romanticism. But Chrischana, part Native American, part Yankee descent, wasn't so sure. Doesn't the sap pressure of youth prevent full consideration? Maturing, we bring a more complex, complete understanding, memory enriched by experience. She had read somewhere that the first forty years of life were original text, the last forty its commentary.

Fire cleansed, she thought again, looking at the debris. Everywhere here is starkly brutally clean. Her gaze read the now open walls of the farmhouse cellar. What had once been the dark mystery of the cellar hole, hidden by the house overhead and the skewed foundation—now open to heaven. Master builders had placed this stonework, precisely, in a bygone era. Once granite, its color now was red. Except for this fire bought ruddiness, the stones might be taken for quarry-fresh; and placed with exactness, as once stones were so placed, each fitted to the shape of its neighbors. No mortar had been used.

She did not want to disturb the silence of her meditation, but she must be attentive to Benaiah. There he was, limby and balancing along a plate atop exposed cellar wall. "Be careful!" She called, "The stones on theya might not be stable."

It had been her plan to come alone, but Balder's son Daniel, her oldest, needed a break from watching Benaiah and Nathan. He had enough watching Nathan, the youngest, and Ben's presence was always a temptation for Nathan who relished provoking the middle boy. Also, she wanted Ben to see the hillside and remains of the place she once knew. Now the boy said nothing in response to her call. Provokingly, he kept right on, placing one foot exactly in front of the other. From Nathan she would have expected flightiness but surer obedience. Now she must contend with Ben's obstinacy.

"Did you hear me?" She called. "Remember what we talked about... You could come only if you were obedient."

Over his shoulder he said, "I *am* being careful. Can't you see? My arms are out.... I'm balancing." But his tone said, *You imbecile*.

Chrischana stamped her foot. "Get over here!"

"Awww..."

"Right now!"

Benaiah flounced down off the plate onto the bed of ash where the ell once stood. He stomped toward her around and over charred timbers, kicking them as he came.

"Listen," she said, taking hold of his shoulder. "I trust your agility (probably betta'n mine). But I don't trust your judgment. Will you walk where I say... or do I make you sit over there on that stub?" She pointed out a fresh stump where the firemen had sundered a maple.

(Stalling) "What's agility?"

"Your powers of balance and coordination. *Well, will you?*"

"I have powers?" His freckled false face brightened.

"You have powers of obedience. We talked about this before. Obey me."

"Whad you say to do again?"

"Go sit on the stump!"

"No you said if I did it your way I didn't have t'sit on the stump."

"That was before y'give me a hard time." She turned and marched him to the stump. "Now just sit theya!"

Sulking, he sat down heavily. A scowl settled, hardening. He watched her step away, heard the crunch of shattered glass and ash beneath her worn boots. In T-shirt, cutoffs and bandanna, her figure receded as she went back to the cellar hole. Ben screamed, "Someday I'll be grown'n you won't be able t'do this to me!"

Dryly the word drifted back to him, "Hallelujah."

She stood on the brink, the massive hearth, beehive oven, and broken chimney with foundation now had her attention. Its bricks, scattered or heaped among the cellar full of haphazard charred timbers, were the off-pouring of an immense chimney that once towered above. A few bricks lay on the ground at her feet. She stooped to pick one up, examining its cleanliness and heft. Could they be reused, she wondered, tossing it down onto a piece of granite. But the brick fell apart like a chunk of dense cornbread. Then, striking the granite with her foot, she found that this foundation stone also broke, if not so readily as the brick. She had yearned to salvage these materials but was now bereft of this hope.

Hush returned to the ruined site in hope's vacuum. She looked back again at the monumental center of the ruined house: hearth foundation, fireplaces and beehive oven. This great brick-and-stone heart/core once provided warmth, cheer, and the preparation of nourishment. Dimly she saw her ancestors maneuvering the great stones into place with the aid of oxen or draft horses. Intently they worked, placing the great stones with skill, laying with unconscious knowledge the individual components of her care. She could not—she *must not* let it all go for nothing. She looked earnestly about her. This place, even scorched and cleared into piles as it was—must not go into other, less caring, hands. She thought of Balder's support check, the lump sum he sent her after learning the truth about Daniel's conception. The money was now in an account of her own... for the heritage of her children. And their children. We hold nothing for long, she thought. It's the passing of the genetic handbasket that matters. What better legacy than a piece of ancestral property? Buy this land, if I can... It will mean a hasty shelter of some kind... But can I buy some of this piece, having no credit, no permanent job?

She shook her head. This burned-to-ashes relic. No—just a hole in the ground. Chrischana smiled halfway. My ancestral relic is a hole in the ground... lined with clean ruined stone. A hole filled with burnt timber and brick good for nothing but powder. And yet—she was suddenly light and lively with this thought. We will have something at last.

If Enan Pale will sell... at terms I can handle.

As she walked around, half-smiling, musing, her middle son sat by the scorched and sundered maples, scowling. If he had been Nathan, he would have peppered her with questions, observations, cheery little subtle

23

attacks on her strictures. But Benaiah's temperament was quieter and he was older, more grudging, and beginning to internalize his rebellion. More like his father Petey, he sat solemnly chewing the cud of retaliation.

Suddenly he pictured himself grown-up and smacking her. If she provoked Dad when he was drunk he would smack her.

But, at once, a frightening feeling came over him. His eyes watered and he scrunched them up, remembering—seeing—how mother had crept into the boys room, locking the door behind her. He could hear the faint click in his head, still. Lamplight had sheeted into the trailer window, silhouetting her; a trembling shadow, softly rapidly breathing. He had whispered, "C'mere, mother." Either it was very late or very early. The drunken cursing at the other end of the trailer had finally ceased, without disturbing his brothers. That night only Benaiah had been awake to throw open his bunk to her. And she had climbed in. He sat now on the stump, remembering her wet face next to his. And his thumb, wiping the tears away.

Ben turned away, hunching his shoulders, trying to withdraw into some sort of hiding. He was frightened of the vengeful thoughts that sometimes sought residence in his mind. *Mother, mother...I won't hurt you. Help me. Please get these thoughts from my mind.*

"You have powers of obedience, Benaiah." She had said things almost like this before. He had powers of obedience, of balance, and coordination. Usually he did not care about such things she spoke of; self-control, goodness, sharing. He could say them by rote, as though repeating lessons for geography. There were mountains, forests, plains, shorelines... all kinds of boring land. There was generosity, and kindness, courtesy, and goodness—things, she had said, of the spirit. "You can obey, Benaiah."

Rap. Rap rap rap. Benaiah heard it from somewhere, knocking. He looked toward the lane which had been so still. What was that? It came again. *There are no doors in the woods, but someone is knocking.*

From across the gulf of the ruined cellar, came Chrischana's tiny voice, drifting toward him. "Hear that woodpecker?"

"Sounds like he's knocking on a door," Ben called back.

"Don't it?"

"Think I'll go see if I can let'em in. Can I get off the stump now, mother? I'll only walk where you tell me."

"OK. Go look at'em, but don't get past the sound'o my voice."

He slid off and, listening, quietly moved toward the trees. The knocking came again and, looking up, Benaiah saw a huge red-crowned woodpecker clinging to a bald patch on a hemlock tree. Rearing back, its pointed bill fell with tremendous force, powerfully thrusting, excavating toward the tree's core. And Ben marveled that a bird, usually such fluttery flighty things, could be so big, strong, and sure.

Later, speaking together of Jasper Mary and her stories, they went up mountain toward blueberry patches scattered plentifully over the rocks. The mighty Abenaki healer had once roamed these hills, eating the earlier generations of this fruit. One of the stories she told the native and settler children was of the mythic hero Culuscap's gift of fire and its many uses for his people. Was it not Culuscap, asked Jasper Mary, who showed us the cultivation by fire of blueberries? Just so the healer passed on the ancient wisdom of her people and of God.

She taught so because each generation wrestles with the same obstacles and difficulties of spirit. The way up and down the mountain is narrow and tufted with puckerbrush. You cannot escape good-and-evil's struggle that you are born into. Even so, between birth and death, there is one thing common to life: the fact of Culuscap's comfort and Culuscap's return. With the Virgin Mary's son, Jesus, you can face anything. This is how I, Jasper Mary, tell it... if you will hear me speak. If you will listen to my stories. Sit upon the scorched stump outside your ruined house, listening to the voice of your ancestors. Do you hear my voice?

Builders in Time

The youthful Balder attained his full stature with marvelous rapidity, and was early admitted to the council of the gods. He took up his abode in the palace of Breidablik, whose silver roof rested upon golden pillars, and whose purity was such that nothing common or unclean was ever allowed within its precincts, and here he lived in perfect unity with his young wife Nanna (Blossom), the daughter of Nip (Bud), a beautiful and charming goddess. [Guerber, H.A., *Myths of Norsemen*]

Balder and Daniel were up on the roof of the children's house, part of the old extended farmhouse; shoveling off what remained of ruined asphalt, prying up rotten boards, and throwing it all into a heap on the ground below.

"Watch how y'walk theya," cautioned Balder to his newly found son, Daniel. "Expect t'find more rot under that patch. Don't want Chrischana suing me f 'negligence if you break y'leg.

His arms full of shingle, Daniel nodded. Sidestepping the patch, he descended to the eaves and tossed his armful out onto the pile with a crash.

It was hot, hot even for August. The leaves over their heads and on into the nearby woods were tattered and dark. The springs of earth were receding under the rainless skies. A torpid quiet sat upon Gottheim. Fire watch, fire flights, the ban on burning, all enacted. Area wells were drying out. Yet, *Simons Ledge* had plenty of water; whether because of the ledge above or the gravel beneath, the plot had an excellent aquifer. Maybe the well had gone dry once since Elda's marriage to Everett nearly forty years ago. Wells went dry in this kind of weather, but that of the old settlers' house beneath the mass of towering rock was not one of them.

While they worked, Balder asked Daniel about his job down at the newspaper. Was the boy privy to secrets too damaging or explosive for print? Was *The Village Voter* in line to be snapped up by some big-city consortium? Did he have a chance to proof copy for what the Ezra Simons had seen on their vacation to (*gasp*) New York City?

Daniel had smiled but slightly over these questions, answering a taciturn no to each. Yes, he had been sweeping, running errands and, lately, doing a little proofreading. He didn't say so, but he thought maybe Mr. Nutting might use him more in this capacity.

Kneeling, Balder pulled up shingles. He was late beginning the renovation. There had been no money to start. He had told Chrischana that the money he had given her was only part of his savings, but it was everything he had saved while working at Gottheim Chair these ten years, at least, after Vietnam. Now every day he was grateful that the money had been just sitting there accumulating, waiting for the son who, without his knowledge, was progressing through elementary school in a desert western city far away. Ambition had been a way of grasping exhilarated at life, but following Vietnam's fires, ambition could never again spur him to life. Only the presence of people to whom he must commit all.... Rebuilding this house had not occurred to him before. Now it was just something to do for the universe, for Daniel, and the others. For Gloria. Using the faculties in a focused, constructive, disinterested way was what life demanded. And human expression of matter could be busy indefinitely in quest of... well, it wasn't the accumulation of debris, or futile grasping after dominance.

He wiped the sweat from his forehead on the grimy shoulder of his T-shirt. Balder picked up the prybar, began breaking up rot in the roof. What a relief. People can beget more people. Once the bank account had seemed almost a mocker—at the very best a cushion for mother's old age, and he would have given it all with relief. But how much better children! People, beginning again and again. You can deny love, discourage, resist, trash it even. But nothing can change its nature. Nothing can alter the pressure of love.

Its channels can change, its water courses. Working on the hot roof, he could see it in a figure flowing out from under the ledge above the house. It coursed under the dry ground, beneath and through the roots, heading for this house. He looked over the roof ridge past the settler's house and imagined its leading-edge, foaming through the trunks, glinting among the stems. After Vietnam, he had hidden himself in the crevice of this tree-gripped rock, and many years later the water came down and out to him of its own accord. Love had been coming. Here, of all places. It was taking up residence in this house. But with Gloria, too? Maybe. He had done what he could to convince her. But finally it was up to her.

Daniel edged down with another shovelful and watched it drop with a clatter. What a relief to see the pile building below. This roof ripping was tedious. Why couldn't he use his Saturday for something besides "wuk." A swim at the Cove with Cindabilla was wanting. Sweat was dribbling around his eyes, down his cheeks. He flung it from his hair with a shake of his head. Daniel trudged back to the corner where roofs abutted.

Balder was already raking together another shovelful. When will this end? When will the man say, "Let's eat," or "Go get a drink"? Why is there so much having to *force* yourself to do things in life? Why can't life just consist of doing nothing? God is great, he knew. Why doesn't God just say, "Do whatever you like; here's food, clothes, house, transportation, live off my bounty—oh, and no more sickness, pain, starvation"? Does God think we can't handle it, or what? We sure have to handle all the other stuff.

He thought about Nellie Sessions. And what she had said about the owners setting wages in all the mills about Gottheim. Balder's comic question about damaging secrets recalled her story again to his mind. All she has in life are those broken arrowheads, bits of rock shaped by hands that are now nothing but soil. Her wrists pain her, all day she feeds glue pin machines for ten cents over minimum wage, and no health insurance, no retirement, no respect. The people around here all work like that, in mills; or cleaning up after tourists. Even mother aches for a steady job cleaning up after them. Place is saturated in alcohol, too. Seems Nellie and Cindabilla's grandmother are the only ones of that large family who don't drown themselves in Budweiser or those toxic sombreros they drink. He knew they were toxic because he made the mistake of sampling one of those coffee brandies one night. When the spinning stopped, he dreamed he was slapping the crap out of Nathan. Those bleary slack faces of her alcoholic uncles and aunts. No wonder Cindabilla talks of getting out of Gottheim before the sickness gets hold of her too.

I'm definitely going to college. He had learned enough in school about self-esteem... and put that together with what he had been hearing and seeing around here. If your boss respects you and your work, it shows in pay and benefits. If your boss thinks you're not worth it, you console yourself into a stupor.

Daniel dropped another load of shingle and splintered wood onto the heap below. It rebounded, and he sneezed as dry rot got into his nostrils. He turned and saw that Balder was having to dig hard, getting the rot out of that corner up there. He was on his knees with the prybar, digging. The boy looked back over his shoulder down at white plywood stacked in the dooryard. They would be sheathing with that. "Except fah the foundation, roof's most important pot of a house," Balder had said. "Roof's no good, rest will rot away, too."

But Daniel could not help wondering why the man bothered with this. Why not just tear it down and start over? What does he need a big house for anyway? That solid part of it—the oldest house—was big enough. He and his brothers had stayed nights just fine in those extra rooms upstairs. The wallpaper is yellow and old, gloom saturates the place evenings.... But Nathan makes so much noise it doesn't matter. Gloom can't survive in a house with him.

Maybe he should broach the subject of area wages with Mr. Nutting. Maybe not. Man's as tough as an old butternut husk, hardly ever speaks. Don't think the editor is one of them... but what if he is? And what if Nellie Sessions is plain wrong?

Balder leaned on his rake, regarding his son. He saw the knot in Daniel's brow, the concentration in his eyes. Boy's sending up smoke signals. Can almost see that smoke shooting to heaven.

Daniel glanced at him, catching Balder's regard. The man said, "You'll be sliding off the roof on that sweat in a bit." The Father grinned at his son.

"Get enough of it, maybe I'll swim."

Balder grinned bigger. Daniel could make him glad responding well to something. "Swimming, huh. Maybe you betta eat first. Let's call it quits fah t'day."

He caught Daniel's half-smile and thought it was almost worth being deprived of his company for the afternoon's work. No way he could stop now, not if he wanted to get this roof on before the fall rains. He was still trying to get the hang of this father-son thing. He liked the quiet companionship of his son, but saw it costing Daniel. *A father's influence could be important, but shouldn't be heavy-handed.* Can't make the mistake of just pouring out all my thoughts and personality on him. Drop a hat and I'd share all my experiences, understanding....

Balder was learning, but he groaned inwardly. Four short years and Daniel'll be gone... Maybe to college, a trade school, whatever he wants. Boy can't see how short time is: Looking, he sees it endless... Maybe so. Balder thought of Vietnam and its aftermath. Yes, time is short. And it is long.

"And her with *four* kids!" said Melvinia, gurgling with suppressed glee. "Should be ashamed of hah self! But nobody feels shame n'more." Her sagging features turned aside in a knowing look.

" 'S truth!" exclaimed Asa Bartlett. They stood together inside the old high-ceiling post office. Asa's hands were full—with his lunch, a flier from the grocery, a packet from the insurance company on his medical plan, some bills, and a *National Geographic*. They were both gossiping away like it was excess gravy scooped up with a thick junk of homemade bread. You could almost see them smacking their lips.

On the way to his box, Learned Gammons poked a narrow face in, saying, "S'what happens when they stot getting ambition. If she just stayed a waitress—good enough f'anybody, good enough f'you, Melviny—none o'that'd've happened. The minute a woman goes out o'town, steps up to being a bank teller and gets throwed in close with a handsome face... Whad you expect?—shake hands'n how'd you do?"

"Lack o'shame," said Asa, his horned rim glasses sliding down his sweaty nose. He shoved them back into place with an immaculate forefinger. His nails were clipped and clean, as though bleached, his crewcut sharp as a razor "This TV culture's gont harm all the little ones. None' o'this went on thirty years ago in the '50's—not like now. Too much shame back then fah that. If we could just bring back shame." Gottheim's amateur historian shook his head, as though mourning over a piece of broken delftware.

The three wise people stood there shaking their graying heads, the prune-like creases of their faces flapping. They knew best. Anybody with sense could see it. If only young folks'd'listen to them. If only the young could see how much betta it was to be all wore down than excited about what they called life's possibilities. If only 35, 40-year-olds'd give up theya notions of fulfillment. Just take to duty and let fulfillment find *them*. Kids'd fare betta. We all gont be dead in a few years anaway. Might's well do the right thing while you have the chance. (Flap flap flap.)

Melvinia had flipped through her mail and stepped out into the glare of Front Street, Asa following. They stood gossiping five minutes more, mail in hand, then went their separate ways: Melvinia to her babysitting, Asa striking out toward School Street. He would go wind the tower clock in the Congregational Church before beginning the afternoon shift at the wood mill.

The Church was one of three, tall and white, all anchoring one end of School Street at shady intervals. They gave an imposing solidity and sureness, a sanctity and peace to this stretch of Gottheim's thoroughfares. Asa approached one of the two—Congo and Baptist, crisp structures painted in 15 and 12 coats respectively, one for each decade since their building. Two other churches in town, an Episcopalian and Universalist, were a trifle peeling and dingy, their congregations thinner and maybe a bit worn at the heels. Only one Church in town had the tower clock, but all pointed their white steeples skyward, pricking Gottheim's greenness, visible from lanes in the Village, and from some distance on the highway.

Asa enters the side door of the Congo Church standing at the head of Front Street looking down its length toward a facing monument at the far end. The Revolutionary War Minuteman stands erect near that point where Front Street veers out toward the highway. The granite statue was placed there at about the time the Episcopalian Church was being mooted by an earnest little congregation that met in a house at the edge of town in the 1870s. It was 10 years after the Baptists succeeded in shouldering their way up with the Congregationalists in a steepled structure of their own.

Asa opens the door to the tower where a narrow ladder staggers up through gloom. He sets his mail on the wall brace nearby, grips his brown bag lunch with his teeth, and begins climbing hand-over-hand into the tower above. He passes the hanging length of pulley chain, next the ladder, weighted with a boxful of gravel. Over a span of the past half week, by degrees, the box had fallen twenty-five feet toward the floor below. As he climbs, the clock overhead begins striking the noon hour. One... two... three.... Asa waits, bracing himself between the dark wooden wall and the ladder, as the deep tones boom out. In the Village below some might glance up toward the gonging. Others will scarcely notice the mellow strokes, and a few will not hear at all. Asa thinks of this, having been in all these attitudes himself. He unwraps his pastrami sandwich and takes a bite, as the hour falls.

Again he begins his ascent, the tower's must deepening in his nostrils. The rhythmic ticking of the clock increases as he climbs. Asa thinks of its sureness as one of his benefits, and comforting. He is paid only $300 per annum to wind the clock biweekly, and has climbed the ladder 3120 times over the years. One time he took the trouble to multiply it out, but that was 20 years ago, when it was one third that number. He has never taken a break from the clock, winding it twice a week in sickness and health. He even wound it during his honeymoon and the week in which Griselda died. Asa is wedded to this work. His wage has not varied in thirty years.

Aside from these comforts of the ticking and the routine, winding the clock yields the benefit of insight. Climbing in the ticking stillness, Asa has time to think. Standing at the top of the tower admiring its gleaming brass works, turning the crank to reposition its weight, Asa can focus on time. He thinks of Time's oddity and riddle, of its strange elusive characteristics. Yet sometimes he forgets about time as he climbs. Sometimes Asa thinks of other things.

Winding the old wooden handle today, he thinks of Olive. Asa is loving Olive Lovejoy.... He guessed that's what it was. Now that Horace has died. He never thought much about Olive before. He had recognized that she was a good companion for Horace, being a firm and definite soul. Her spirit is more solid than human flesh. So many are ill-defined, unstable

31

and unsure. They are as changeable as the color of Hutchins Pond when the varying sky moves over its waters. He has seen the pond in every color, from the deepest heartbreaking blue, to live green, golden, silver, pewter and black. There are even times when it's colorless. The varying wind gives textures too numerous to mention. Griselda was like that. Olive is not so entertaining but, now that he is nearing 60, Asa is content with that.

Being married to Griz—*I had enough entertainment to last two lifetimes*. Olive probably felt the same about Horace before he settled down and got on with the business of loving her. Asa chuckles in spite of himself. It took heart disease and cancer to settle the boy down. The way he wanted to use his time at the moment—that was how Horace used it. A very entertaining guy.

But Asa wants only so much entertainment. He wants to work, to read, go for hikes, berrying. He particularly likes a focused rummage through documents. All a bore to Griselda. Distraction was how she filled her time out of work, even once or twice distraction with Horace. Sick with anger and sorrow it made Asa. Sick in his level fastidious heart. The messiness of her life was a terrible weight on his orderly soul. He tried to speak of this with her, but she thought him merely self-righteous, blaming Asa for trying to constrain her blithe spirit. Said it was his duty to loosen up. "Quit making me the bad guy, Asa. You'n this town. You're so good'n pure. Don't you realize how that makes it on others?" Every time she said these things it set him on edge. He was 20 years understanding her attitude: the blithe spirit in her was one of self-righteousness.

Oh, but they had some good times together. Asa loved her better than anything, even history. He loved her like she should have been loved: with all his goods and patience. And it was sure to take little of the latter, but he was ready to love Olive that way. In youth he overlooked Olive, craving Griselda's spontaneity and fun. Now he wants the definitiveness of Olive. That and her brightly painted fingernails.

With a groan, Asa unbends from the task of winding the clock. He has winched up the gravel-filled box for the next half week. His aged muscles have taken their painful shot of lactic acid, and he is fit for another three-and-a-half days. The idea of this job for a pittance was Asa's. When it fell vacant thirty years ago, the church wanted to electrify the clock. Now, Asa pops his brick-red head out the little window next the Roman numeral XI in the east-facing clock. He remembers wanting to save the rituals and romance of the great timepiece. Back then, he had a telling premonition about that proposed move to modernization.

The four clockfaces' windows let in the dusty light but he opens them to let in air. If need be, you can set the great pointing hands of time from here. Anyone chancing to glance up from below will see the tiny disembodied head of the historian, peering like an imp face from the great white dial that is set roundabout with black Roman numerals. "How fitting," remarked Eloise Patadoe once, upon seeing this. "The historian as imp, watching from his tower clock while tiny mortals walk to and fro, forgetting." Asa, if he had heard, would have retorted that it was not enough to scare history into the ignorant. Only by becoming history do you learn from it.

Asa Bartlett saved the Congregational Church Tower by means of his twice-weekly hand labor. His faithfulness keeps it from the ravages of automation. In the 1950s and 60s, when convenience became the overwhelming standard, its peril to antiquarian timepieces was little understood. Friction, resulting from the attachment of the motorized chain to Gottheim's clock, would have ground its precision gears away. By spending a little time here each week, Asa preserves the works that may continue to animate the town's timepiece for centuries. Since that ignorant era of the mid-20th-century, the brass works of clocks all over New England, the Midwest, the South, and in California, have been destroyed by electrification.

Sitting in his gleaming mountainside office looking out on the green slopes, Julius Golding appreciates Gottheim's village clock. The ski magnate is a cultured man, aware of the venerable history of tower clocks. He likes thinking of antiquarian clocks ticking away over the small-town face of the nation, gifts from the old heroes of materialism. From the start of the Industrial Revolution in England, until after the turn of the 20th century, the heroes donated tower clocks to ensure promptness in their employees. With a faint gleam in his eye, Julius reminds himself that eventually materialism destroyed the necessity by providing cheap ubiquitous wristwatches... which, in turn, he supposed, elevated the town clock to its current status of icon, an austere reminder of earlier ways and more picturesque bucolic times. For Julius they epitomize the calm solemn beauty of the traditional New England village.

Cities, towns, villages, and colleges have their prosperous patron saints of heroic materialism, someone in the Andrew Carnegie template: one who employed largely, cheaply, and in unsafe conditions; but then disseminating altruistic culture throughout the community. Mitigated hypocrisy, he supposes. Culture abounded from the coupling of capital and labor, in the form of libraries, museums, in donations to civic organizations. Yes, Golding credits labor, but his firm belief is in capital as the primary force behind any endeavor. He ticks off the names, all timber and mill families, who, for more than a hundred years held preeminent positions in Gottheim. The tower clock—with its chiming of the hours, the quarters and halves—reminded everyone, subliminally at least, that these people had the real sway in town. Townsfolk at the turn-of-the-century were also reminded by a glimpse of the mill owner in somber three-piece suit, watch fob glimmering across his expanse, further evidence of his keeping the hours of the community. Julius looks out on green mountains, thinking: Not the sun, but the man with the money determines when work will begin.

Times have changed, he knows. Gottheim's mill owners have steep competition for that preeminence now... in the persons of himself and his brother Harry.

Each winter he looks out through falling snow in these mountains, out from this perch on the rim of Western Maine. He sees necklaces of iron and steel, of concrete, brick and glass, adorning some of the monolithic bosoms of the Meguntics with new chairlifts and snowmaking lines. Necklaces set with the gemstones of trail groomers, hotels restaurants shops condominiums. He reminds himself that it's all capital-intensive, everything in continual need of refurbishing or replacement or addition... And he wants to add mountains to the collection.

Golding is fit and tan from outdoor activity crammed into his full schedule of flying and franchising. He looks out past the green slopes into the more distant north where lies the great lumpy blue counterpane of the Meguntics: but just now he thinks of what is going on in the south behind Jasper Mountain, down in the Village of Gottheim. Clouds of dust are rising, jackhammers pounding away; there's blasting and the endless rumble of dump trucks loaded with fill. More trucks will come, heavy with concrete and steel; stucco, lumber and glass. Already there are hardhats working in steel-toed boots, two-way radios in their hands. If all goes well, builders will be busy in Gottheim. After stalling for a haggle over politics and property, townsfolk will permit a business boom at last. Julius allows himself the luxury of a gleaming eye once more. Here's the trickle-down some have been dreaming of.

The knock at his door is so tiny, timid; so slight that at first it does not register. When it comes again, he turns from the view back to his polished kidney-shaped desk. "Come in, Amanda," he says. "You don't need to knock—ever."

His niece opens the door softly, softly enters, quietly closes it behind. "Hello, Uncle Julie." But her small white face speaks to him more eloquently than the words. It reveals that she is quietly glad to see him. He has nieces and nephews, children of his own, who speak familial greetings—but not as Amanda speaks them.

Amanda is the small living daughter of the Goldings' dead sister, Frances. Frances died last summer in attempting to locate the unlit runway of the Gottheim Airport, shortly after dark. His headlights on at the end of the runway, Julius was waiting below. Waiting to guide them in. In the east stood Mount Will. Looking off toward the lights of the village, he never even glanced at the dark bulk in the dim overcast. His thoughts were on the resort sponsored concert of Celtic music that they would all be enjoying later. All the Goldings would be there with interested townsfolk. He waited that night, past concert time, in mounting uneasiness. Uneasiness turned to dismay, and terror as he realized Frances was not coming. They had talked on the phone just before takeoff from the airport in Beverly. Nevertheless, he then hurried into the village to call, in case she had turned back after takeoff: calling only to discover from her oldest son that she had indeed departed in the long-overdue Cherokee 180.

Only Amanda, an eight-year-old at the time, made it down in the drizzle. There was a story in town that a dark angel led her downslope through the trees, over rocks and streams. Her sister told a reporter from *The Village Voter* of Amanda's initial account, which Amanda herself no longer remembers. She's back from the experience now, a surer quieter child. But she was always the quiet Golding, and Julius no longer feels apprehensive for her. He has come to feel more apprehension for himself.

The necklaces on the side of this mountain still matter as much as before. In fact they matter too much he is sure. Collecting them has become an obsession, a narcotic, occupying his psyche and senses with their oversight and increase. There is nothing... what *is* there to be desired?— truly desired?

Sometimes Julius thinks of Edwin Arlington Robinson's poem about Richard Corey, the wealthy and influential townsman. Yes, Golding cares for his family; more than ever, in part because of Frances' dying, in part because true desire has so ebbed. Why is it that even family can do nothing to banish this rasping emptiness, this obsession with trying to fill...? That fictive Maine townsman, Richard Corey... who glittered as he walked and all the townsfolk looked at him... But it couldn't stop the fatal placement of that bullet.

Looking down at Amanda's wistfully smiling small features, he feels a faint tenderness welling. But it subsides on his recognition of it... Yet he will not let its fleeting dissuade him of its reality. Amanda will have his unalterable affection, if he fails to feel it much himself. Feeling is not everything. There are other truths one can be faithful to... somewhere.

"What can I do for you, baby?" he asks the girl standing before him. She is dressed to go swimming. A pale shift with leaf pattern covers her swimsuit. Stray wisps of hair escape her ponytail.

"Will you take me swimming? I want to go to the town beach, on the pond."

"Poor girl. Am I all you can scrape up for company?" There is much to do this afternoon. He glances at the rolls of architectural prints stacked on his desk.

"But you're the one I want, Uncle Julie. Please?"

Deeply reluctant he hesitates, then says, "All right. We'll go down to the pool."

"But I want to go to Hutchins Pond and see the kids from my class."

Turning away toward the blue view, Julius hardens, but not visibly. He does not like to see the grubby locals swimming at the town beach. He does not like to be looked at.

"All right." He speaks slowly, turning back at last. He'll wear dark glasses, take a book. "The pond, then. We can pick up sandwiches on the way."

Amanda smiles a soft confident half smile.

The man walks away from the stack of lavender rolls piled on his desk. Julius Golding climbs Mount Will every day. But the only angel he ever sees there is Amanda.

Rhetta Bearce looked out her kitchen window. There sat Decatur's Diner— vacant abandoned decrepit—just beyond her otherwise elegant gardens. She looked with distaste at the dim hole that led to the dining area, at the brown outline where kitchen walls once abutted the exterior of the faintly rusting maroon and silver dining car. Through the hole she could make out a contour of an old booth, faintly backlit by a grimy window. Had it not been for her irritation and disgust she might have lingered gleefully over the pathetic impression of the diner's dereliction. But just now she was furious over its mere presence.

Lyman Bearce, her old sawhead of a husband, had the thing set there solely to vex her, to put her precisely into this state that she now enjoyed (as he would have put it). That was the south side. Did he expect the garden to get up and go elsewhere for light? No. He relished her vexation so much that he was willing to blight the prospect of the beautiful house and its surrounding gardens and grounds.

Those sweet neat rows, clod-lined and floral bordered, just coming into longed for fullness; chockablock with leaves and heads that Rhetta had planned for and designed on paper; each year changing the pattern and elaborating this form or that. What she most enjoyed was to adapt one of mother's old quilt patterns, whether snowflake, thistle and shamrock, hens and chickens, anything lovely. Winter she stood at the bedroom window, gazing down on snow and visualizing vegetables, showy flowers; remembering and projecting summer sights from the high perspective.

Now, in the heat of August this greasy monstrosity, this old *train wreck*, was shadowing the color and beauty of Rhetta Bearce's lacework. Oh *how*! Just show me how to get back at Bearce and rid my plot of this ugly—competitor. There, the word was out. Once she thought of Decatur's Diner as ancient hussy and rival for his affections. But no more. Rhetta rejoiced over its closing as no one else in town, not because of the old rivalry but because its passing would ultimately sadden Bearce. *And he did it to himself*! She felt the twitch of a wicked smile play at her lips.

Years, maybe decades, had passed since she had mourned time he spent there conducting his business. His brothers both enjoyed the Victorian offices on Front Street, but, before this boom, Lyman had always preferred the diner's counter. Yet now that the space was wanted for some silly new boutique or other, the endless cups of coffee and powdered donuts, cigarette smoke and grease were out. It would be a sacrifice, she knew. He liked the smell of the place almost as much as that of ripped pine.

She turned her eyes from the sight of the old diner, drifted through the eclectically furnished rooms, and out onto the piazza (as it was called in the old days) to tidy her floral rattan wing chair and matching ottoman. Here she had her cozy cool summer corner set up as she liked, screened in with the storm windows put away. Once the kids were gone, Rhetta discovered that she had been building a nest here over the years. Now it was as comfortable and nurturing as she could have liked had she given thought to such things in her active youth. This was her place inviolate. The rest of the house was more or less a museum, a three-story mansion with mansard roof, complete with cupola and gilded weather vane; painted paneling, columns, piazzas with balustrades, even porte-cochere entrance. It would have to be decorated entirely for the period then, of course, but this place was bound for the National Trust when they were gone. She smoothed the old antique quilt upon the back of her chair, straightened the stacks of *American Heritage* and horticultural magazines beneath the waxed tabletops on either side of the chair. She stood with an ache, slowly, and walked her perfect posture back through the perfect rooms into the kitchen. Hildy had cleaned the place to a T. But, failing to notice, Rhetta stood once more over the sparkling sink, looking out the window.

Ugh. Maybe I can get Hezzy Kimball, or maybe Kenny Carter, to move that thing... Both strong men, able to stand up to Bearce's ire. She sighed. Lyman would just order it right back. And she would have it moved... again.... What good gossip! Turning ever more eccentric and quarrelsome, the Bearces are at it again. Do I really want that?

No, and yet... The dignified Rhetta Bearce giggled. But it came out as a cackle, alarming her with its untoward echo in the room.

Cackling?

A shadow fell swiftly down across the window, and she gave a small involuntary gasp. There it is again. That old owl. Horrible scruffy alien thing! She had not seen anything like it for hunting—in daylight! Rhetta glanced at the Black Forest cuckoo clock against the green tiles above the stainless steel refrigerator. Two o'clock.

She went to the closet in the pantry, got a broom then went out into the heat of the garden. The woman looked over her neat rows, intersecting lines of carrots and beets, broccoli and cauliflower, four colorful strains of cabbage, six kinds of lettuce and much more. But the owl had disappeared. Rooting around where she couldn't see? Great for keeping rodents down, good for keeping out jays and crows. But this aberrant owl tears out the plants themselves.

Mrs. Bearce walked among her vegetable designs, looking for the great horned owl and signs of damage. Why has Elda Simon persisted in repairing this bird's fortunes? The menace has been shot twice by various village people but the girl mends its wings each time. What is the matter with someone who can't recognize a favor of fate when it visits? God knows we need such favors around here—the way Gottheim's been going. All that entrepreneurial elation, with its noise, dust and ugly new superstructures. And, yes, she admitted to herself, a loss of prestige for Bearces. She did not like this new acquaintance with eroding significance, now that ski people were in the ascendancy in Gottheim.

She had come down through the garden toward the diner, but now she stepped from its shadow toward the marigold border, looking off down past the house. There was the gleam of Hutchins Pond, and toy village rooftops and steeples amid the comforting foliage. But there dust was rising, and a distant rumble. Unpalatable food for her affronted senses! An eerie *vaBOOM!* threw sudden echoes across the valley and up the hillside at Rhetta. Blasting!! Trying to place the foundation for one of their hideous simulated Gothic structures, no doubt. Or was it to be stylized Italianate or Greek Revival? They change the design as often as she picked up a week's edition of *The Village Voter*.

She whirled. Where is that owl? She went back through the intricate rows, stepping gingerly, hoping not to startle it up. The old thing might attack her as it had Asa Bartlett. But Mrs. Bearce wasn't afraid. Suddenly she stood at the gaping doorway of Decatur's Diner. Might as well have a look. She set the broom handle against the metal skin of the

38

diner. Years had passed since she had been inside. Rhetta set her hand on the sticky door frame and jerked it back, glancing quickly at the grime coating the frame. On hands and knees she climbed past the iron wheels sunk in the dry August field. The sun, shedding itself savagely on the metal exterior, had turned the diner into an oven. She pulled herself up awkwardly and looked around at the dingy linoleum-covered tables, the worn counter and plastic covered metal stools.

There's where Asa Bartlett used to sit with his father in the old days. Later, he came alone, mornings, after Griselda went to work. There was a selfish one! *that* girl. Griselda Gammon Bartlett. The gay girl grew ever more selfish as the years wore. What is it about selfishness... always popping up just when you think you've got it licked? Rhetta had found it a negative strength of her own psyche in this endless moiling over Bearce's Bearcisms. The man was as obstinate as—as herself. She coped with the challenge through escalation. Sometimes she actually believed she could top him. But, in moments like this, thinking of Griselda—she saw herself (the cackling still ringing in her ears).

She had become a boxy-shaped older woman with wavy short hair, perfectly coiffed; her body in that state of ineluctable deterioration—headed for the bone bin, no detours for historic preservation. No keeping it lively, fit and glamorous, as she had managed with the house. Yet, for all this disintegration, the spirit within (its negative aspects, that is), seemed ever more powerful. Wasn't selfishness once only a tiny nuisance motive, barely on the periphery of consciousness and easily quashed? It was fast becoming an invigorating reason for being. How much of my relationship with Bearce is this continual one-upmanship? Is there anything else to this union? Are we simply united in our mutual monolithic selfishness? Maybe I can escape this almost continual self encounter if I no longer have him to war with.

If she were severed from him it might render her harmless. Stop the cackling, at least. Standing here, sweltering in Decatur's Diner, she tried once again (as so often before) to visualize divorce. But, again, it was plain as the white August day. Financial settlement, its aftermath and enforcement would only intensify the struggle. God! She would never be a harmless little old lady! She would endure this mounting malignancy forever. Till death do us part. There's a settlement impossible to argue over!

Bearce, Bearce. How did it come to this? We loved one another! We thought we did. Doesn't it amount to the same thing?

Turning to leave the diner, Rhetta started back suddenly. Confronting her were the great yellow eyes of the horned owl. She gasped as the big female blinked once and coughed up a dark viscous ball.

Glancing down she saw a tiny dried heap of them littering the floor, furry undigested discard of the owl's insatiable appetite. She looked from this refuse to the owl's enormous sharp talons—clutching the edge of the diner's order window.

Mrs. Bearce shuddered inwardly. The owl had nearly blinded Asa last spring. But Rhetta Bearce refused to show fear. Staring straight into its flat symmetrical face, she said, "Why don't choo go back to the night, waya you belong?" It was her low voice saying this, and she decided to agree with it. "Yes. Go back where you belong."

Its face a frost of feathers, the great horned owl stared back at her. Then, to her deep amazed relief, the owl turned its head and lifted away. With a beat of its great wings and slow winking of its great owl eyes, the raptor swept past. Out through the door of the diner it lurched, sweeping heavily over Rhetta's garden. It lifted up past the dormers and mansard roof, coming to light on the gilded device above the cupola. The weathervane was a replica of a fallen white pine. It had been her first anniversary gift to Lyman.

He loves his white pine, she thought ruefully. His money trees. No, she corrected herself. Not just for the money. Lyman loves white pine. He takes care of them, always loved their long-armed beauty, the way the strong boughs hold themselves ready to heaven. He loves them in every stage of growth, from a wispy seedling.... Her eyes swept the place. And he loves this wretched old diner. Not because I hate it, but because he loves it.

"Go on!" She called to the owl from the doorway. "Go!!"

She watched from a distance as it fell sweeping down. The owl flew off into the great dark pine woods bordering the north side. In the vacuum left by her cathartic cry, Rhetta Bearce sat down on the gritty floor of the doorway, peaceful. For a moment she surveyed the garden. The shadow of the diner was shifting.

About to slip down into the dry grass, she noticed the cough balls lying near and picked up two. They were soft and dried, and, after a brief examination, she slid them into the pocket of her smock. Mrs. Bearce had an old birch burl bowl that she kept for such natural curios. Periodically she changed its contents, adding new things. These would make a nice addition to the tiny bird's nest, galls and colorful fungus she now kept in the bowl. From time to time she would feel the softness of the cough balls, remembering the owl's great horned face so near.

Beneath Mason Mountain, a tent sagged among the tangle of bug-eaten green. The Twitchell camp sat beside the stream where thriving mills once stood. Dark and weathered ostrich ferns, growing next to the pooled and sluggish stream, indicated where fiddleheads emerged in the spring. In the shade-dappled woods one could see the water level fallen owing to August drought. An extended spell of waterless weather showed in the dark and droopy green, and low water.

Here Chrischana's children bathed and washed out their under things, their jeans and socks. Wilting before the fire, the little family cooked their meals. But now a ban against burning was on, so they ate peanut butter and fruit from the Front Street Foodliner. Submerging milk in one of the stream's pools, they scarcely kept it cool. Chrischana had jobs babysitting and cleaning for rusticators. The money Balder had given her for the boys' support was still sitting in the bank, waiting upon her hope of Enan Pale selling at least part of the burned-out Twitchell Farm.

The old house was no more, and the land little more than stone. But there were still some large maples in the old dooryard, and the tall sugar maples, bristling downslope below the lost structure, held promise. Maple syrup could sell almost like liquid gold. She hoped to buy tubing, buckets, and an outdoor evaporator in order to process the sap next spring. Twitchell Farm Maple Syrup. It had a quiet sound, for a modest business. The sun will coax hidden life from underground roots by day, nighttime cold staying the flow until next day when it will rise again. The boys can tend the process too, boil the sap, watch it thicken. If they'll lift their feet, they'll earn—and learn—a lot from this. Chrischana almost grinned a secret sweaty grin.

All the dishes were in the stream on a sandbar before her. She scoured them with sand washed down from Mason's rocky sides in spring. Good cleaning agent, sand. The boys wash their jeans in it too. No pollution, no phosphates when there's lots of sand.

A distant sound... of engines... approaching through the woods.... In cutoffs and T-shirt, her brown braid lying along her breast, Chrischana stood looking over her shoulder toward the sound. Downstream and opposite, Nathan looked up from the pool where he sat submerged to his armpits. He had heard the engine before Mother, but was busy digging for artifacts, his fingers burrowed in the muck. Among his finds since moving to Mason's Mills were sand-smoothed bits of colored glass, bits of chipped stone that he thought were arrowheads, and some flakes of clear mica. Now, when he saw the dark gleams of the square vehicle jouncing through foliage, Nathan clambered quickly from the pool and splashed over to stand by Mother.

The shining Land Rover pulled to a stop at a discreet distance from the domestic scene, and two men, casually dressed, got out. At first neither were familiar to Chrischana. It was time now to face the fact of her trespass. But she was reluctant to leave this place. They were happy here and tired of moving, setting up camp anew each time. This place was to have been the last stop before home.... Is there a home?

The short, bespectacled blond man came straight to her, full of energy and zip. Something familiar about him, after all. He would suggest in a friendly way that there would be no need to call the authorities, provided.... The other man was tanned, darker, aloof; his face aquiline in profile, obscured in sunglasses. Avoiding glancing her way, he looked over the monstrous hewn foundation stones of the old mill and dam. He surveyed the surrounding terrain, the lay of the stream among rocky shoulders. The zippy younger man surprised her by extending his hand. He actually reached for hers before she could think to offer it. His grip was firm if brief.

"James Fay. Beautiful stream, Ms...."

The brother of Gloria, Balder's girlfriend.... She found her voice. "Twitchell, Chrischana Twitchell." Levelly she met his gaze, which glanced past her at once. She recognized him as the man who was always finding his way, unpleasantly, into the pages of *The Village Voter*. She felt Nathan nuzzling at her side, but she was not about to introduce him. James Fay was in a hurry. The other man was keeping his elegant distance.

Nuisance time, James Fay was thinking. A squatter. Just what we need to hold up the project. He had summed her up at once, noting the slogan on her T-shirt. *Imagine water*. Imagine no squalid squatters, he thought, saying again, "A beautiful setting, this stream. An old mill site, I understand."

Waiting, Chrischana said, "Yes."

"We're going to buy it," said Fay, not bothering to elaborate or soften.

"That so? Who owns it now I wondah?" She was inquiring politely, to pass the time. Mr. From Away caunt hurry me out of my dignity. Be interesting to see how busy-little-man puts it to me.

He thought better of his lack of elaboration, which might be useful in nudging this woman into place. Some other place. "You know Enan Pale. He owns a lot of these old places, sells stumpage off them."

"Hey!" exclaimed Nathan. "That's the man we want to buy Twitchell Farm from, Mother!" Nathan did not take his eyes off this sleek stranger. Fay was immaculate in chinos and open throat shirt. Nathan was fascinated by the thin gold chain around his neck, and the heavy gold ID bracelet on his wrist.

Chrischana smiled at Fay, rocking Nathan a little where she stood.

"Place on Blackwell Mountain that burned?" Fay was surprised, doubting they could afford anything.... But you never knew. Perhaps this is a happy coincidence. Taking them at their word instead of their looks is one way to deal with the situation.

"Thing is," reflected Chrischana, "He don't seem t'be interested in selling. Won't even see me. Probably thinks I don't have money—but I do." She smiled her half-smile.

Fishing in his breast pocket, James Fay came out with a card. "Take this to his office and say I sent you. Mr. Pale will see you."

She leveled her gaze at him again. "I'll do that, Mr. Fay. In fact, we'll go now." And she thought, I'm sure Mr. Golding will appreciate the privacy. She wasn't sure which Golding, but it certainly was a Golding.

"You do that!" James Faye looked with distaste at the dishes lying in the amber water on the sandbar.

Theodora raised eager unseeing eyes and set the receiver back in its cradle. She began pacing among the Thomas Mosher pieces in the open room, lacing and unlacing her slender fingers, fiddling with a loose strand of hair. Theo went into the dining area and ran a thoughtful hand along the perfect curve of an isolated Windsor chair. Gloria Fay was coming to dine, luncheon, next Thursday. Now there was planning to do, and it must be a memorable meal, absolutely gracious. She must make friends at last with James's sister.

Let me see.... Asparagus and potato soup? Not for a hot day. Something shrimpy, green and cool? A salad, iced tea? Simply fresh fruit for dessert: pineapple, strawberries, apricot, a hint of ginger.

Standing by the buffet she fidgeted, opened the drawer, pulled out two cookbooks. Will we be friends? We *will* be friends. Be positive.... So much in common. The International Institute for Coordinated Experiments. And James. What else? Gottheim. We both care for this humble old place.... We're going to make Gott'im shine. Some of the old fogeys are against it... but once the noise and rumbles subside—there'll be a cinema, more shops, a Bohemian coffee house. But it's more, a new spirit, an up-and-coming attitude! And everyone involved! That's what it's all about.

And love. She had glanced into the mirror over the buffet, saw her eyes shining. James Fay. We are so good together. Kind man, not like the ones who.... A Baptist! Of all things. Who would have thought I would ever consider being submerged in a tub—in front of a church full of people! Weren't Baptists rednecks down South? But there are classy black Baptist congregations—people with real intellect, leaders in the country. Weren't their churches instrumental in fomenting Civil Liberties?

Of course it's bigger than a tub. The Reverend, or whatever they call their ministers, will be there in the water with me. And others will be baptized and we'll all be robed....

Will we be engaged? The baptism will signify something... beyond dating. We're definitely dating. Surely Gloria will acknowledge that! She must acknowledge it merely by excepting my invitation.... I'll be baptized for God's sake!

This is all the stability Theodora Prescott has ever searched for. Being married, finding God in this way, will do it. No more looking here and there, high and low, like in the minister's sermon. Throw out a shelf full of New Age books, Eastern thought, fad psychology.... maybe even IICE. (James hates IICE.) Remember that brush with Catholicism? But this is it!

...What are doubts...? She wandered into the kitchen. Just think of James and a future with him. It settles you. Engaged, married. Yes. Or— no? Goose. Just wait. It will all appear at some point.... Come together. And this lunch—it will bring friendship, a type of intimacy with James's sister.

She noticed the kitchen, how it gleamed after Melvinia's cleaning. Theo knew she was lucky to get her after the diner closed. Melvinia Sessions does not mess around. She got the job done—if she did keep Theo in her place. Melvinia hated uppitiness in anyone. She makes cracks about people from away, mocking them behind their backs, commenting dryly to their faces. They must guess she doesn't think much of them. Well, she values practicality over—learnedness. Theo made a point to be respectful of Melvinia, dreading to think what she made of her. She didn't dare mention rebuilding Gottheim to her. Melvinia roared at such ambitions. "Reg'la Disneyland, this new Gott'im! When's Goofy coming? Donald Duck gont live he-ah too? They ski?" She started ticking them off on her fingers: "We got nevah-nevahland, Frontierland, Tomorrowland, New England. Meguntics had nothing until IICE took up with Goldings. Whoopee! Gont have a good time at last!"

Theo had laughed in spite of herself. She always did. Whenever the older woman got going, she saw her point as plain as pie. That's me, she thought.

Uniform in her flagrant inconsistencies, Theo. Whomever she was dealing with in this moment, that's where she found her identity, her definition. She was convinced of anything you put to her—as long as you stayed in the room. As long as her nose was still in your book, your editorial. When Balder rebuffed her efforts to bring psychological evaluation to Gottheim Chair, she had had to return to IICE for further encouragement in implementing them. Balder never did fill his out, and then he left to work in the paper mill. Only be convinced yourself, and you had her heart entire. Spend the afternoon and you could build your palace in her. In the evening someone else would have the throne.

James Fay saw much of this. She was his, he did not doubt. But what a watch she'd need. It would frustrate him, he knew. So he deliberated. There was time.

"You got that right," said gap-toothed Elmer Robbins to the older Lyman Bearce. Cup in hand, tugging on his ball cap, he moved away from the coffee machine to let large Robbie Robichaud have a turn. You-got-that-right-Robbins, Elmer was sometimes called.

People were coming and going in the early morning around the coffee pot in one of Buster Bearce's oil, gas, and convenience which were sprinkled throughout the county. It was just down the highway from where Decatur's Diner stood until recently. The store was cramped and dim and crammed with little convenient items.

"We don't get that rain," said Elmer, "fires gont get out of hand fast."

"Gusty's got get those permits tightened down," returned his boss Lyman Bearce, referring to the state capital, Augusta. He took a gulp of coffee and smoothed his great white beard. "No more permits till rain comes."

Robbie, the logging contractor and pulp truck operator, interjected. "Those trains is what's setting things to blazes—lighting that brush along the tracks."

The men around the coffee machine agreed. There was a letup in the heat today, but rain was still badly needed. All was tinder dry, the ground either like concrete or dust flying away. But fires showed, and volunteers were constantly on alert.

"Been in the woods lately?" Robbie continued. He was a big man, in his late fifties and dressed in soft green work clothes. "You can feel the static in the pine needles when y'walk."

"Evahbody wants t'know when the dust gont settle," said Elmer, referring to construction in the village. "I tell 'em when snow flies."

" 'S'about the size of it," returned Bearce. "Nothing'll stop the developers but a glacier. Tearing down's going on till you don't know the place."

"Least we got a cap on strip development, with that agreement the town got from them," said the contractor.

"Don't bet on it," returned the lumberman. "We put a check on Jaspa Mountain, but theya's plenty others coming. If you think folks won't sell along the highway, you're full o'shit. Money's too big."

You should say it, thought Robbie. He implied his thought by saying, "What's going in waya Decatur's was? Thought that'd be up and selling something by now."

Bearce actually smiled. "Just have t'wait'n see."

Robichaud drew back, faintly affronted, staring at the lumberman. "No secrets in this town. All comes out in town records, finds its way into *The Voter*. Nothing slips past."

"But you ain't heard nothing yet." Freckled Elmer smiled, feigning knowledge he didn't have.

Robbie thought he recognized that smile, and began to think Bearce had no buyer yet. Old bastid probably wants too much for it. He swallowed some coffee and changed conversational course. "That group of IICE's— what's it called—with all the meetings? Gut big changes in mind for the town."

Lyman Bearce almost chuckled. "You'n your rig got nothing to fear. Like to see 'em change the way you haul logs. Little girl, in heah come telling us—been heah generations—how to *fix* Gott'im!" He did not refer to Gloria Fay by name, and he had nothing to say about IICE and its community alliances and committees. "Gott'im needs fixing! Hell, she's cute, her'n those frigging little studies. Next thing she'll be telling us how to run sawmills. Maybe she's another Theodora Prescott."

The listeners around the machine guffawed but Lyman Bearce drank his coffee and looked disgusted. Theodora Prescott's furniture mill was a disgrace to all the mills around Gottheim.

"Like to invite Miss Fay to the veneer components mill'n show her how we bend wood." Elmer suggested this with a sly grin. "Wondah how she'd do under a jolt o'that juice?" He referred to the new technology for bending hardwood.

"You been hanging out with the boys fom the paper mill," said Robichaud, thinking protectively of his daughter Drusilla. *Either that or it's your fathers in you.* He recalled the story of a Robbins who stole settlers' children and sold them to Indians for spite. "Maybe you talk like that because you're afraid someone will call you good."

Elmer chastened his sneer into a grin. "Good's one thing I caunt be accused of!"

"Got that right!" someone mocked. The men around the coffee machine laughed.

Robbie Robichaud walked away. Lyman Bearce turned to watch him go out into the sun.

The two young women sat on the deck of Theodora's condo, looking out over the Meguntics through sparse leaves. The view of mountains was framed by tall gray birches and quaking aspen. Beyond the fluttering leaves, mottled mountains stretched beneath speckling clouds toward the mysterious heart of the state. The air about them was sweetly warm and dry. They had just finished the light lunch and were sipping iced coffee and cream.

Gloria sighed. "Just look at it. This is why I love it here." Her gesture took in the heavenly scene.

"And to think I've lived here all my life," enthused Theo. She so wanted the other to see her absolute fidelity to this place. (...In all but that abortive half term at Vassar.)

"Yes," said Gloria, dismissively. "But you know what I've noticed about people who have never lived anywhere else? They seem practically immune to this beauty. It's like they don't see it.... not Balder, though," she added.

Oh, there was a topic with which her hostess could impress Gloria. Theodora knew as much about the mechanic as anyone. After all, he had been in her employ for several years—until he went off to that awful paper mill; and they had practically been childhood chums... sort of. Gloria was attracted to Balder, had dated him earlier in the summer. But who wasn't attracted to Balder? Something had gone out of Gottheim Chair since his departure. The whole place seemed less substantial now, more rickety. Endangered. As though his absence revealed the company's decline.—Or actually precipitated it? Revealed it, caused it?—*Oh, I don't know*.

What she was certain of was her mounting unease, increasing sense that the place was a figment, doomed to ultimate—imminent?—collapse. Great-grandfather's once nationally prestigious manufactory! Gottheim Chair had always been there, the bulwark of her life, as fundamental as the woods or mountains. As a child she knew its magic, wandering its labyrinth of passages, compartments, strange great halls of machinery; discovering its hiding places. But, as an adult, she took it all for granted. Now she had offers, people wanting to buy—for its location. *To demolish it*! And, cringing every time she considered it, she was tempted.... But, if she allowed someone to obliterate the mill, dissolve its workforce, put up a ski shop or condominium... it would empty her life... point to the awful vacuity of her existence. What would she *do* without Gottheim Chair? What would she *be*? (—Maybe James's bride? If only—)

Yes, often she gave the mill only minimal attention.... Then again sometime she gave it *too* much, obsessively planning changes that weren't apt, without really understanding—anything to be involved in her ancestral concern. It wasn't until the void of Balder's absence that she realized how much the mill was part of her identity. My *raison d'être*! All coming to an end? Oh Balder, can't you see—they want to tear it down!

It had all been moiling around in her mind for weeks. The new relationship with James was comforting, hopeful, and Gloria was here at last... but these things would surface unexpectedly. Naturally, like organic scum on a stream or in a well. Now, slowly, she responded to Gloria's statement about Balder. Her tone was careful, measured and out of character. "Yes, Balder sees things... to some extent. The beauty he sees. But some things he misses entirely. And other people—well...." Thinking of the jobs that would be lost if the mill went, she added, "People here work so hard. Actual workaholics. So they can't always notice the beauty."

"Alcoholic, too—they aren't making enough money here, you know." This response from Gloria was a trifle pointed. She stopped, then went on. "But Balder?—miss something about the mountains?" It was both leading and impatient. Theodora's feeble grasping after insight did not interest her, not when the woman paid her employees so little. *She practically pulled up to the door and <u>drove</u> Balder to the paper mill.* Gloria could be fastidious in her low-key display of respect for Theodora. She would not crush the woman's self-esteem (what there is of it) with a reckless demeaning of her. I can't abide that. I will be bored donkey's days if it will spare someone so fragile a little humiliation. People accused you of patronizing, but how else can you be kind?

She said, "But you are right that he can miss—well, like when it comes to the interests and needs of women in the 80's. Let's face it, he's a Neanderthal at his dressiest."

Theo could not bring herself to fine-tune what she was getting at. To do so would reveal her insecurities. She couldn't do that until she felt... until she discovered just how acceptable she was to James's sister. The cozy feeling she had hoped for was eluding her.

She swished the ice cubes around in her glass, thoughtfully. Suddenly she burst, "What can you make of his going to work in that place? He never cared so much for money before, and that's the only reason they work there. He might find mechanical work engaging, but that's not it. Not in that place." She reached for the pitcher and began pouring more iced coffee.

Gloria said, "He wants to renovate that old house of his, and wood mill wages are notoriously low—at least they would be notorious where I come from. Isn't that why they're workaholics—so they can survive?"

The implication was rude... but perhaps unintentional... yet Theo took it in her usual way; as though it was not meant for her. In company she'd gloss over a slight... only to feel its force later when alone. Then it would undo her. But now she agreed casually, and picked up the topic.

"Renovate *Simons Ledge*!? The whole thing? He'd be better off tearing down all but the central house. He should take off all that clapboard. I think that's an original log house under there. It could be a real piece of rustic Americana."

"He does intend something like for that part he calls the settlers house. But he's also got these ideas for the rest of it... a real familial setup that makes my head spin thinking of it." She stopped.

"Really?" Theodora held still, expectantly.

But Gloria would not be prodded. She could not bring herself to share a confidence with a woman whose mind was like a restaurant table after a party of eight. Whatever her relationship with Jimmy! No intention of involving myself in *that*.

The pause embarrassed Theo. Rushing to fill the silence she said, "Balder has a son now, I guess, and he's all worked up over parenting... like a kid in a candy factory. Who wouldn't want to be loved like that after being alone so long? We all knew there was something to the Chrischana-Balder thing, but thought it would progress to marriage.... as things did in Gott'im back then. People didn't get pregnant or if they did and didn't marry, the girl had to leave in disgrace. If he had known, he would have married her. It wouldn't have occurred to anyone that she wouldn't want to! But, not knowing why she left.... well, he never made it to college like he planned. Can you imagine someone with a broken heart taking refuge in Vietnam! He could have been designing state-of-the-art furniture mills, walking around in a suit with a roll of blueprints under his arm. Can you picture it?"

Gloria grinned over the conjured image, but a private look passed into her gaze and she turned from Theo's eager face toward the shadow-dappled array of mountains.

Theo turned away too, disappointed over the other's aloofness. *We will never be sisterly. Never.*

Evening. Theodora is on the deck again, standing at the rail, a glass of white zinfandel beside her elbow. She must have her wine now for James will be here soon. He is a faithful abstaining Baptist. She looks out toward the hushed contours of evening's rest. But, like the trembling leaves of quaking aspen beyond the rail, Theo is restive, her thoughts a turmoil of old faces.

The faces of her father and his cronies, the mill owners of yesterday. They mingle with contemporary faces, older now, the ones owning the mills today. When she was a little girl, they came to the house in Gottheim—the old faces—to play cards, smoke cigarettes or cigars, schmooze. Only they didn't call it that then. It was simply the old-boy jokes they shared between them, grinning. I bet they are at it still. Only they never dare include me. How could they? Theodora Prescott, mill owner. It's a silly oxymoron.

She swallows the wine. *But it is true... what I heard as a child, playing beneath the card tables....*

Apparently her memory had submerged it... until Gloria's remark of this afternoon... coming back to her now, its pointedness growing until it pierces. They don't need to include me. I'm included *en famille*. It was all fixed decades ago. Like the wages of the workers. No one would make more than what the mill owners, together, decided. The stewards of the community....

Leaning over the rail, anguish in her thin gut, Theodora trembles. She jerks herself up, knocking the long-stem glass with its contents down into the junipers below. It's no different from the publicized squeeze put on pulp truck operators by the paper mill. No—it's worse than that. That was done by strangers, absentee owners. These employers are related to the community—my relatives, some of them, for godsake!

My relatives, me. Demeaning the labor of people.... –There's practically no one here not related. Among generations of locals, if not by blood, then by marriage. Why do we keep doing it to ourselves!?... Can I look them in the eye... Lyman Bearce, Enan Pale, the others—and say it?

Theo feels her face twisting, bleared with tears. All my little plans for improving Gottheim Chair. For lifting the employees up on some fantastic cloud. She can hear Melvinia's happy mockery: "When's Goofy coming, Donald Duck?" The shame of it piercing through her thoughts, making a shambles of Theodora's mind. Balder's scorn of her silly plans— sticking to her like burdock and nettles.

Teary-eyed, she looks up at the rustling popples. Unceasingly rustling. She turns, withdraws into the townhouse, closing the French doors with a click. Anyone looking up was bound to see her there, toiling in tears... someone bound to hear her crying. If only I could flee, anonymous.

Can Gloria have known?

She stumbles through the living room, wiping tears. Did she find out somehow?... Someone telling her? Unthinkable... even with all our studies. No one would tell. Who knew to tell besides the conspirators?

What if... oh God, I cannot confront Lyman Bearce. Someone powerful like that? What would he do if I did?

Throw me in the booby hatch, that's what! And they would all back him! They'd get into the files at IICE, or ferret it all out somehow, and *throw* me to the loonies!

"Woman's finally gone off her rocker. We always knew. Caunt count on a thing she says. What's needed is pity: Theodora Prescott—

madwoman!"

In woods beneath a shelf of Jasper Mountain towering above the Simon house, Benaiah Twitchell discovered a monolith: horizontal, long, and maybe seventy feet high, merging with the steeply wooded slope behind. It was possible, the old settlers knew, by circuitous route to bypass the ledge above and come down from remoter reaches, to walk the great rock and gently descend to the forest floor above the house. Surveying it, Benaiah did not discern the monolith's vast and mysterious connections with the giant soaring distant and far: far beyond the house, the rock, and his own young thought. He saw only the great face of this rock, split here and there with slender trees, and topped with more bristling forest. In places it trickled water from some secret source. To him the great rock was of storybook proportions, the grandfather of all stones. In moister days a stream ran under it, cooling and full, falling down toward the pond well below. Even today, in the midst of the driest season Gottheim had seen in three decades, there were pools, soft dark earth and green things growing; because of those trickles from the rock. He looked in the damp spots and saw the split imprints made by the dainty feet of deer. He also saw their round droppings in the streambed between its rooty banks.

To Benaiah, reader that he was—and Daniel read to them, the great rock was like something out of *The Hobbit*. He thought of the road to Rivendell and of Mirkwood. Trolls might have been formed out of rocks like this one. Following between the streambed and the giant rock, he saw the rock sloping down toward him, and discovered that he could easily climb the slope to come out atop it. From there he looked out in the direction of the house hiding among the trees, toward the pond and village, yet he saw only trees. He turned away and wandered over the surface among the popples, maples, beeches, birches, until he came to a tight group of three trees. He walked around them, speculatively, thinking he might build himself a deer stand.

Benaiah shimmied up one stem, grabbing a branch, hooking it with his arm and then a leg. He hoisted himself into the tree. Now he climbed higher and looked out. There was a corner of the pond and roof of a mill. Distantly, he thought he heard the drone of its separator. And dust was stirring here and there. Remotely, the clock in the tower above the Congregational Church struck the half-hour.

Working on the project over the afternoon and next morning, Ben made progress. He dragged bits of two-by-four, scraps of plywood; carried hammer and nails—all from Balder's rebuilding project. He had rope to help him climb, and haul up the scraps and tools. For hours he worked, hoisting and hammering. Sometimes he stopped and looked out into the trees or down to the rocky leafy mossy mushroomy floor. Excited, he thought of deer bear coy-dogs raccoon bobcat fox, all coming into range. You could really do something here, in these woods.

Little by little he had got used to Gottheim, and to the woodland that once terrorized him. He remembered the way he had paced the woodland track, hoping for Mother's return—when they first came to Maine and had to camp in Abenaki Notch. Trees trees trees, nothing but trees. No telling how long you could stay lost in them... endless maze, every turning like the last. There was no way to tell here from there. Hardly any houses to be seen— when any house was safety, security. From the window of the Bonneville he looked for houses, seeing miles between each one. A long road from Phoenix had sharpened the little Twitchell family's longing for home, for Mother's grateful Gott'im, as she called it. But, when they found it, to Ben it was no place at all. Trees. Only trees... and rocks, and the fear of being lost.

But now Benaiah saw houses everywhere. They lined the road, packed and populated the rural world he was coming to know. And the country was becoming a city to him, filled with what he wanted, things to do. The woods held out the promise of exciting encounters.... Especially if Balder would let him use his hunting rifle this fall. It was a beautiful nut-brown 30-30, and Benaiah was aching to try it. Maybe, if Balder saw how hard he worked on this deer stand.... well, the man was sure to let him use a gun.

Balder likes to see people doing things for themselves. Don't like to see'em lying like lumps in front of TV. Summer reruns of The Ninja and Knight Rider aren't awesome to him. Mrs. Simon took care of wild animals, but Ben knew for fact that there was deer meat in the freezer. Balder got his buck last year. Even Mother got deer when she was young.

Having just sweated it into place, he stretched out on the small scrap of plywood but found it far from level. Phooey! But—good enough. He peered over the edge. Two scraps to hoist up, then back for more to make the railing, a place to rest a gun barrel.

He sat up, leaning against the trunk. Ah. My first little house. I can bring my blankets up here, make money raking leaves this fall then buy a Coleman stove. Cook breakfast right up here!

Benaiah squinted out the sights of an imaginary rifle. He began sighting along the forest floor, carefully aiming.... He touched the trigger.... What's that in the leaves? He held his breath. It was a deer. No, two deer! A red one, and a white.

Posey and Sugarloaf!

Always he had hoped to see them. Softly they approached, browsing on the leaves. And he looked on. He watched for several minutes, until they knelt among a clump of seedling fir. Resting, they lay, chewing chewing chewing.

What would they do if they saw me? he wondered. Bet they'd let me near.... Posey and Sugarloaf.

He leaned out a bit from the platform, calling softly. Posey looked up, watching momently. She kept chewing, turned away. Sugarloaf looked, too. But the fawn turned to white china, staring as though a statue, with eyes like pink glass.

Every time he went into the woods below Simons Ledge he brought something from one of Elda's tins. But he had never seen a deer nor had a chance to offer anything. Now he felt in his pockets for peanuts. He had filberts, too. So, still looking down on them, he held out a peanut, saying softly,... "Peanut Posey, peanut." And she pointed her face up at him. He saw the delicate fluttering of her black nostrils, the mild white rings around her eyes. She was nervous, but, if he was careful....

He turned and began feeling his way down, sneakers pressed against the trunk, the rope cutting into his palms. All the while he spoke softly of the peanut. Maybe Posey will even smell Mrs. Simon on the peanut. Didn't she say molecules of things and people stick to other things? And that's how animals pick up scents. Makes sense. (He smiled over the homophone. Daniel would.) "Peanut Posey, peanut."

His patience paid. Standing now, the deer briefly stayed as he let loose the rope. Softly he approached, holding out the treat.

Gently, Posey picked the peanut from his fingers. He held out another for her fawn. The small white deer stretched for it, and Ben looked down on him, studying his form. The great pink eyes, pink insides of its ears, white bristles softly trimming the delicate features. How thin and strange its limbs, like dainty sticks. The nervous innocence of its spirit appealed unconsciously to Ben. His eagerness abated.

He emptied his pockets to the deer and brushed their coats with his palms. Sugarloaf seemed attentive to his mother, as though connected by invisible threads. Taking cues from her, it was as if the fawn had no thought but Posey's thought.

All of Benaiah's own thought was set on them. In feeling their noses with his palm as they picked up each nut, touching the hairs of their hides, he thought of their molecules mingling with those of his hand. Seeing them with attentive eyes, the image of deer imprinted him with their truth. He might have gone into the forest with them, a deer inhabiting Benaiah's body.

Why would anyone want to shoot a deer? No one could pull a trigger on Sugarloaf.... would they?

But he had eaten meat from Balder's deer. Even Balder had pulled the trigger on an eight point buck last year.... I was building—*I* was going to shoot one. It's true what Mrs. Simon said. Posey would wind up on the dinner table.... Sugarloaf end up a statue—stuffed. All because he was white as a sugar cube and a good target.

Still rubbing their sides, Ben thought very carefully. *What if Sugarloaf wasn't white?* Couldn't his coat be dyed? Maybe made two-tone, like camouflage to hide his hide. He smiled over the double meaning. It was something Daniel would think of, and Ben did because of his brother's influence. "Hide your hide, Sugarloaf," he whispered, rubbing him.

The boy looked through the stems and understory of young hardwoods and firs. He listened to make sure no one was around. He looked back down at Sugarloaf, struck by the contrast he made with the greenery. If he could carry the fawn away from this interwoven greenness, off this great rock (even if it was buried in woodland far from the road).... Benaiah wanted to bring Sugarloaf down to their bedroom at *Simons Ledge*.

Now, seeing that the nuts were no longer forthcoming, the deer knelt down again among the seedling fir. Ben saw that they wanted to rest. Softly he stole from them and headed for the sloping end of the big rock. When he was down by the streambed he quickened his pace and made straight for the Simon house.

What would she have that I could use to color his hide? He had to hurry, do the job today before they disappeared somewhere up on the mountainside. Think dummy, think. Maybe food coloring in the kitchen cupboard? Mix them together and make a muddy mess? He had experimented making frosting once back in Phoenix. For sugar cookies. And Daniel had laughed at them and asked if he had used Ritz dye. Sugarloaf will be so ugly that no one will want him even if they could see to shoot him. But how do you apply it?

His mind busy with possibility, Ben came down toward the house. You could see it better now that Balder had hacked away some of the old lilacs and vines. From the roof of the children's house came the sound of hammering. As he approached, Ben could hear Nathan's incessant nattering, as Dad would have called it, but muffled and indistinct. Brat was probably upstairs driving Balder up a wall.

Once inside, he made a quick pit stop, then crossed to the knotty pine cupboards. He pulled himself up on the sideboard and opened the cupboard door. He peered inside and began rummaging among small containers of sweet basil, dill, oregano and chili powder. Where were some things of food coloring? Doesn't she ever bake cookies? He hardly heard the approach of the others, though Nathan was squeaking away about dorky Cabbage Patch Kids.

"Need help?" asked the man, seeing Ben settle back in disgust on the countertop. What choo afta?"

"Food coloring," was the terse reply.

"Caunt 'memba last time I saw food coloring. Might be some up top, though." He reached up into the highest shelf, behind the dusty jars full of macaroni and dried elderberries. "Food coloring!" He handed down a small box containing colored vials.

"What's *that* for?" asked Nathan.

"I was curious about that, too, but didn't think it polite to ask."

"Nathan knows nothing about that!" growled Ben. "I'd tell you but *he'd* mess up my plans."

"Caunt have that!" said Balder cheerfully, grinning at Nathan. "You ain't been to the barn t'see what mother's got out theya today. Ain't had a chance, we been talking all morning." He raised his voice as Nathan headed for the door. "Don't go touching those raccoon kits. They look cuddly enough, but you dassn't."

"OK," said Nathan, slamming the screen door as he went.

Ben slipped down from the countertop. "I was building a deerstand up there'n I saw Posey'n Sugarloaf'n had this idea to help'em." He stopped to see how Balder was receiving it.

Arms crossed, the man leaned against the sideboard, his thoughtful gaze on Benaiah's freckled face and green eyes. Stroking his dark beard, he said, "Yuht.... Go on."

"Well... they're up there in the trees, resting on that giant rock—the one with trees on top and a brook under it?"

"Great rock."

"I could dye Sugarloaf so hunters don't shoot him this fall. If I mix these colors, they turn brown." He shook the coloring box.

"Well... lots oh' things come to mind about this plan and I can see you're in a hurry t'get back up theya—but I got my doubts about the permanence'o this dye. First rain come along might wash it off. Clothes dye'd be betta, but we have to buy some. Time we got back they'd be gone."

Ben's face fell as Balder continued. "That don't mean you caunt have it on hand, case they show again sometime.... But consider this."

The blond darkly bearded man moved away from the sideboard and began to wander about the kitchen, occasionally stroking his beard or talking with his hands. "Seems like you seen something special about

Sugarloaf. ... But you was up theya building a deerstand, getting all set to get your first buck."

"You got one last year," said Ben, watching him.

Balder grinned. "Deer's here partly coz other critters got eat. Eating out of the woods means seeing your food before its dead'n watching its death throes.... Instead of picking up a package of meat at the market."

"But he's special, like you said. So is Posey." He turned and began taking lids off the tins on the sideboard, filling his pockets with nuts.

"Yuht. We know em'n that makes'em special."

"They act... so... gentle...." He wanted to say more but didn't know how.

"Trusting, too. They can tell how we feel about 'em."

"Yeah," said Ben, awe lighting his face.

"So naturally we want save'em. Don't want no black barrel aiming down on them." Still talking, he went to the refrigerator, rummaging for sandwich fixings to put on the sideboard. He got bread from the bread box and began making sandwiches. It was as though he were thinking aloud as he went on addressing all to Benaiah.

"Maybe everything's got its destiny. Not that every step's cut in concrete on into the distance. Theya's what you might call leeway—f'what you will. Take Sugarloaf. All white. It happened, so we got take it into account. But he's not just some albino fluke o'nature *the end*. He's an albino buck born to Posey on Jaspa Mountain in Gott'im Maine with friends by the name of Benaiah, Balda, grandmother, etc..... take into account that he's born in a world that wants to fix him in Time by claiming a li'l of his glory, to show it off a bit. ...Stuff and mount him to make their own li'l lives seem more colorful. But there's us, the others that want to see him run free—in beauty. Maybe t'nevah get a glimpse of him again. ...Or, maybe see him once in a while high on a ridge, pure white and crowned with a mighty rack. It's all this he was born into."

Ben was listening hard, snared in the complexity of Sugarloaf's life.

Balder continued. "We're scared to have Sugarloaf end up dead, stuffed, others gawking at'em, shaming his glory, stealing his life. Because we love him."

His gaze upon Balder, Ben nodded.

"His maker might've felt the same when making Sugarloaf. Maybe feels like that about everything made and while planning what to make.

"Maybe They was sitting at the kitchen table talking, the Maker and His Friend. All manner of creation flows off them during the conversation: spiders, worms, lilies, clouds, peas, nuthatches, chickadees, bumblebees, red foxes, ravens, voles, asteroids, planets, suns and some of that gaudy stuff like palm trees, frangipani, scarlet macaws'n crocodiles.

"He's saying, We'll give the people free will so they can decide what they'll do. We don't want to make puppets, do we?

"She says, but if we give'em free will, it means letting them do what they want in creation in accordance with its laws. And we could give them Time to be builders on it with us.

"He's glad She says this. So He says, They can learn about us that way.... Things like what kind of spirit to have when they go get their food.

"But then one of'em says, That means designing, creating it in beauty and just handing it over. What if they in't trustworthy? Should we just give'em a white deer'n let them shoot it, stuff it'n stare at it? Let that neat deer get all moth-eaten and dusty?

" 'N the other one comes back with something and they go on like this, back-and-fourth polite like, f'the equivalent of one trillion years or so. At some point during the conversation, the Maker has a … a small… — takes from his pocket a hard something in His hand. May be like a marble. Sometimes he rubs it gently with two thumbs, thinking strong and tender thoughts about the coming creation. Then it grows a bit."

Balder looks over at Benaiah to see if he's still with him.

"One day His son coming, stops by and says, Ma'am, Sir, you still talking about that?

"Whole lot'o nodding, What do *you* think?

"Considering, There's *something*... but let me think it ovah a while, and the son goes his way to a favorite thinking place, some rock overlooking the water somewhere, or a big rock in the woods, comes back a few thousands years later, saying, What you need's someone go down theya and mumble around with 'em, show'em we're heah. Y'caunt just get a guitar'n start with a cool riff unless someone shows you how and where to put your fingers. Waya's the inspiration? You show me how to respect creation'n I'll go down with'em.

"So they all agree'n off he goes, comes down—out Mary's womb in Bethlehem.... Kinda like Sugarloaf come out of Posey on Jaspa Mountain."

Balder scraped excess mustard from the knife back into the jar. He looked over at Ben, having stopped and started on the sandwiches several times. "You knew they mounted Him on the cross—? Good Friday, Easter and all. But that's waya the destiny comes in. Where Sugarloaf's and all our destinies come in. Ben, someday I might walk into the lobby at Jaspa Mountain Lodge'n see our white deer mounted theya. But. He'll be gone. And I'll just be looking at his fine clothes."

Shaking his head, Balder stacked the sandwiches on the plate. "That don't mean I won't be sad. I'd be awful sad to see him standin' theya.

Maybe that's his Maker, showing us how it feels."

Balder looked at the boy. "You believe that story, Ben?"

Slowly Benaiah nodded. His eyes had been looking far away, but now they looked up at Balder. The boy nodded again, saying softly, "I do."

Balder grinned. "I was hoping."

He pushed the sandwiches toward Benaiah and went to the door, saying, "Gut to get your brother." His hand on the screen door, he turned. "By the way, Mutha might just have something to say about that deer stand of yours being on this side of the mountain." He thought a moment. "She's probably too shy to say it, though. I hunt in townships north of here. You can come with me this year—if you want."

He pushed through the screen door, letting it slam behind. Ben saw him disappear into the glare.

Greenhouse Gott'im

Dear Editor,

Following our joyous encounter with Gottheim's Jasper Mary Day, we decided to search out the sights of her life for ourselves. Imagine our horror upon discovering that awful tire dump at the site where her treasure is supposed to be hidden. This immense and hideous hoard is kept behind a wide strip of trees, but does that matter when millions of dangerous old tires are piled up behind it in monstrous black mountains? How this has been allowed in our beautiful little Township of Quaker, and sanctioned by the DEP, is beyond me. You've written about greenhouse gas in your editorials, well, what do they suppose will happen to the air if those piles catch fire? Also, imagine the groundwater, our precious well water, being contaminated with oil from a meltdown there.

Why, may I ask, is Ceylon Segar permitted—nay, *encouraged*—in this outrageous misuse of the property by the very department supposed to be protecting the environment? We appeal to the authorities (both publicly in this letter and in a copy to their offices) *to think*! This part of the state is less and less the paradise we supposed on moving here. It's enough to turn us into rabid environmentalists! Make no mistake, Mr. and Ms. Legislator. We shall sue if anything happens to those tires!

Jamie and Frederick Sludlinger
Quaker Plantation

Dear Editor,

People in Gottheim have known me all my life—my relatives, neighbors and friends. They know the kind of man I am, really. A man who helped raise money for the Knights of Christos Christmas fund. I donated labor and materials to help rebuild the burned-out places of my fellow townsmen when their own houses caught fire. I served on your boards and committees, volunteering many hours to help keep our town viable. Working together in these various organizations and activities, we joked and laughed, told stories of town life, and just plain knew each other as you can't help doing in a place like Gottheim.

It was a terrible verdict, taking away my name and freedom over something I am innocent of. It was not premeditated murder that put my wife Albinia under concrete in the Pine Hill condominiums. Everyone knows that Albinia and I had a good enough relationship. We did have a passionate relationship, but she would not want to see me sitting here in Thomaston for what happened between us that awful night. I know this beyond doubt, and am asking you to consider the situation in its proper perspective. You know there's no real murder in my heart, just as Albinia knows it there where she is in heaven. I am certain she has forgiven me, just as she always did.

Yes, her death was terrible, but understand. Domestic violence is not the same as violence between strangers. We are, were, flesh and blood people no different than any couple. No different than any of you. And with strong personalities such as ours, there's bound to be passion enter into what would have been regular arguments and disagreements. But you can't make that the same as violence between people who don't know each other, aren't married and so forth. You all know I loved Albinia and would take back what happened, if I only could. It was an accident. I was scared and so did what I shouldn't, namely the concrete. A mistake and I'm sorry. I should have called the police immediately.

God knows my heart and that I am now a born-again Christian, forgiven by God but in need of forgiveness by my neighbors. Please folks. You know me. Have worked with me, eaten with me, had good times together. Let me hear from you in my hour of need. Look into your own hearts and see if you can recognize me and Albinia there in your own relationships. She wouldn't want you to turn your backs on me.

Ithiel Whitman
[State Prison]

Dear Editor,

This is just to thank the people of Gottheim for the neighborly assistance in the crisis we have with Uncle Cyrus Brook in Jericho this summer. We're grateful for the gift of water from Hutchins Pond since the brook all but dried up this month. Seeing the water truck pull up at the town office loaded with your good clean water (which we can't get even though we're on the Arossagunticook River) really lifted our spirits here. The folks outside Jericho Village proper were all set—that is, the ones whose wells didn't dry up. The rest of us are glad to see water again.

We might even have to postpone the opening of school because we can't support the needs of the building till we get water again. The hydrologist from the US Geological Survey has blamed the water failure on last winter and spring when we didn't get the necessary rain and snow amounts to keep aquifers up where they need to be this time of year. The unusually dry weather has near dried up Uncle Cyrus at its sources, at least till we get good rain. Since the middle of July we've had only 0.15 in. when normal for the same period would be 0.60. But it's been a year or two since anything was normal, and we're hurting now.

We've never seen it this low. Just hope and pray the good Lord knows what this is all about and see we get our rain this fall, if not sooner. And the people all said amen.

Alfred Tuttle, selectman
Town of Jericho

"Trout's hurting," said Hannibal Poulin to Pete Prince and Balder Simon at lunch. "Layin'low in pools where they ah easy pickings fah raccoon, mink, crittas like that.... In't enough water to float a frog, some places."

They were up on deck outside the new co-generating conveyor building, above Arossagunticook River, overlooking on either side the twin towns of Guildford and Spain. Their hardhats were off and the stinky breeze blew on them, carrying off sweat from their paper mill labor. The steam of papermaking poured off, blowing down valley between the two towns. High overhead thin smoke, from a combination of bark and chipped tires, burned off into the atmosphere high above the houses and businesses. The scrubbers would have eliminated the smoke entirely, but there were bugs in the system just now.

"In't but half of it though?" agreed Simon. "What's spawning gont be like come fall? Fishing'll be down two years. Look't that water down theya. Evah seen it s'low?"

Looking down from five stories where they could see lavender brown shallows beneath the scuzzy surface, Hannibal Poulin shook his dark head. He had a beard and it waggled as he talked. "Nevah. They said this watershed's worst hit in the state."

"We usually get less rain in the mountains, but you'd think snow melt'd make up for it." Simon said this and took a bite of his liverwurst sandwich. "Not this year."

"The mill keeps it low on purpose, does it?" asked Pete Prince. An apprentice millwright to papermaking, he was new in the state as well.

Poulin answered, "They prac'ly own the water. Got to balance the amount available with what's needed for waste treatment'n storage. They like to have four months worth stored to get through wintah."

Prince took a swallow of Coke and wondered aloud about the number of squirrels on the road. "Keep hitting those things. Drive along the highway and suddenly, *thunk crunch*, there's another dead one in the rearview mirror." His face was ravaged, but there was humor in it and widely spaced light eyes, greenish. He was a likable guy with a Midwestern accent. Something familiar about him Balder thought, as the man continued. "You're driving, see one coming, try to brake, but the damn thing can't make up its li'l pea-sized mind whether it's coming or going, crossing or not crossing. But you're doing 55 with one of those honking huge logging trucks on your bumper. *Thunk crunch*, another smashed squirrel. They go like that all year?"

Simon grinned. "Usually see a lot o'that in the spring, early summer. Theya young squirrels don't know no better. Theya was a bumper crop'o acorns'n beech nuts built up the population last year. Now, with the drought there's not much fah them to feed on. Last spring theya was a record litter count. Guess they feasted'emselves to the brink of famine." He grinned again.

"Fire danger's worst thing," said Poulin. He had opened a carton of milk and, after a swallow, blotted his mustache on his grimy shoulder. "Color's gont be off this year. Maybe it'll keep the leaf peepers off the road though. Those buses is worse'n pulp trucks any day. Tour bus drivers just don't know how t'drive two lane mountain roads. Saw one almost run off the highway last year when he wasn't expecting that passing lane to end."

Prince raised a skeptical eyebrow. "I dunno. Those trucks look like they carry a whole damn forest full of tree trunks. They call 'em pulp trucks: you get a load dropped on you in one of those curves—you're mashed to pulp. *Thunk crunch*."

Simon grinned. "Where you from? The desert? Cleveland?"

"In fact," he answered, smiling, "I lived both places, one time or another."

"My wife's name is Twitchell. Our kids are under her name 'cause it's a common-law marriage."

Peter Prince was sitting across from an alcohol abuse counselor in the large grubby room of a house-shop on Main Street in Jericho. He had been in the mountains only a short time, and this was his first real friendship. He had met Hermann Gottesman at an AA meeting two weeks ago. Hermann was a vast, powerfully built fat man, balding, with a ponytail and a surprisingly tiny voice. In aiding his fellow alcoholics Gottesman found a meaningful outlet for his somewhat desperate passion.

He ran a cafe in Jericho, downriver from Spain, an oddity attracting disaffected high school students, kids seemingly uninterested in cars, sports, dates and clothes, with a bent toward self-expression philosophy books art or other weirdness. Gottesman was adamant about keeping out the drugs, even cigarettes for the underage, but he provided an otherwise free atmosphere where kids could talk and drink sodas or coffee and play games like chess and Scrabble, but also pool and ping-pong. Over in the corner were Pacman and Atari for the electronically inclined.

It was 10 a.m. and the two men sat across from one another on dilapidated couches in the midnight blue *Kids Cafe*. The door was open and a beam of sunlight fell into the dark interior, full of dust motes and smoke. There was also dingy light from the front and side windows. Peter Prince was referring to the vast void left in Chrischana's wake when she ran from Phoenix with the boys; leaving him alone with the strange idea that she no longer believed him sincere in his repentances: "Sometimes I can't blame her, and sometimes I hate her for leaving." He exhaled, staring up at a smoke ring slowly rising to disband. He took another drag on his cigarette, saying, "After she left I'd binge, and hate her. Before she left, I'd binge... and then hurt her. Hell, Hermann, why do I have to say these things? All this goddamn honesty stuff.... Yeah, I figured I could handle it and my hurtin'her days were over.... but then I think, Wait, I said all this before, felt all this before... and it always came back again. The uncontrollable rage. So, I admit it to myself. Shouldn't that be enough to make it go away?— confess your sins and all that?"

"Should it?" prompted Gottesman, solemn-eyed and bespeckled. He had a degree in psychology and another in philosophy from an early stage of his career to the bottom and back again. Since then there'd been training in substance abuse counseling. Now he was a committed 12-stepper who had salvaged existence with the aid of Higher Power. After his last detox seven years ago, in New Hampshire, he had come to Jericho following a detour home to New York, found this boarded-up derelict storefront, rented and equipped it with used appliances and furniture, put in a bed for himself in a back room. On top of one of the many bookcases lining his wall sat a large piece of pegmatite, stone blocky with huge grains of mica, feldspar and quartz. He called it his Higher Power, not out of superstition, but as a symbol of what was above him that he could not see. Desolation in his formative years had blocked such beliefs from him. Hermann Gottesman was immensely strong. It had taken a long acquaintance with alcohol to convince him of something stronger. His habit was stronger than himself, taking everything from him. Now, every day, he had to rediscover that there was Something stronger than either of them.

Peter opened a fresh pack of Viceroys and lit one. He exhaled and said, "Before I found out... while I was finding out that college wasn't for me, I was assigned a short story I couldn't get out of my head. Can't remember the author but the title sticks t'you like a burr. 'A Good Man Is Hard to Find.' Story about this 'good Christian woman' who called strangers 'good men'—even one who was about to kill her. Her own son she condemned to death without a thought. That's me, that's my mother." He said it with bitterness.

Hermann nodded. "Flannery O'Connor's story. Acclaimed, but has its flaws. Parts of it are unconvincing. Other parts are quite chilling." He took a swallow from the liter bottle of Coke that he kept by his side. Now, looking at the haggard but handsome face of Peter Prince, he understood that the green-eyed man was in line for destruction... if he left the course he had set in stopping at Alcoholics Anonymous. If he turned around in the middle of this road, he would be destroyed.

"Hermann. I have an awful twisted—twisted feeling sometimes. Like I feel myself slipping... mentally. A godawful rage. I think something evil is just around the corner, waitin' to nab me—sometime. Other times—it completely slips my mind. Then I think, That evil guy's not me. He's gone forever.... And I feel like, Hell, I'm here in Maine—I'll just drive over to Gott'im and drop in on Chrischana'n the boys. Just for a visit." His gaze had been drifting around the room, slipping now from Hermann's almost tonsured-looking balding head into his eyes. "What do you think about that, Hermann?"

Hermann's answer was prompt. "I think it's a very good sign that you're willing to ask someone else what they think. You're beginning to get that you don't know everything about this disease. That maybe you do need counseling." And he thought, without saying, You're still flip-flopping back and forth between remembering and forgetting this fact. He had seen Peter Prince's bull-necked bravado more than once. The nature of self is glib, making self-understanding a very slippery business. You wanted to lecture, tell clients what's what, but it wouldn't communicate.

Prince ran his restive fingers over the frayed arm of the couch. Humbly he said, "And your counsel would be?..."

"To wait. Wouldn't you expect a great deal of emotion being mixed into a meeting like that? That it wouldn't really be just a casual undertaking?"

"Nothing casual about it," he admitted. "It'd be a big thing for all of us. Like going through the de-barker over at the mill." He formed an o with his lips, breathing out another smoke ring. It rose, wafting toward the light of the open door.

(Editorial): We don't usually comment on the national, international, or planetary in this space. We try to stick to the hometown issues, keep things simple. What kind of place is Gottheim? How can we help make it better? Should we keep Front Street as our Main Street in Gottheim, or should we allow a mini mall on the highway, complete with post office, to replace it? Do we want directional signs uniform and small, clustered, or strung out along the highway. Do we mount a campaign to keep chain stores out, or should we encourage their presence to provide the nearby, lower-priced alternative? Are we maintaining perspective and balance on the local environmental and economic fronts? These and other subjects most often occupy this space. This town and its neighbors are properly our sphere of concern, and we look to our community if we are to be happy and well, raise our children safely.

Yet today we want to shift the focus outward, wider; perhaps look down upon little Gottheim from a distance, and then look out around us to the atmosphere surrounding our tiny community. We may have to blink back tears caused by the smoke of spot fires. Up here we can plainly see that Gottheim is tied to every place else by what is normally invisible, namely the atmosphere; or in other terms the climate, which in times past was beyond our human intervention. Mark Twain's famous quote notwithstanding, it is time we started doing something about the weather.

Us, do something about the weather? What can we do about the weather? Maybe you're wondering, even saying aloud, the crazy editor wants us to do something about the weather. Is it bad enough that wells are dry and fires burn and crops wither before reaching fruition? We can do nothing about these things, yet the editor of *The Village Voter* wants us to.

But the editor is not crazy enough. Considering the equally ruinous deluge of two years ago, we must get a lot crazier and suggest that this wildly inconsistent weather is the result of the greenhouse effect. El Niño and the North Atlantic oscillation are held to cause the fluctuations, and studies are of course ongoing. But there is evidence showing that these have been dramatically influenced by global warming. The Legislature as a whole is unwilling to mandate the curtailment of emissions until findings are definitive.

In this space, we put it to you that crazy is our current course of doing nothing "until findings are definitive." There will be no definitive findings until global warming effectively strangles our planet. The president and legislators do little, under pressure of industry lobbyists who obfuscate the issue with talk of definitive findings.

Gottheimites, there is something you can do about the weather. You can write your congressional representatives. You can trouble the sleep of senators Cohen and Mitchell, of representatives McKernan and Snowe. Send them scrapings from the bottom of your wells, ash from the burnt-over sides of Twitchell Mountain. You can ask them to represent Gottheim and the State of Maine instead of the suits walking the corridors of our national capitol. Let the gentle persons from Maine understand that we here in Gottheim want water. We want rain. And we expect them to do something about it. J.W.N.

Dear Editor,

I won't ask why you printed that letter from Ithiel Whitman, proclaiming his innocence of murder by strangulation of my twin. You would only answer that the First Amendment guarantees every view an expression, that as editor you have an obligation to present them, no matter how reprehensible, so people can make up their own minds. That's why I fully expect my page space after Ithiel Whitman's sickening self-pitying plea.

Your editor's note at the end of these letters states that you have the right to refrain printing any letter. In other words, you personally chose to display his fabrication, that slandering use of Albinia Bisbee's name—someone who couldn't come up from the grave or down from the skies to protest these lies.

He justified battering because the evil in him makes him think everyone is alike. My sister was a good person, but the evil in Ithiel always accused her and provided an excuse for the beatings.

So, Ithiel, you say we are all exactly alike. We all work raising funds for worthy causes, we all help put on Jasper Mary Day each year. All the people in Gottheim meet, eat, and have fun together. And we all quarrel with our spouses and lose our tempers. We all abuse each other, strangle each other, and entomb one another in concrete.

If it says so in The Voter it must be true. Isn't that so, Mr. Editor?

Elvegy Bisbee Blanchard

"Look at these thins."

Cindabilla is provoked. She is walking with Daniel through her withering pumpkin patch, kicking at the puny specimens with the ball of her bare foot. One of the little things bounces on the concrete-like earth, its withered stem and dry leaves rattling.

"Clouds is comin'but d'you think it'd rain?—maybe that light stuff fell yestadee, pretend rain. Enough to make you mad's all. Theya irrigating like mad round heah, trying to keep evah thing fom drying on the stalk. But if your brook's dried out like that one back of the farm—kiss it g'bye!" She gestures beyond the corner of the barn where her pumpkins lie ruined. "Look at those leaves out theya. Evah seen leaves go fom green t'brown before the end of August?"

Daniel says little, walking beside her. Tomorrow's return to school occupies his thoughts. He is ready for it, even eager to walk the concrete floor hard beneath its waxed linoleum; glad of the straight ranks of metal lockers, all identical, uniform. The heat and laxity of summer, along with its contrasting discipline of work, part-time work at *The Voter* and labor on the Simon house, bores him. He is hungry for assignments and the challenges of the classroom, the glittering eye of a Mrs. Medford and the dry stare of a Mr. Clough. This year he is going to work for them; this year go straight ahead without looking aside at his classmates' dubbing around. That's what they call it. He calls it goofing off. Last spring they tormented him. But hazing's over now. He has earned enough respect to get by. He will be expected to goof off with them, make a game. No being goody-goody, no actual studying, no being nice to teachers. Well surprise, you guys: goody-goody is caving to your pressure: Be good by being bad.

He could spare himself the trouble by hanging with the honor society types, the kids who know they're college-bound. But their's isn't the company he enjoys. It's like they've been dunked in bleach, squeaky clean. Give me the real kids, Cindabilla.

You can study—invisibly. He did in Phoenix and had friends. Hit the books and mind your own business; have fun at lunch, after class, but quietly learn. I can do it here. Don't volunteer anything. Won't raise my hand in class, ever. His dialogue with teachers will be in the essays, reports. They won't get him to speak in class and he'll see the disappointment on their faces, but they'll get used to it. Daniel Twitchell goes quietly about what he wants, balancing the forces in his life.

Life outside learning is not so simple; not at home with mother and his brothers, especially when Petey was there. It's not simple with Cindabilla anymore, either. He has been trying to get her to go back to school with him. She wants nothing to do with Hazel Newell High. She's got to see that the only way out of her life is education. He tries hard, but can't seem to put it convincingly. To Cindabilla, high school in Gottheim, Maine is a dead end.

Plaintively, still kicking pumpkins, she says, "Daniel, sellin'these thins was gont pay f'my education! Now I got no money t'get out of Gott'im."

He says nothing at first. Daniel is relieved that the pumpkins aren't working out. He has seen enough of urban life and is aware of its dangers. But maybe lack of money won't stop her. Cindabilla is determined to leave.

He watches her fidget, pick at the vines with her toes.

"Can we go down by the road? I'm supposed t'meet Mother...."

Together they approach the overhanging branches of the big maple where, a couple months ago, a great horned owl fell out of the branches, agonizing. Thinking of this, he says, " If you leave, what's it gont be like fah Babette 'n Gram? Uncle Ferddy might stot giving them a hard time again." It is the only argument he can think of at the moment.

Cindabilla shakes her emphatic head, her ginger ponytail waggling. "Daniel, I'm not about to cut my education in order to babysit grown-ups. Why don't Babs get wise? I told hah, when I'm gone, Ferddy'll stot up again. Caunt prove I shot 'em, but he knows. He won't hurt Gram. Babette's only one he'll hurt—unless he kills her'n gets someone afta." She thought a moment. "He might hurt his kids if he had any. Fucking bully. Shit f'brains. Thinks he *owns* Babs, like she's his truck, o'one of his guns. Like suddenly, coz she's close, a woman caunt be her own, control her own looks, thoughts, anathin. Like, if she does, it takes something away from him. She's got do evah thing his way or she's a traitor. I tell hah get out of Gott'im before he kills you. She shakes her head, says I don't know Ferddy, that he'd track her down. I said Ferddy don't know nothing but Gott'im and he's scared to go look for hah. But she looks away, says she's scared, too. I'm telling you, Daniel, I gut get out of here fah I get like that!"

They are out on the road where the rounded old heads of mountains are shouldering, protectively. Daniel looks toward their darkly crowned summits. The sky here is smaller than it was out around Phoenix where the mountains stood distantly. Weeks have passed since he seriously thought of Petey intruding here. Most times he thinks that in Gottheim the Twitchell family is hidden, secure. That the world lies out that way, far beyond the river-split hills. That Petey would never come to such a remote place. But Daniel recognizes Cinda's description of Ferddy in Petey Prince and wonders, Is there a difference between them?

Ferddy seems permanently lost in the bottle, submerged. Dad has some goodness about him.... But it seems like he's going to stay out of the bottle, then sooner or later falls back in.... Ferddy has Gottheim to anchor him, tie him to his true identity. Without Gottheim, he'd lose what definition he has.... Petey can go anywhere because he has no place to be out of, no place he cares about. There's no Gottheim for him, like Mother has. Now, Cindabilla has brought it all back, how Pete mocked Mother's memories of Gottheim.... He looks over at the girl.

Under this scrutiny she turns to face him, exclaiming, "*What*?!"

"... Nothing...." Struggling inwardly and unable to confess, he shrugs. *I don't want you to go*. Maybe I should say it.... But she already knows.... Made enough arguments, objections. She knows I don't want her to leave Gottheim.

Dear Mr. Fay,

You raised enough dust into the atmosphere, into our homes, nevertheless, we wish to extend congratulations upon the Jasper Mountain Resort Association's recent construction project. We regret, of course, that the design of the building is stylized, but at least the materials appear somewhat authentic.

As you know, most of us on the Planning Board are members of the Architectural Heritage Foundation, so it is natural that we object to aspects of your latest proposal for the so-called Gottheim Inn. The design is out of proportion and construction materials don't meet the standards we agreed upon. Stucco? Think, Mr. Fay, think! This is a New England village, not a Floridian mall. You say you have spent a lot of money to design authentic structures? Well, you're going to have to spend more—to make them clapboard or *brick*. We've yet to discover an original Yankee village containing so much as a smokehouse made of stucco.

Why is there so much difficulty executing your promises? Count your skier visits, sir, and see if you can't translate them into the brick you spoke of.

Sincerely yours,
Rhetta Marie Bearce

Blindness takes time. It's what Elda surmises while hiking around the crest of Mason Mountain on a September afternoon. She is trying to follow a deer trail. The dark boughs of hemlock brush her thin shoulders, arms and hips, as she passes. It is the soft caress of woodland upon one of its caretakers. Her backpack empty except for the litter of lunch, Elda is on one of her rambles, having no other purpose in mind for this drab Sunday afternoon. Her old hands are stained purple with late blackberries. Whatever she finds unlooked for on her way is welcome, especially as a distraction to thought. She has been tracking changes in her vision. Such as a difficulty in reading signs and seeing detail. There are spots everywhere— exactly where she wants most to see. Yet the great leap into darkness is.... It doesn't happen.

Once blindness started happening she gathered courage and read about its various forms—an emotionally difficult task in itself.... Maybe if she got a much stronger pair of reading glasses from Brown's Variety? Biting her lip and frowning she considers that the optometrist in Guildford might be able to help her... if she could stand to sit in some chair in a darkened room and be pronounced upon.

It must be macular degeneration and not cataracts. That would fit.... There are two kinds, one especially terrifying, escalating to complete blindness.

... There would be no cure, for either form.... the thought of cold instruments acting upon the delicate mechanisms of sight was impossible to contemplate anyway. She would prefer prayer to such professionalism. A woman like Elda Simon might have to be led out blind, leaning on a stick.

Downslope a woodpecker hammers in treetops. Earnestly she searches for it down through the trees.... Something's different. Something's changed since I came here with the owl in spring.

A raucous cry overhead takes her attention. Wings spread, dark pinions flaring, a raven swooped toward the woodpecker, driving it away through treetops. Through tiny new clearings she sees it come and go.

That's it. Loggers have been here since the Twitchells vacated.... but not with wholesale cutting. As she comes down, she sees two neat plots, widely spaced with lanes leading away. More?... A network signifying development.

Taking one of the lanes and coming to a yet wider lane, Elda follows through trees, gloom upon her. Here! In the heart of history! The old mill and abandoned settlement of the century past, disturbed in its profound rest. Some would be glad to see it happen, a new kind of life—not Elda. She mourns.... All gone in a blind evanescence of *dollars*! Mason's Mills, gone from Gottheim—never to be heard from again! She is shaking. Oh, what is happening to me? Never let these things bother me. Not like this.

A gleam through trees? She turns slightly, trying to see with a still unpracticed peripheral vision. A car, parked... people!...

Too late for Elda to make a retreat, the young couple approaches, one waving. Too late to slip back into the trees, be the furtive creature she is at heart. Oh, for the puckerbrush now.

"Mrs. Simon, Mrs. Simon!" A woman's voice calls, glad and light. They come near, and she sees their blond heads. A man and woman in their Sunday best. It dawns on Elda that this is Gloria Fay, the young woman Balder was seeing—was it a month ago, two? Who's the young man—her new boyfriend?

"Hello, deah," says Elda. "Good day fah walkin'."

She bucks herself up for the encounter. She can act as normal as anyone.... If you just keep it up for a minute or two, you can escape without much awkwardness. Then you get the peace of your own thoughts again... no matter the quality of those thoughts. They are preferable to small talk with strangers. She sends out her shy smile.

Gloria had seen the figure with its bandanna, recognizing the mother of Balder. So much time had passed since that evening when she saw the white deer, and Mrs. Simon with the gun. Too much time... since she had seen Balder. *Balder, oh Balder.*

Gloria hurried toward her, leaving James Fay to catch up at his own pace. But not before urging him in an undertone to be friendly.

"Of course," he had returned, but in an afterthought adding (jocularly), " Sis, I need a bit of befriending myself—for Theodora, you know. You can warm up a little. She's been upset lately, nervous. I don't know why"

"Well okay, since you're so sure about her."

Gloria introduced them and the three spoke of the weather, quickly exhausting the subject. With her usual excuse about the animals' feeding time, the older woman began to move on.

Gloria blurted, "How's Balder, Mrs. Simon? We've both been so busy—haven't talked much lately. I heard he was working on the house?..."

71

Clutching her purse in one hand, she ran two fingers beneath strands of hair blowing across her eyes in the slight dry breeze.

" 'Bout got the new roofs on the old parts, I guess. Finishing up shingling now. Get it good'n snug fah wintah."

"Yes!" said James Fay. "Roof on by winter. I'd like to get our roof on myself. Right here, in fact. Mason's Mills is going to be a unique subdivision. One with a friendliness families rarely find today." He spoke quietly, with a childlike enthusiasm. "We're going to maintain the integrity of history here. Might even dam the stream again, re-create the old mill pond. The children can skate on it in winter. Sis and I are each going to build here, as well." He smiled at Gloria. "That is, if I can talk her into it."

His words warmed, and he began speaking of his philosophy of development. "It's the ideal that we've always known—as New Englanders. (We're from Boston, you know.)"

He gestured. "We plan a small common here, as in a village. Everyone will own a small lot and hold adjoining lands in common. It will be private yet maintain the sense of community so essential to families. Hiking, skiing, skating, horseback riding, they'll have it all...."

Mrs. Simon's gaze had already glanced away. Still smiling politely, she started edging past.

Embarrassed, Gloria interjected with a question about the Simon house.

"I'spect you just betta come see fah y'self, deah. He'd be glad t'see you coming, mentions you fom time t'time." There, thought Elda. Must be what's on that girl's mind. I can go now.

She smiled, slipping away, leaving brother and sister to their new plots. Elda felt sure she would not enjoy the ground around one of her favorite haunts again. Maybe... maybe the young man's plans weren't really—how could she judge it outside her lights? But where was the historical integrity she longed for? Was there benefit where benefit should be? Who were these families going to live here, not a Mason, that's sure. Though their ancestors once built the mill, they could no longer afford to live in such new places. But there. Life had to continue. Young families, whoever they were, had to live someplace. And Gottheim was a very good place to live.

But Elda's thoughts on the subject were nebulous and unsure if deeply unconsciously felt. No bitter thought long inhabited or motivated her. Simply, Elda Simon would be gone from Mason's Mills. No one would know of this natural withdrawing, this leaving to others what their from-away dollars had, in legal tender, purchased.

Not all Gottheim's citizens will look at it this way. Everyone has a point of view. When Eloise Patadoe, artist and homesteader, reads about the new Mason's Mills in *The Voter*, she will fume, maybe even plot with innocent good humor. She'll comment that James Fay will put a bronze plaque there, fixed to the old granite, commemorating the old way of life, nostalgic. Children will climb on the monument, pretending to be Indians and pioneers—no. More probably earthlings and aliens. Whatever it is kids will be playing in the late '80s and '90s. In the year 2001.

Leaving Gottheim

Sunlight kindled in the mountains as two teenagers crept along the train's length. There were cars loaded with logs, with finished lumber or with wood products—all bound for away. There were tankers and trailer-loaded cars, and empty freight cars, from points north. Early on a school day, and no one else around, a boy's voice went on earnestly, hurried and hushed, pleading with the girl to change her mind. Asking her to remain in Gottheim.

Dressed in denim from head to foot   blue denim, jacket and jeans, black canvas sneakers—all brand new, Cindabilla Sessions crept along the siding, Daniel tagging after. She slipped down off the gravel into the wildflowers and weeds to wait. On her back was a new nylon book bag, also bought new for school by her grandmother. But the pack contained a change of clothes, toiletries, sandwiches, and a small piece of feldspar, studded with dark garnets—a memento from the old quarry on Uncle Tom's Mountain.

Daniel Twitchell wore blue jeans and the leather jacket Peter Prince had given him last Christmas. His ball cap shadowed his Native American gaze. He plopped down beside the girl, one hand gesticulating while the other held biology and geography texts to the his chest. Gone is the habitual guarded or solemn look of him, replaced by a face puckered with concern. And still his quiet voice pleaded.

Now she was counting out the contents of her pockets, and he began emptying his own, still protesting. He blamed himself for not bringing some savings to bequeath her. If she went through with this scary plan to arrive cost-free in Boston, she would be needing every cent. But Daniel had not been thinking of anything remotely like this when he climbed out of bed earlier. He should have known something was up when she arrived happily and unexpectedly beneath his window at Simons's Ledge. It was well before the school bus was due to lumber up the hill. If only he had not allowed himself to be hurried away from the house. He might have brought food *and* money.

"It's betta this way, Daniel," she was saying. Goldenrod dust got into her nostrils and she sneezed. "I'm not stayin'heah, and theya's no way to Boston without that punkin money."

His brown eyebrows shot up. "I'll *give* you the money to take the bus to Boston. We... we could get Eli Simms to take you to the station in Portland—or Berlin. Simple'n safe!"

"Daow! I'm going this way, Daniel. Now shut fuckin'*up*!"

Daniel sank back, silent and disturbed among the asters and goldenrod and pearly everlastings.

But Cindabilla was on her knees, nervy and alert for the movement of the great empty boxcar above them. The train must be moving in order to preclude some official's keeping it back—should she be discovered climbing aboard. She had studied these movements over the past weeks, aware that the engine ahead was set to pull the train off the siding for the haul down to the eastern seaboard.

Now, with a piercing screech and jerk forward, a clanking and rumbling passing from one car to the next, the train above began to move. Heart thumping, Cindabilla leapt up. Her backpack bouncing, she scrambled onto the rail bed and began running alongside the cavernous boxcar, trying not to trip on the ties. Grasping the track of the car's great sliding door, she hauled ass, flinging herself up onto the gritty floor. Clambering to her feet she turned to wave but saw Daniel running below. His eyes were wide and glistening as he grabbed hold. Hauling with his free arm and clutching with a leg, he gained a hold. Cinda pulled on his belt loop and Daniel rolled across the filthy indented floor, still clutching his school books in his arm. He lay there panting, spread-eagle and groaning, feeling the jerk and roll of the train. He turned his head and saw the distant backs of houses sliding past.

She stood over him now and he rolled back his eyes, looking up into Cindabilla's gaze. She did a bit of footwork to keep her balance, grinning down on him in wicked glee. "Going t'Boston, Daniel," she said. "Fuckin'goin't'Boston with me."

In the Simon house they moved about like ghosts, quiet, yawning. In the bathroom upstairs, two boys leaned over the sink, brushing their teeth. Balder padded around downstairs, tucking in his flannel shirt, looking for his work boots, yawning and stretching one last time. He found the boots by the couch and sat down to put them on. Out the front windows he saw the colors of the sun still stoking in the east and trimming high leaves with new light. He went into the kitchen where Elda was heating oil in the iron skillet. It was their week to have the boys, get them up, fed, ready for school. They had to be down at the end of the lane before the school bus, alive with kids, lurched to a stop.

Balder opened the bread bin and took out a half loaf of wheat bread, went to the toaster on the sideboard and tossed in a couple slices. Mrs. Simon began cracking eggs into the crackling hot skillet. Her mind was on the wood mouse in a nest just under the sideboard cupboard. The tiny orphan might fit comfortably in a thimble, so small was the creature. Elda was in the midst of nursing it, and would rather be over there crooning it a tune... but first these had to be fed. Soon they would be out of here.

Balder took the steaming kettle off the back of the gas stove. Maxwell House instant was already in the bottom of his cup. He poured boiling water over it and the fresh coffee smell roused him. "Want some?"

"Got mine," she muttered, grabbing her cup from the back of the sideboard. "How's toast comin'?"

"Two more slices'll have it." He popped them in and went to call the boys. Nathan and Benaiah were already downstairs, but still sleepy and subdued. Nathan, Balder knew, would soon be bouncing around. He watched their bent backs where they rooted under the couch for sneakers.

Nathan was saying, "What's Dad look like, Ben'ah?"

"Stop asking me that, geek."

Balder tucked away the scrap of conversation for future consideration. "Waya's Daniel? Your brother's usually down first, now school's on."

"Still sleeping!" sang Nathan.

"Well go wake'em!" returned Balder, grinning. Nothing like a Nathan to get you moving in the morning.

"Yes Sir!" yelled Nathan, saluting. Like a deer up a slope, he took the stairs. Balder heard the boy issuing mock orders in a high-pitched voice, the sound of Daniel's door banging open. His grin widened. This family organism! It had almost as much movement as an active battlefield, and a lot less tension and grief. Place could use a few more critters, he thought. His mind went to Gloria. She had called him. At last.

He heard Nathan slamming around upstairs, but missed Daniel's answering comments. Nathan's squeaking accelerated, more doors banged. Then, suddenly, silence. Balder stood at the foot of the stairs. Nathan appeared at the top, his hair still tangled from sleep, bare toes curled around the lip of the top stair, socks dangling limply in either hand.

"Can't find'em," he said. "I looked in all the closets. Maybe he's hiding in that other part?" He gestured in the direction of the attached children's house.

"We called downt'Sessions. Cindabilla's gone, too. They'll probably turn up at school, but choo might want call theya later—find out f'sure."

Balder stood by the drainer of the dishwasher in the Farmingham Royal Tavern and Inn, talking to Chrischana. On seeing him come through the screen door, she had stopped work. Steam rose from the stainless steel washer as she stood drying her hands on a towel. Stepping back to glance at the ticking grandfather clock through the kitchen door, she said, "I'll call ovah theya in about 20 minutes. That should give 'em time t'get to homeroom." She mopped at her forehead with the dish towel. "Sorry you had t'come down heah for that, Balda. Late fah work in't choo?"

Balder grinned. "Got your Maine way o'speaking back, complete. Know that?"

She nodded. "Sometimes I lapse though."

"Well, look," he said. "I ought be apologizing to you. I was scared whole way down heah you'd want yank'em back from me. Guess you can't just tie kids up, chain them to the bedpost, huh? They got legs and can get away from you." Again he grinned.

She smiled a half smile. "I feel sorry fah you. You're just getting started. Can't see all that can go wrong yet." She grew grave and said thoughtfully, "The beard's getting longer. How long you gont let it grow? Till you get the hang of this father thing?—but you are doing a good job, Balder. Really." She could have reached out to touch that beard.

Unsettled, Balder sensed it. She understood about the beard without being told. Or, maybe Daniel did tell her, though he couldn't picture the boy saying so. How tempted he would have been by that touching gesture, even yesterday. But two things had happened to make him... set a distance between them. He damped down the grin and thanked her. Then he said, "Your names are all Twitchell.... was that always the case? Guess I nevah felt right asking Daniel this...."

She looked away. "Well Balder—his name was—is Prince." She looked back at him. *Be honest, not ashamed.* We... had that commitment but, no, we never did marry—legally. On the other hand, the law did consider us common-law married I guess."

"Uh huh. Well, like I said. I wondered."

He excused himself on account of work, said goodbye, stepped out the door and down the steps to his pickup. After getting a jumpstart off the Chevy before coming down here, he had left it outside idling because the battery was low. There were jumper cables under the seat for after work.

Someone in the parking lot at the mill would give him a jumpstart. Maybe Peter Prince.

It was something to think about on the way to work, anyway. That, and the fact that Chrischana would have to be told. Balder didn't think she knew yet. The man. The one who must have been cruel to her... causing her to flee back home. Here. If not in Gottheim then somewhere nearby.

Driving through the village he thought about the other thing. Gloria had called last night, inviting him to dinner... which he declined.... then turned around and invited her to supper. Supper at *Simons Ledge*, this week, his week with the boys. The silence at the other end of the line had been long and intense. That silence had troubled, refreshed, and intrigued him— in that order. Then she said yes. Glory was coming.

Out on the highway, Balder opened it up. Ahead, some tour buses trailed one another into a curve. One, two, three of them. Leaf peepers. And the foliage doesn't look that good, either. Lots of leaves—here and there—already gone. A pretty spotty picture for them. But the tours come anyway. Once they get those things booked in advance.... Jeepers creepers peepers! Glory's coming!

Cindabilla slides the lock shut with a click. She closes the commode inside the tiny compartment and sits down, her heart pattering. Now she gets to her knees on the toilet lid to look at herself cross-eyed in the mirror above the little stainless steel sink. Ballooning her smudged cheeks, she blows out a long breath. Cinda gives two squeaks and sinks down, sighing. But she stands again, turns on the tap and bends to drink thirstily. The train lurches, and she sits back, relieved.

Daniel should be holed up in the lavatory in the next car. He *had* to make it past the conductor. She smiles at the thought of serious Daniel hunched up on the flush. He's got enough time to think about it now. Probably kicking himself, smacking his forehead. Wondering why the fuck he hopped a freight with Cindabilla Sessions, bad girl from Gott'im. So exciting! She begins humming John Cougar's *Jack and Diane*, more excited than she has ever been. It's only beginning: *I'm going to New York City!*

Pulling away from the station, the train builds slowly toward the rhythm she has become accustomed to. It's smoother than the freight, much smoother. The hours they spent on that rattling old clunker. Seems like days. But we bypassed Boston, never stopped! New Haven, that was the surprise.

They had peered from the doors of the rusty old freight car out on the crumbling old cities and suburbs moving past. She was amazed by the vast clutter of buildings, highways, streets, rail lines, masses of slow or stopped cars; the unbelievable glut of wooden houses concrete steel brick glass. Houses jammed together, mile upon mile, hundreds of thousands of houses, millions? Where's earth? It's disappeared. How did these masses of tiny people come to live like this? No way you could give'em all a reverse nod. No way whatsoevah.

... But, there would be no need to say hi to everyone here like you did in Gottheim. No way they'd know who you were to get mad and say "stuck up." Maybe that's why people can rob murder strangers, just jump out of the crowd and... so easy. All faceless. Heard that word faceless, now I know what it means. All those people and all those houses and all those cities everywhere. At home people don't kill strangers, only people we know. See Daniel, she'll say, already my education's on.

She dusts the rust off her denims, dusts off her arms, shoulders, legs. Cindabilla takes off the jacket Gram bought for her, inspects, brushes off its back. This new outfit. I'm *dressed* for New York City. Dreamed of that place ever since Aunt Sally came back from West Germany and told of Greenwich Village, the lights of Times Square, Statue of Liberty, Empire State Building, World Trade Center, Grand Central Station....

She stands to wash the rust off her face and hands. It must be a gift that that dirty old freight car wasn't going to Boston after all. When it stopped, they climbed down, crossed double rows of tracks, came to an Amtrak station, climbed on this train for New York. The lavatory was her idea. "It's all worked out fah us, Daniel. All we got do is stay locked in till they call Penn Station or Grand Central, whichever comes first. Then we get off, no ticket necessary."

After the fruitless call to Hazel Newell High, Chrischana left the clean stacked dishes of Farmingham Royal Tavern and got into her old Bonneville 500. She fired it up and pulled out around parked tour buses to start looking for Daniel. First she drove out to Sessions to talk with Hannah, Cindabilla's grandmother. Babs and Ferddy were at work, one to the spool mill, the other to the town garage, but Hannah would be her best informant anyway.

"No, no, they in't heah," said the old woman, peering at Chrischana from behind a few greasy strays of gray hair. "Cindabilla was up fah light, though. Heard hah root round in the kitchen. Left awful early. Say they in't been t'class this morning? Well, I'll just saddle Jimmy'n rattle around the puckabrush, see what I find."

Chrischana drove back to the village, poked about the streets and lanes, parking lots. It looked like these two were up to something, darned if she knew what. It wasn't like Daniel to skip school, but he was close to Cindabilla whose name was synonymous with truant.

She drove out to Bearce's lightless convenience store. Young Wilbur Twombly was at the cash register, no one else around. "Seen Daniel Twitchell or Cindabilla Sessions in heah? The boy kinda dark, she's got a light ponytail?"

"Two kids missing fom the high school?" Wilbur, hardly more than a graduate himself, had almost dropped out once: He could read already and had planned on becoming a rock star. Yet he had persevered, randomly, and ended up with a summer school diploma, just a step or two behind his class. Today he was on at the store. Nights were gigs in the area.

Chrischana stared at his long acne-pocked face. "You heard this already?" She glanced up at the lit face of the clock above the counter. Almost ten.

He shrugged. "It's Gott'im, in't it? Haven't seen 'em. But if I do?— send 'em back to Hazel Newell good'n propah."

Robbie Robichaud stepped in, large and in workman green, ready for coffee in the cramped little store.

"Hi, Mr. Robichaud. You seen my Daniel'n Cindabilla Sessions, Hannah's granddaughter?"

"Whad they look like?" He grinned. "No, ain't seen 'em. Why— they skipping school?"

"At least," she said, trying not to let worry into it.

"Oh, they prob'ly went to work in the woods!" He grinned more and Chrischana smiled.

"Well, give Elda Simon a call if you heah anathin." She stepped out the door.

The tower clock was striking ten as she drove along Front Street again. Could be they're hiding out at the Cove—smoking cigarettes and dreaming big on something together. She started to turn the Bonneville around in the Foodliner parking lot. Asa Bartlett, the clockwinder, was coming out, one arm wrapped around a bag full of groceries. She leaned over, rolled down the passenger window and called out, "Seen my Daniel?"

He walked over and leaned in his dark red bespeckled head, the bag crackling against his sweater. "I heard they was missin'," he said, shaking his head. "Prob'ly playing hooky, s'all. *You* nevah skipped school, I spect. That Sessions girl—no wondah. You know her mother was high on drugs night she give birth t'Cindabilla. And they say that Etta's father himself was drunker'n a stone night *she* was born. Runs in the family!"

"Gut go now," snapped Chrischana turning her face away. She frowned out the windshield and Asa stood away. The woman drove off, muttering.

The big Bonneville 500 bumped along the dippy lane that led

toward the Cove. She rounded the curve of an elder thicket and a brown half moon shoreline came into view. There lay the sheen of Twitchell Pond. They had camped here early in the summer, when the water was still too cold for swimming. There was the tree, a great knobby white birch, ancient, massive and full. The spreading branches upheld its great dark green crown. Mostly, birches in the area were tall spindly things. But this one, with its many spreading limbs, had always reminded her of a tree goddess, one of those dryads or nymphs or whatever they were. Like a great she-being about to step away and wander waist deep into the water. Sleeping beneath her branches, they had heard rustling leaves, lapping water. They sheltered here after disaster at Deep Hole, when the walls of Abenaki Notch closed in on her.

The pilgrim Chrischana got out of the car and sat on a hewn log. It was a bench in cross-section, flat on top, and curved like the shoreline. An ancient seat for the rituals of generations of young Gottheimites, carved with the many initials of teenagers now grown up. And teenagers gone, too. Idly she wondered about them, tracing the old engravings with her finger. K.C., romantically tied to W.B. Did they grow old together, wither, lie in the same grave? Maybe the soil they became together was now part of that graveyard across the pond, Twitchell Cemetery. She looked across the glimmering expanse toward the opening in trees, where the brown lawn sloped to the shore. Have to grow old first, Daniel!

She shook her head. Skipping school. Daniel and Cindabilla were far from dead, but Chrischana herself was quietly inching up on it. She shook her head again. Dead already? It's only skipping school. Small's my power over my own mind. Daniel is holed up somewhere, safe, but this mind rattles off on extremes.

Where in the name of God *are you*? *Where*?! She crossed her arms, wearily bowed her head. Resting, sighing deeply, her brown braid hanging down, she closed her eyes and asked for something with words.

On the highway into Gottheim she saw Abner Chapman. He was walking the shoulder, his sun darkened face a pucker of grim concentration. She pulled over, got out, approached the man in his now faded fatigues. She doubted whether he had been to the Army-Navy store since his tour in Vietnam. Coming up behind him, she coughed while still several yards back in case he was unaware of her presence. "Morning, Abner. Got a minute?"

Startled and wild-eyed, Abner turned. But he saw it was Chrischana, an old classmate and friend. She had stopped to speak to him a few times since her return, once buying him a cup of coffee. He knew she had children. Now she began telling him about Daniel. He may have seen them because he was about on the roads, early and late. Habitually Abner walked the highway, the streets, sometimes in anguished concentration, sometimes alive to the doings about him and ready for conversation. At those times his eyes would relax. Or, he might be like a ghost on his feet. Maybe he had seen something though—sometime?

In the doorway of Buster Bearce's convenience store across the highway from them stood Robbie Robichaud's twin sons, Alvin and Ansell, watching. They had come into Gottheim to Kimball Supply for bar and chain oil, a new set of files, and were now on their way back to the woods, coffees in hand. "Theya she is," said square-faced Ansell to his identical twin.

"Might we could beat the bushes when we go back fah'em" answered Alvin.

"Might," Ansell agreed.

By the time they got into Alvin's pickup and pulled out toward Copenhagen, Chrischana, disappointed that Abner knew nothing about the missing kids, was on her way back up to Elda Simon's.

The older woman had just come in for a cup of tea, looking to revive herself from morning chores and a brisk ramble in search of wildlife in need of her ministrations. She had also kept an eye out for Daniel, returning distracted by the sight of a deerstand—half built—up on the rock above the house. Water boiled out over the bag as she tipped the kettle, releasing the strong scent of orange pekoe and other black teas. Was that Chrischana's kerchief passing the window?

She went to let the younger woman in. "Find 'em yet?" She had missed seeing the furrow in Chrischana's brow.

"No, but it's not certain theya together. No one in town's seen 'em. Was hoping they'd come back heah... somehow."

Elda shook her head, saying comfortingly, "Have a cup o'tea with me, deah. Maybe we betta call Balda?" She went to the canister on the sideboard for another tea bag, feeling guilty for dwelling on that deerstand. Here was Daniel, missing, and all she could think of was that stand. Who could have put it theya, half-done? Seems twas one of the boys. That job of hammering showed the hand of a child.

Chrischana stood by the gleaming wooden sideboard, absently watching the little woman pour her a steaming cup. She took it, saying, "Let's not call'em just yet. Still early. I don't believe harm's come to'em."

Elda nodded, sipping the hot tea. "He'll probably call on break, anaway."

—

Asa Bartlett sat in Olive Lovejoy's kitchen, eating an egg salad sandwich. She sat across from him, large, solid, talking. Her red fingertips fluted the air from time to time, speaking along with her words. Light fell through the double windows above the sink, aglow with dust motes. The flecked Formica table top was set for two, trimmed with Jell-O salad, thick slices of tomato, a wedge of head lettuce and a pot of tea. Now that Asa wanted to marry her, Olive had given over her care of the developmentally disabled. He didn't think he'd be able to live in a house full of disabled people—or any other kind of people. All he wanted was Olive. Their plans were up in the air like the dust motes and Olive's red tipped fingers, but she spoke of going up on the mountain to do domestic work once the season got underway.

The disposal of dwellings had not yet been settled, there being two houses between them. This house of Olive's was a three-story turn-of-the-century Sears catalog house. It had polished hardwood floors and rag rugs, and leaded glass bookcases flanking a stone fireplace overlaid with oak mantelpiece. The matching oak floor molding was eight inches wide, three inches around the door frames. A solid oak banister ran from the ground floor to the landing. In the kitchen, where they sat talking, linoleum with hand cut insets gleamed across the floor at their feet. Built among traditional New England houses, its wavy concrete block exterior was once an affront to the classic or gingerbread aesthetic of the purest. But some of these traditional houses had themselves been converted into bed-and-breakfast establishments and set to work. The function afforded their owners to keep up the appearance of prosperous ease. But many were new owners from elsewhere, aware of both the commercial and historical value of these structures, and pleased to cater to the tourist and seasonal trade; join the class of small-business persons who could, with a bit of capital, earn a living in Gottheim.

In the country setting, white and tiny in the distance beneath a low mountain ridge of Jasper Mountain, Asa's extended farmhouse overlooked the pond. The farmstead, comprised of the big house and bits and sections of other houses from a bygone time, had been in Asa's family for generations; the not so gentle hardly fertile slopes steadily farmed since that first clearing soon after the incorporation of Gottheim. Asa was the one to give over farming full time, after the passing of his father in the 60s. He kept it in hay but the livestock were mostly gone and there was a healthy assortment of cats to keep the place clear of rodents. This mill worker's careful craftsmanship, and attention to historic authenticity, combined to keep the house as neat and austere as any 1800s connected dwelling could be. In spring nine huge maples yielded numerous quart jars of syrup. When hung with spanking-clean galvanized covered buckets and seen from afar they resembled jeweled giantesses in the sun.

Asa and Olive were inching up on retirement age. Now they wondered aloud if such a condition really existed—retirement. However much they talked of it, the question always came back: "What'll we do then?"

Olive's earnings had gone in Horace's illness, but Asa had carefully and scrupulously set something by for the event, yet neither could imagine not working. What would give the day its shape and supporting activity? Asa had suffered bouts of depression, over the course of his fruity life, and understood that work kept thoughts occupied, holding the undesirable ones at bay. Whatever the pace, trotting or plodding, his plan had always been to die in harness. Now, to the clinking of flatware, cups and plates, the loving couple talked of these things. Slowly a plan emerged.

Either of these two houses could make an ideal bed and breakfast. Both would. "I could do all the handiwork, keep'em repaired inside and out. Yardwork, neat and trim out front," he volunteered. "We could have our own private areas, keep us separate from the guests'.... Think of a house providing a living, making money!" He pulled his apple crisp toward him, sliced into it with his fork.

"Well, it's the local economy now, Asa," Olive said, then took a sip of tea. "You couldn't imagine selling mulch hay—whole crop—even five, six years ago. Now developas all want it fah landscaping. The power company, wanting so much fah that new right-of-way."

"But think of us employin' people! Imagine givin' orders to people round heah? I dunno."

"You'd hire a contractor, wouldn't choo? Do it that way. People want work. Melviny'd love working with folks she knew, stead of strangers. Could maybe persuade Decatah t'do breakfast, one place. I caunt do both, you know. He'd have to sharpen up a bit, though. Learn a little fancier way o'cooking. Maybe Chrischana'd work fah us."

"You heard about her boy? Him'n Cindabilla missing? Wondah if they found them yet."

She nodded. "I betta get back on the phone, find out. I been callin' all morning trying to find out if anybody seen anathin."

"Yuht, betta." He stood to kiss her. "I gut wind the clock before my shift!"

It was a long day. Although Chrischana had not yet reported Daniel missing, the Gottheim police were already keeping an eye out for the boy and Cindabilla. One of the officers thought there was cause for concern:

Late last spring there had been two attempted stranger-abductions in the town of Percy. Someone in a new Bronco had tried to entice adolescents into going for a ride. Teenagers were a fixture, walking the shoulders of highways and back roads. How else could they get around? If you've got no car and want to see your friends outside of school, you have to walk. Few parents have time to drive here and there, ferrying kids back and forth. That's why late bus has always been provided for in the school budget. Afterschool activities would be impossible without it. Though things have been quiet since the too unsolved incidents, the culprit must still be at-large somewhere. The Bronco's license, known only by color—black numerals on white—was in-state.

At noon Chrischana talked to Balder but encouraged him to stay at work. It was still too early to suppose this was anything but truancy. She was determined not to be alarmed. But Balder, unaccustomed as he was to child-rearing, was worried. Woods around Gottheim were as large as the states of Rhode Island, Connecticut.

"No need to worry," returned Chrischana. "Cindabilla is some woods wise'n crafty in't she? No use making a big deal out of something bound to turn out insignificant. It's not dark or cold enough t'worry. Let'em have theya li'l rebellion... then wail on'em when they show up." Crisply she reminded Balder of his own youth. She could feel his grin coming over the phoneline in response.

"Wait it is! Can I be first t'wail on 'em?"

"I betta do it. You'd be too easy on'em. Leave it t'you to console 'em after."

Hanging up, she recognized her relief. If others can be so easily persuaded that this is normal, maybe it is. She looked at Elda Simon heading for the door. Something needed attending to in the barn. The older woman stopped to smile in her transparent but slightly absent way. She was wearing her usual T-shirt with flannel shirt and dungarees with rolled up cuffs, low sneakers.

"What will you do now, Christy?" She thought to ask it.

"Now?... well, I'm going to thank you f'your kindness." She gave the old woman a grave half smile. "I'm grateful for what you do fah'em. You are a good gran'mother."

Her hand on the knob, Mrs. Simon stopped, embarrassed, surprised. Grateful and guilty over the kind words. "Why-thank-you-Christy." She scooted out the back door.

Shortly after four o'clock they learned what happened. Having spent the afternoon searching and talking to townsfolk, Chrischana came in on

Balder's heels. The smell of the pulp mill was still on him. The three converged in the kitchen as the phone rang, and for an instant they all froze. Then Balder reached for the receiver of the old black wall phone. He twisted its cloth covered cord. "...Yuht.... Uh-oh. Okay. Don't worry, we'll get'em."

He hung up, expelled a breath, and lifted his blue gaze. He looked steadily at Chrischana, saying, "Mystery solved, but it don't look good." Frowning, he would step close and hold her, but instead he stayed by the phone. "That was Olive Lovejoy. Talked to ol'man Kimball's niece. 'Memba ol'man Kimball, Israel Kimball? Was an old man even when we was kids—hermit lives in the tower of the oldest Gothic, up on the side of Crazy Knoll?"

She was quiet, her nod almost imperceptible.

"We knew even then that he looked out that tower fom time to time, seeing all below. Place looks out over the edge of the village waya the railroad runs. Seems he was looking down from theya this morning, saw two kids—one all in blue, long light ponytail—fling theya selves into a moving boxcar. That blue one.... That was Cindabilla."

Her face dim and fallen, Chrischana sagged against the table.

"We gut go downt'police." He said this quickly and started toward the door in an effort both to rouse and keep from going to her. She followed him out and he called back through the screen. "Give them a call, Mutha, let 'em know we're on our way."

Elda, still standing by the door, watched Daniel's parents go around the corner of the house.

They were underground for an hour, hopping first one train and then another in a convoluted attempt to get from Penn Station to Grand Central. The first thing Cindabilla wanted to see was Aunt Sally's Grand Central Station, but she was diverted by the vast subway system itself—transfixed by its screeching tumult, powerfully tunneling disappearing trains and their miraculous charging reappearances. All a steel-dark mystery, the fascinating idea that you could forever ride hundreds of miles beneath the surface of a vast city. Carefully they studied a free subway map, carefully chose their trains, yet missed their stops and connections, bemusedly. And found themselves interminably riding, observing the underground culture of great halls, scurrying passengers, springing train doors, token machines, and musicians with open instrument cases gathering change. The graffiti! Yet, both agreed that the most impressive (and scariest) encounters involved the swiftness of the train doors. The pace and movement of the underground culture awed them, but the speed of those doors, they agreed, might forever separate them if they did not take care.

But at last they stand below the gallery stairs of the great main concourse of Grand Central terminal, staring up and about them, transfixed. Somewhere on the edge of Daniel's consciousness hovers the phrase *sensory overload*. His gaze rises and falls, trying to take in the vast textured movement of rush-hour commuters, briefcases in hand; the early 1980s floor-level glut of vendors and displays which trouble the old elegance of 20th-century New York; the far vaulted ceiling where constellations glimmer, the great *beaux arts* arches letting in light beams where dust motes float in Heaven's light.

The hustle and echoing roar of the busy concourse fills him and dimly he becomes aware of Cindabilla at his elbow murmuring over and over, "Nevah nevah nevah nevah...." Seeing her pale gaze wandering over the scene, Daniel longs only to cover his ears and shut out the overwhelming hustle and roar of Metropolitan commerce; its cacophonous waves crashing without rhythm, its intelligence decayed to babble, with purpose or plan undiscernible from the torrent and might of confused speech.

Long moments he stands by her, acclimating himself, watching others move this way and that. What's it to do with us, except as...? We are overcome in a sea. His gaze fixes on an island, the central information kiosk, crowned with a great cubic clock. One brass face for each of the four sides of the six directions, it stands above the hurrying heads. He stares at the pointing hands of one yellow dial. Five o'clock.

Daniel shivers. They're sitting down to supper now, at *Simons Ledge*, eating together at the kitchen table, finding out what went on all day.... Wondering where he is. But his own day has worn itself away in travels, in this... pursuit. He went after a girl. A girl who goes after—? He looks at her wide eyes again, her open astonished face. Oh yeah. He remembers. Her education. She wants to learn the ways of the world. Well, this is the place to do it. He thought he had learned them in Phoenix.

He thinks of Mother, his duty to her. She's got no idea where he is. None!

And beside him, Cindabilla's still murmuring, *Nevah nevah*. But, suddenly the sea casts a limb at them. No longer just spectators, they must take mindful part. A man materializes, purposely. Disheveled, swart as Daniel. If his eye is a fixed vacancy, his hand is out to them.

Daniel bends to Cindabilla's ear: "Run Cindabilla run." His school books still under his arm, with his free hand he clutches at her. They turn and patter up the marble stairway, brushing the dividing brass rail. Peering out from around the corner, panting, they look down on the swelling sea. With a squeak Cindabilla sneezes and pulls out a wad of lavatory toilet paper, blowing her nose. "Look't that, Daniel," she says, holding out the wad. "Black snot!!"

He pulls back, grimacing.

"Heah," she commands, handing him a clean wad. "Blow into it, see what you get." She looks at her palms. "My fingers is filthy, too." (Pointing down,) "Imagine how many hands touch that brass railing each day. Or how many have held this." She holds up a patterned brass subway token. "Millions! I eat something now, I eat with all theya hands." She thinks a moment. "Daniel! These black boogers ah fom the subway. It's filthy down theya!"

He obliges her by showing her his snot, but he's thinking, Couldn't we have found this out from a book?

Looking around, Cindabilla sees a sign. *Park Avenue.* She opens the map. "Look't. This's East 42nd and Pock Avenue." She points out an intersection on the paper, saying, "Heah's Times Square. All we got do is go out like this" (gesturing). (Counting)... "Four blocks to Times Square! Forget the filthy subway. Let's go."

But Daniel does not move. It's suppertime and they've spent too much of their money on subway tokens. The peanut butter, lettuce and mayonnaise sandwiches, made by Cindabilla before light this morning, are long gone. Dazed Daniel puts a restraining hand on her arm. "I think that was a homeless man that came up to us. Cindabilla, what are we doing!? It's suppertime."

In scorn she looks at him. But thinking a moment and smacking her thigh, she says, "We'll do what *he* done—panhandle." She says it significantly, as though she has studied and knows what to do because of it.

But now Daniel is thinking that he himself was homeless—before Balder became his father. The Twitchell family was homeless on leaving Phoenix. They had to camp everywhere they went. He had seen on TV in Phoenix that homeless panhandlers came out when the President emptied the insane asylums, but he couldn't imagine so many insane people. And he couldn't imagine anyone walking down Front Street with his hand out. No one would have the nerve.... But this is how it's done in the city.

"Cindabilla, I think we should go back to Gott'im—*now.*"

"You go. I'm going to Times Square'n see all the lights when the sun goes down." Off she walks.

Daniel stops. Then, troubled, quiet, he follows. He must keep his wits alive, watch out for things. Anything. Anything could happen. Hurry. Don't lose her in this people sea.

Navigating it, he calls after the retreating lithe blue form, its long ponytail swinging. Daniel threads out toward the Park Avenue ramp.

"Cindabilla!"

But he needn't have worried for once outside Cindabilla stops, astonished by her first sight of the great city: staring amazed out through the great notch where buildings stand on either hand, towering up in abstraction of the hills back home. Glass, concrete, brick-and-stone, steel; the endless ranks of great Gotham's façades rearing up like mountains. She is dwarfed, as the mountains at home do not dwarf her. The greatness of it! What masterminds! All straight lines, order and clockwork. Gone the chaos of Sessions' kitchen. Oh the city!

Now the sea of people gives way to the sea of fuming traffic, yellow with taxis converging and diverging, choking the ramp in an effort to deliver commuters for their race to the suburbs. Or to gather suburbanites to the pleasures of the city. Down the Avenue stretches a string of traffic lights, red or green, toward infinity; more cars, lit buildings, banks of gleaming windows, shadows and movement and standstill and hummingness and honking. There are dwarfs and giants here, demons and angels, and mechanical workings undreamed of till now. How in the name of everything that works, can this great city work? How do all the sinks and toilets and lights and stoves and heaters and and and... how! No TV show on Earth could prepare you for it. Place's crammed, compacted of people. People living their lives on top of one another. Doomed to produce neighborliness at a level she would've thought impossible. Block wouldn't stand for the population of Gott'im. Even a building would not.... Maybe just the first two or three floors of that pale monster building over there?

Beneath the monstrous colonnade of Grand Central Terminal, Daniel catches up to her. She does not see the despair in his usually solemn eyes, the dream of desolation troubling his brow. But he says nothing to her, knowing himself powerless to dissuade her. All he can do is watch, as he has done since his day began, since his life began somewhere in the American West when he was born to an unwed mother. He *must* accompany Cindabilla, follow her around until a thought worth thinking, plan worth executing should find him.

"Don't look s'sad," she says. "Look out theya. Didn't choo evah see it like this? In Phoenix?"

Dumbly he shakes his head, aware but scarcely seeing. He wants never to take his eyes off her. She might fly down the stairs, disappear, become a molecule in the polypeptide chains of suburban commuters. And, down there—along 42nd St. was it?—a different type of New Yorker might emerge, one with a more predatory agenda. Can't you tell how desirable innocent *young* you are, he thinks miserably. Can't you see that people here might not have the same sense they have in Gott'im? A sense telling them not to hurt or use other people? They don't even see you here unless they want something from you.

But Cindabilla, map in hand, is heading for Times Square. There is nothing to do but follow.

At 11 o'clock and still alive with the dark shapes of people, the street outside was doubly lit with neon reflecting from puddles laid down by a cold drizzle. She had seen the lights of the Square that did not look like a square. There was nothing to compare with it in Maine, not even that time in Portland.

Their jackets hung down from the stools where they sat, but they'd never be dry before their hamburgers were eaten. Daniel was reminding her that they would have to return to the wet streets and she was saying that they could return to the terminal for shelter. He would have agreed, but it was at cross purposes to his talk which was a constant flow of petitions and reasoning.

Never talked so much before, she thought. If he would just settle down and shut up, maybe sleep in a corner somewhere—then they'd have peace. It had been a long day like a night of partying at home: long, convoluted, full of dangerous thrills, detours, and observations of hard-driving attempts at gratification. But, then again, it was completely different. And now, as though he was Uncle Asher under a mountain of reefer smoke, she couldn't get Daniel to shut up.

He reminded her that it had taken them four hours to get up the courage to try panhandling enough money for supper. He listed the times and circumstances under which they'd been accosted to trade Daniel's leather jacket for heroin or crack. He recounted the propositions they'd had for sex from the "weirdo fucking freaks," as she called the prima-techs and gays. And more he recalled, before ending his recital with the scene of a mother trying to sell her baby. Daniel had yanked her away before she could find out what would become of the little thing.

Once the warm food hit her, Cindabilla could hardly keep her eyes open. She heard her own voice answering his repeated entreaties. "All right, call'em, if that's what you want, Daniel. I give up!" She said it to shut him up, but she was thinking, I'm still gont see the Statue of Liberty, go up the World Trade Center. Aunt Sally said you could see all them pretty buildings lit up from theya, like church steeples all across the city.

They walked back on 42nd St. in the rain, avoiding encounters, a woman railing and ranting at nobody. She seemed to be following them, but maybe it was just a coincidence. Once inside the terminal, Daniel approached the payphone and inserted one of his last quarters.

"Should'o changed that," she reminded him. "Phone only costs a dime." Then she sank to the cold marble, leaned back against the wall and closed her eyes.

"Yuht!" Balder snatched the receiver up, began twisting the cord.

"Father?" He heard the voice saying, *Father*! It was the first time Daniel had called him anything but Balder; no, it was the first time he had called him *anything* directly. Daniel's voice was distant, tentative, tired. Safe! But now he was saying there was but one quarter left.

"Way-you-at-Daniel?" He peppered questions, grateful and full of hope. Now, grinning at Chrischana, Balder forced himself to slow.

She had stood from the table at mention of her son's name. Exhausted and relieved, she wanted to knock Balder into the front room, snatch the receiver, babble and holler at the boy. But, as more of a grimace, she returned Balder's grin and sat down again. Turning her coffee cup, Chrischana leaned into the one-sided conversation, trying to hear Daniel's words.

"Okay," Balder said. "G'me that number." Scribbling, he repeated it. "Okay, stay theya, right by that phone. I'll make arrangements to wire you bus money'n call you right back."

He hung up and immediately began calling Benjamin Biddle, the pharmacist and Western Union provider. "Roust Biddle out, get him to send money to the New York City bus station," he said, looking over at Chrischana.

She jumped up with a squeak of despair. "New York City!"

"Look," he said, dialing the New York City area code after his brief conversation with Biddle, "Just talk to him. You'll feel betta."

The tone of her speaking wavered from stern to soft murmurs and back again as she talked with her son. Her eyes relaxed. Her gaze drifted away from Balder. To Daniel she heaped admonishment, repetitious instruction. Told him how to handle himself in the terminal that night and on the way to the bus station in the morning. Made him promise to stay out of the subway until then. Take no arguments from Cindabilla. Don't look anyone in the eye, get straight on the bus, etc....

Balder held out his hand for the phone. Reluctantly she parted with it, stood near, then wandered into the front room where Elda was slouched in the chair before the flickering television. Sleeping. The box in which the tiny wood mouse nestled was at her side. On the mantelpiece, the Simon's nut-brown clock with gold hands ticked away, drawing Chrischana's attention.

Almost 8 a.m. Was this nightmare really over? Were they really safe, returning home after all that uncertainty? Yes. It looked that way.
They waited down at the lower level, looking for the approach of the train to take them to the Port Authority bus terminal. The long night in Grand Central was over and, hungry, bleary-eyed, they were submerged in the crowd of commuters.

Suddenly came the train, shrieking to a halt. Packed among commuters, they edged forward, Daniel clutching his books, stepping warily into the car lest the swift doors slam. Safely aboard he sought out Cindabilla among the trench coats and suits.

"Cinda," he called, "Cinda!" He pressed through to the glass of the closed doors.

There she stood on the platform, a small slow smile on her face. Even as the train moved, she backed away, her fingers raised above the edge of a denim cuff, wiggling at him.

Boldly Cindabilla waved, dwindling into the distance. Happily triumphant. Then she turned, instantly submerged in the reforming crowd.

Bird Hunting

He felt the lowering day about him, gray and stern, with wind to drive more leaves away. Its cold breath pierced Balder's mackinaw. He stood in the lane looking up through leafless twigs at the turmoil of sky above. *There*, he heard it again, the honking of Canada geese. But he couldn't see them yet. Must be a ways off up the hill. The woodland swept upward, obscuring his view, dense as a shut door against the hillside.

He stood a while, waiting to hear them again. Now his mind went to other things, recalling that Gloria had backed out of supper with the family at *Simons Ledge*. She had to hold her ground. She was holding it, leaving him alone.

Daniel turned the corner from the road to the lane, drawing Balder's gaze. The boy walked the lane toward him, head down, feet scuffing through colored leaves.

"Father," said Daniel, drawing near. "I saw the geese, coming up the road. Like you said we would, come fall." The wind blew back his hair, scrubbed his face, solemn and still. The brown eyes were serious and deeper than before. Balder looked into them, then away. Now he looked back again.

"That li'l girl...." said the man above the wind. "Pray fah her—out theya in the ol'world."

Daniel nodded. He needed more.

"What's the strongest thing on earth?"

Daniel shrugged, turned up his collar.

"Strong to hold the world together. Love."

The two heard honking again, looked up to see the straggling v through the crosshatching of twigs. The birds passed high over the bare branches, sounding.

Balder looked at Daniel's face, still raised in scanning for the geese, quiet, troubled. "Can you do anathin fah Cindabilla? Keep her safe, provide, make her life go right?"

Daniel hesitated, shook his head, kept his gaze high. His eyes still pretended to be after the geese, averted because he could not rest them elsewhere.

"Just recognizing that, you're on the way t'helping her. Maybe praying she'll come back's not it. But that she be safe'n warm, learn what life'd teach her. It'll help, just that prayer. Let the girl go. That's love."

There was no response. Then Daniel nodded, still looking up past the naked twigs and stems. He was glad that Balder had spoken—knew he was hurting.

Balder said, "You coming to the house?"

"Not yet."

Daniel watched Balder wane, going toward the house. It struck him that his father was a lonely figure, not the happy man he seemed. The figure turned the corner, disappeared.

Reaching the back stoop, Balder stood looking into the woods from across the backyard that he had cleared not long ago. He was thinking of Peter Prince. The man was gone. At least Balder had not seen him at work these last—was it a week? Two? Was he out sick, or just in another part of the mill? Maybe he went back to Phoenix. He had never told Chrischana about meeting Peter Prince. Too much going on. But now, is there any need to tell her... if the man's gone? Might drive away her peace. She's almost happy now. Got her own little place, small, but her own. She's busy, contented, goal-oriented.... *Better find out where the man went*.

The wind drove down a flock of leaves, the scent of wood smoke coming with it. Balder stepped out into the yard to look up at the new roof of the children's house. It looked straight and snug now, made to satisfy. But that feeling was temporary. There was still much to do, inside and out. Over the winter he would refurbish its inner rooms. Working on the house was something he could do for everyone, not just Gloria, but especially for her. He never knew what a human being might do.... *On the other hand, you might never see her again*. He might rebuild the entire house and her never set foot in it. But someone will shelter here. Sometime. Something small like this was all anyone could do; and you could pray.

Benaiah crept through the woodland below what he called Monster Rock, as silently as he knew how. He tried to be quiet, expectant, alert. Weeks had passed since seeing the white deer, and the weather had changed. There had been a frost, everything coated in white, like you'd expect. Dark leaves and brown, all trimmed in soft white on the ground. Winter was going to be something, their first *winter*.

He had been working hard against waning hope, hoping to see

Sugarloaf the white deer again. In a few weeks it would be deer season, and Sugarloaf'd be mincemeat. Mother had assured him that the fawn was too young to qualify, but Balder had warned that as a curiosity Sugarloaf might be a temptation for some would-be hunters.

Now it was only October and bird season. But Ben could not rest assured. Some idiot with a bird gun might just as well shoot at the white target. He clenched his fists and dug them deep into his jacket pockets. It wasn't fair that all the rules in the world wouldn't stop the hunter if he wanted that deer. They did what they wanted if they thought they could get away with it. *Is that fair?!* Angry, Ben walked on through fallen leaves.

Then, he saw the orange and was on alert. A hunter in blaze orange hunched several yards away in a clump of evergreen, not moving. Probably a bird hunter waiting to ambush some innocent bird. Ben stood quietly, deciding what to do. He could make a bunch of noise and scare it away, ruin the hunter's chance.... But then he'd have an angry man to deal with, one with a gun. Well, it was worth it. Suppose he was after Sugarloaf?

Yet the hunter did not look very large. His back was to Ben, the feathery branches obscuring most of his form. And there was no gun showing, no telltale barrel cradled in the crook of an arm. Quietly Ben moved closer. Now the tousled head was visible beyond the little clump of evergreens. There was no mistaking that rat's nest. Nathan. But it was no wonder he had not recognized his younger brother. Nathan had never sat so still. Maybe he was sick. Or dead. Or taken over by aliens.

Ben shivered as an eerie feeling came over him, almost as though he were slipping out of his body. He felt hairs rise along the nape of his neck. Suddenly his arms seemed too loose in their sockets. Fidgeting, he suppressed a rising urge to shriek.

Nathan turned his tangled head. Seeing Ben, he raised a finger to his lips then pointed up into the branches above his head. At first Benaiah saw nothing but stems and twigs, a broken branch or two.

Suddenly he saw it. An owl. A tall owl, with two tall tufts on its head that gave it the appearance of a broken branch. Now the tufts looked like horns to him, devilish. He saw that its coloring was textured and tweedy, contributing to its camouflage. It sat on fierce clasping talons, perfectly still. Was it sleeping? Or aware of them, pretending?

He came and knelt softly beside his brother. Together they stared, remembering all they had heard about a great horned owl terrorizing Gottheim. And, before she had healed it and set it free, it had been in grandmother's barn. But now it was here in the wild, uncaged, a fierce bird of prey. Huge. The boys were watching, mesmerized, their minds immersed in its lore. The bird would eat *anything*. It would eat them if it had the chance: an ear at a time, the fingers off their hands. It could puncture them full of holes and they'd stagger bloody from the woods. Or lie rotting, picked apart at its leisure. It was... —Stephen King's owl! Whoever Stephen King was. Nathan and Ben weren't sure. They knew he lived somewhere in Maine, and that this owl had come out of him. "That owl's right out of Steven King," everyone said. The man probably opened his coat, opened his chest cavity, and this owl came flying out to snatch puppies, cats, little kids.

The boys knelt there gaping upward, their muscles taut. Suddenly, from far above, came a startling harsh cry. Their heads jerked back. It came again, a double cry. Falling through the upper branches toward them came a set of wings, black and open, fluted. There came another, behind the first, swooping. The owl's eyes started open, staring at the boys, yellow. Winking once, it turned its tufted head and started up, great wings extending. They beat. Down fell the owl toward the youngsters, and they fell backward, screaming.

Heavy, but quiet as a great moth, the owl swept off as the two great ravens flew like shadows through the upper story. Harrying and harsh, the ravens were after it, crying with protective joy. Out of here! they seemed to say. *Our territory! Beat it!!*

Staring from a thicket in wonder, the Twitchells watched the shadows plying upward through the heights above Monster Rock, passing out of sight. Only the ravens' cries came back to them, distantly.

"Did you *see* that!" shouted Nathan. "They chased that ol'owl right outta here! I thought for sure he was gonna pick our eyes out! Didn't you, Ben'ah?"

"No, I never thought that, you dork." He was still staring toward the heights. Then, satisfied the birds were gone, he sank back, allowing his legs to sprawl. "That was Stephen King's owl, you know."

"Yeah'n we saw it. We saw Stephen King's owl." At school he could tell about it and, at supper tonight, they'd all hear. Ravens had chased the owl away.

On the drive up the river from Guildford to Gottheim, Balder considered. Did he owe something to Peter Prince? Prince was not surly or provoking or cocky or lazy, at least not much cocky. He avoided the idiotic scatological subculture in the mill, men whose brains were from the groin down. If they had brains: Balder wasn't sure. Sometimes you had to work alongside all kinds in a place like Adirondack Paper, but he didn't have to spend break with them. Also, you had to watch yourself, choose the right approach to some people.... They don't stand for display of ego. Some people couldn't help it, though, and wore their foolishness like a brand. Peter Prince wasn't much like that, not a bad guy. You might even feel like tossing back a few beers with him. And here I am, a union brother even, all cozy with Peter Prince's two sons, never saying a word.

But he had terrible suspicions about this likable man. In fact, once he had been *sure*... before actually meeting him. But no one had come right out and said anything to confirm those suspicions. Yet—he must have abused her. To the point where someone as responsible as Chrischana found it necessary to run away. And there was Ithiel Whitman... the likable man who killed his wife.

The highway slid along under the wheels of his pickup, smooth new asphalt lined with high pines. New roadway, courtesy of a ski magnate's connections with state officials. A view of the Arossagunticook opened up, some raindrops speckled his windshield. He went through the radio stations looking for something good. Sultry "Bette Davis Eyes" came on.

Peter Prince was working in the bleachery. Balder had seen him there today. The man was still going through his apprenticeship, spending time in various parts of the mill. He was here, but still keeping away from Chrischana. She did not know that Peter Prince was in Maine.

Balder had avoided dealing with all this till now. Chrischana's reasons for returning had been no business of his. She would have told him if she wanted him to know. Balder hated getting snarled up in emotional revelations, relations. But, also, he wanted to love Gloria with his whole heart, and little moves toward Chrischana would only strengthen the bonds he now had with her. He had one foot in the world of her family, one foot out. You never knew what might destroy the balance and bring you tumbling down slope toward... Chrischana. Even the fact that he saw her nearly every week... while seeing Gloria never.... Distance, placing emotional distance between himself and Daniel's mother, was the only way.

Gloria's great face and eyes, those teasing laughing features, her ways making him light.... Sometimes it all went dim. ...But I want to be faithful to it, to her. How long does love continue? I still love Christy.... and what is Gloria doing now?

Peter Prince got tired of asking himself nearly the same questions about Chrischana. Some subtle inquiries, put to the bartender at Farmingham Royal Tavern late one night, told him what he needed to know. Chrischana Twitchell lived in some sort of camp near an old burned-out farm. He knew what it meant to her, that old place of her childhood.

The old Twitchell Farm crowned the top of Buck Hill, a spur of Blackwell Mountain. Blackwell was low but vast, visible for many miles along the river and highway paralleling it below. With the telltale clear-cut draping its shoulders, it was one of the baldest mountains around (that side), but it was wild, wild as the territorial bear inhabiting it. Moose, fox, bobcat and deer frequented it, he supposed. There were old twitch trails and roads from the days of settlers. Blackwell Mountain was monumental and drear in autumn. Peter thought it might be desolate in winter. How could anyone live here alone? But her family had, generations. Was there even any water up here?

Peter Prince had come up from the dust storms of Phoenix, suburbia edging its desert and provoking those storms. It was an artificial place, sure; totally dependent on precision engineering to bring water to its new sun-loving populations. There were also questions about the water rights of Natives, the depletion of underwater reservoirs, and schemes to divert the Colorado River in order to fill swimming pools. Peter sometimes wondered how long it could last. Even so, he liked Phoenix. He could have lived there the rest of his life. His passion was biking the desert.

But he had traveled cross-country on his Harley-Davidson, towing his tools in a small trailer. It had been necessary to sell Chrischana's vintage Hog in order to make the move, but she had left him no choice. What was he supposed to do—cuddle up to chrome when what he needed was her love? It was all of herself she had left him, but its sale made the necessary traveling money. After all, she had appropriated the family Bonneville for her trip back East.

Now Peter lives in Jericho, Maine. He drives a pickup leased in Waterville, sporting a Maine license plate. His apprenticeship has been served, and this is his week on the night shift, southern schedule. He has not shaken the feeling of disorientation imposed on him by that backwards rotating schedule. And today, a cloudy sere fall day, finds him parked in thorny puckerbrush below the summit of Buck Hill. The surrounding foliage is russet, what's left of it, and he is hidden, waiting for the Bonneville to come wallowing downhill and veer left where the narrow hill road turns on its way down mountain. He watches from the brambles as the rusted old boat lumbers sedately toward the next curve. He sees Nathan's tousled head popping this way and that, jouncing in the backseat—probably irritating the hell out of Benaiah. Daniel is harder to disturb. A slow smile comes up from somewhere, as Peter Prince remembers his sons.

She is taking them down to the school bus stop on Lower Intervale Road. From there she will go on to that job washing dishes at the Inn. He knows a lot about her life here already, though he has been watching only two days. He has yet to see her new home on the hill, however. Today is the day for that.

He starts the engine and pulls out of the brush. Turning up the narrow old settler's road, he wonders how she will get in and out this winter. No way the town crew comes up to plow this dirt road. Maybe she plans to live in town?

Smiling, he recalls following them up as far as the turn yesterday. He stayed far enough back that they would not have recognized the lone person in the pickup coming behind. "Twitchell Twitchell." He says it under his breath. He shakes his head. You can't get away from it like that. You know me better. "Or should I say betta?" He mutters it.

He has tried to joke with Hermann Gottesman over those soft Maine r's. He has a subtle sense of humor but is a hard man to move. Impossible, in fact. The huge man with the tiny voice is solidly immovable and he doesn't think much of... well why *does* Hermann reject the joke? Yeah, yeah. He probably thanks it a slur. He thinks I get sloppy and lack respect. And maybe he's right. Maybe I'm just a wad of useless shit waiting to be flushed down God's toilet. The devil in me would like me to believe that. You cannot joke Hermann off, reason, intellectualize, fake him out. Don't even try wheedling. But there are times you have to rebel. That was how you dealt with inflexibility. Pure rebellion will get you where you want every time. And what I want now is a glimpse into Chrischana's life. And I want to see my own goddamn kids and *that's-what-there-is-to-that*!

Gottesman is full of shit if he thinks these things constitute rebellion. These are goddamn rights. It's not rebellion when it's your god-given right. Ask any patriot. Ask the Founding Fathers. Read it in the Bill of Rights. I'd rather throw the goddamn tea into the goddamn harbor than pay goddamn taxes without my goddamn representation. He smiles.

The hill is steep, the road narrow, deep-ditched on either side. He is coming out of the woods now. The whole clear-cut, draped across the triple summit, is spread out above him. For a moment he gapes at it, stunned by its barrenness and breadth.

They don't fuck around with those trees. When they cut something down, they cut it down. He recalls the pulpwood and chip piles at the mill, understands now how they can be so mountainous; sees again the glut of magazines spread along walls in newsstands and bookstores in Phoenix. There are magazines for every interest except picking your nose. He himself has two subscriptions for motorcycle magazines and knows of half a dozen more. But culture has to thrive, you have to get paper somewhere. Be nice if it grew on trees instead of being trees, but so far, it's the best material they've come up with. Glossy paper is unbeatable for quality, and that sheer seductive look.

The dirt road surfaced on Buck Hill, and curved to the right. It dipped and humped its way through more thickets. He pulled up and got out, following a dwindling track on foot. He passed an opening to an abandoned log yard where skidders had, not long ago, landed pulpwood and saw logs. It was vast as a suburban mall parking lot, empty, with a plain gray floor of weathered tree leavings.

Prince continued rounding the curve, and now he saw through spindly stems. The trees ahead had a withered look. Scorched. He looked up their lengths, surprised. Blackened trunks were crusted in stiff scorched leaves. Leaves that had not changed color and fallen as leaves should.

It's not natural.

Why'd she want to live in this blasted out wilderness? There's nothing up here. If there was water anywhere around he'd eat his saddle bags. At least in Arizona they know how to make a desert bloom. They even make massive aqua reservoirs with wave action so people can play. He shook his head. She's gone out too far to come back. *Gott'im!* You left Phoenix for this?

As he advanced, the scorched trees parted. His gaze grazed an old truck camper to settle on the twisted pile of corrugated roofing. He stepped over the rubble to the great gaping cellarhole, recently purified by fire. In its midst he saw the massive hearth foundation. He looked to the fire-clean stones lining the great hole, pieced together like a jigsaw puzzle, fitted with a skillful hand. He thought, *Whoever built those walls knew what he was doing.* Walking around the cinders along the foundation, he looked down into the jumble of broken bricks.

This is the farmhouse she was raised in. He ran his long mechanic's fingers through his unruly hair. Its strands fell immediately into his eyes. He looked back over his shoulder toward the lane. Nearby stood the camper supported by staging. *That's where she lives now.*

He walked over to it, put his head on its ribbed aluminum side and, hand up to shade, peered into the jalousie window. Covered. He walked around. On this side stood narrow tanks of propane. He shook his head. They all live here?

He stepped around and looked toward the cellarhole. Again he was shaking his head, but his spirit was sinking, his rebellion seeping off.

This is the best we can do? After what, 34 years of living? Is this to be your life? Why don't you come home with me? Can't we do it? Can't we make it work—get rid of the violence somehow? Will there ever be anything good for us?

Peter Prince looked up toward early-morning clouds. His wide shoulders drooped. He sagged a little, realizing that this was all he had given them. A house destroyed, a camper on a clear-cut mountain. Today, it made him very sad. He would go back to Hermann Gottesman now, seeking counsel.

But tomorrow, tomorrow all this would make him very mad.

She was wandering in her dusky dawn garden, stylish and matronly in a soft felt hat and worn tweed jacket with velour trimmed pockets and collar. It was early Sunday morning. Rhetta Bearce had come to terms with herself over the blighting derelict on the south border. She could wait it out, knowing that Lyman Bearce would not keep the grubby old diner out here forever. It might remain a year or two, or even three, but someday it would be gone... whether by his hand or hers. And maybe the peace of their determined coupling would never be disturbed by it. If she possessed herself in patience, blocked pettiness, someday soon it would not mean so much to Bearce to have it outside his back window. She had to take into account his secret sentimentality. No one in all Gottheim knew this about him. No one but Rhetta Bearce.

Stepping around toward the corner of the house, she looked back at the garden, now nothing but a pleasing pattern in neutral hues, with only the perennials remaining inground. She started around the corner where white columns framed the western piazza. Now she noticed the powder blue Saab coming up the drive.

Who's this?

The car pulled around the semicircular drive and stopped before the white steps. Ever composed, Mrs. Bearce moved toward it without hurry. She thought she recognized the flighty manner of the younger person getting out. Theodora Prescott. Calling at, what? She looked at her gold wristwatch. Twenty minutes after six on a Sunday morning. Strange indeed. Even Bearce was still lying in bed.

With staccato footfalls, seeming to agitate the very air of the calm morning, Theodora hurried over. Far below the hill, its tiny roofs visible now that leaves had fled, Gottheim was shadowed and tranquil. Part of the glimmering pond showed. Later, church bells would sound out of the valley of ponds.

"Good morning, Theodora," Rhetta's voice rang out crisply. "Nice to see you out'n'about early." What can the little thing mean by it? But Rhetta kept her curiosity checked. The young woman will reveal the reason for this soon enough.

"Good morning," gasped Theo. She seemed relieved to find the older woman outside. Clearly Theo was agitated. She dropped her gloves, then a silk scarf fell, fluttering. She managed to hang onto her purse, Rhetta noted, and bent to help her pick up the things.

"What is it, deah? You're obviously upset." No use pretending not to notice. The bird-like thing seemed about to fly. The girl looked up suddenly, as though about to seek a perch on one of the mansard dormers.

"Oh Mrs. Bearce, you're a strong person, tell me what to do!" Her hazel eyes were frantic, and the small receding chin quivered.

Mrs. Bearce touched Theo's elbow, concealing her surprise. "Maybe we betta go inside'n have some tea. You must calm down, Theo, if you waunt to communicate. The kettle's already steaming on the back burner." But Theo hung back. "Come on now, I insist."

Looking fearfully up at the long elegant windows, Theo stammered, "Mr., Mr. Bearce—"

"Don't choo worry'bout him. He's still sleeping up in the corner room. Won't heah a thing!" Explaining that the front door was locked, she took Theo determinedly by the elbow, guiding her along the slate walk around to the side. Theo was soon seated in the dining room with the teapot and a plate of raspberry cheese pockets before her. Rhetta poured her a cup of tea and sat down facing her across the fluted curve of the mahogany table.

Meekly, Theo followed her every movement, barely responding to Mrs. Bearce's conversational overtures as she gathered the little repast. Now she fluttered nervous fingers over the cup and saucer, speaking in an undertone, as if fearful that Lyman Bearce would pop up in the doorway, glaring. Whenever she hesitated Rhetta reassured her. It would be another hour before the man got up. Maybe two, she added as one seemed insufficient to calm the girl.

Mrs. Bearce noted with satisfaction that the room's warm and tasteful furnishings seemed calming to Theo. Her gaze wandering from the fabric covered cornices above the windows down along the elegant treatments of rose, seafoam and teal, Theo's eyes relaxed a bit. The marble topped buffet with its groupings of tapered candlesticks above rich dark wood seemed to diffuse a soothing pleasure in her birdlike features. Rhetta did like this sensitive girl. Theodora would come out all right. She always did seem to recover from her upsets... though their financial consequences must often be classified as large embarrassments. At least she could afford it—though it was a wonder how.

Yet, listening, Rhetta Bearce began to be alarmed, though she did not betray her feelings to this daughter of her late peer. What is this girl saying?! The townsfolk, every laborer, has back wages owed—for decades!? Is she out of her mind?—but it's no good being influenced by the child's hysteria. Be calm and try to get at what lies behind this gibberish.

"My deah," she said, taking hold of Theo's wrist. "Eat a bit, and drink your tea. Then I waunt the whole story carefully, a sentence at a time. Rationally. Don't that tea smell good? It's that rich flowery Plymouth Company tea, y'know. I love this tea."

Nibbling the pastry, sipping her tea, Theodora obeyed.

Mrs. Bearce said, "Numba one. Tell me exactly what's this... charge you make?"

Theo gulped. "That the mill owners have been working together to keep wages low. Forever. At least, since I was a little girl."

"How'd you know this, Theodory?"

"Well... I heard them talking. At cards'n such. I was under the table playing, and they'd be smoking, dealing cards, talking. Firming it all up. I heard them several years in a row. I'm not misremembering. It's not one of those fake things. At least I know it was not just one time. They met like that once a year—to confirm it, I think."

Mrs. Bearce looked sharply at her. "You're quite sure you 'memba it truly? Not a dream or anathin?" She held Theo's arm, looked directly into her eyes. "Sure?"

Woebegone, large-eyed, Theodora nodded. "It happened."

"But, what made you come out with it now, afta all these years?"

Theo fidgeted. The cup clacked against the saucer in her trembling fingers. "Something... a friend... said jogged my memory, that's all. I don't even remember what.... Please believe me, Mrs. Bearce."

But doubt hovered, hesitating in Rhetta's thoughts. If it was *anyone* but Theodora Prescott! Suppose she came up with this after some hair-brained session at IICE? Maybe under hypnosis false memories were evoked. And Rhetta could not help remembering all the fiascoes Theo had embroiled herself in. The older woman turned away, just a little, her elbow on the table, her gaze out the window where dark boughs were visible beyond the sheer curtains.

Theo sank back into herself. *Oh what had she done, coming here?*

"Tell you what," said Mrs. Bearce at last, turning to her. "I think now... well, you've told me this, Theodory. So, you can relax because you told someone... connected with this... theory—"

"But it isn't." Her voice was low. "Please don't make it seem—that."

"All right. Yes. I'm sorry, but you must realize that conspiracy is too strong a word. People in Gottheim ah not conspirators, Theodora. And I need time fah this news t'sink in. Can you content yourself with having told me... fah now? You said I was strong, so let me chew this ovah a time'n you rest. Okay? Don't expect me t'jump right up'n stot something." She stopped. "How long you been in this state?"

"Weeks. Only days? A month? It just sort of built up. I couldn't stand it anymore. Can't sleep... feel like I'm being hunted. It's awful, Mrs. Bearce. I haven't even told my boyfriend. He's devout and I'd be too ashamed." She paused and a look of horror came over her. "It would have come out in a session at the Institute if the season weren't over."

"Gracious!" said Mrs. Bearce. That was all they needed—psycho-babbling gossip! At least, she decided, it didn't start with IICE. "And you say a Bearce was there? Lyman or his father?"

"Well, both, I think." She nodded. "The Bearces where there." She said it emphatically. "Most if not all the mill owners were."

Rhetta looked toward the window again. "We're going to... have to consider." She was unable to say more. For, surfacing, came the disturbing suggestion that she herself had suspected something like.... From—long-ago. Theo's tale was jogging her own memories.... Kerosene lit lamps, cigarettes, talk.... She came from an old lumber family in a logging hamlet up the valley into Abenaki Notch... now extinct that hamlet. Nothing there now even to show there'd been such a place. Her father and grandfather had been lumber barons, too. But what possible good would it do to bring all this out now? She tried to picture what it would mean for the town, *for Bearces*. No. Not just yet. She couldn't.

Rhetta looked at the quiet creature before her. "Feeling any betta now?"

Theodora heaved a slow sigh, then brightened perceptively. "Yes." Her gaze slid away and, with something of exaggeration, she hesitated as though rummaging about in her psyche for evidence. "Oh, I *do* feel better, Mrs. Bearce. *Thank you*."

Gathering her things, she stood to go. Rhetta walked her through the elegant rooms to the front door with its flanking divided lights. Together they walked down and stood in the drive. Rhetta could not feel relieved herself until she extracted a promise of silence from Theo. Then she tucked the young woman into the Saab and watched the car diminish as it passed down the drive and out into the road. She would see Theo again later, at church. Or—no. Theo hadn't been to the Congo Church lately. Rhetta had heard she was dating someone—oh yes, that impertinent Mr. little Fay. The developer with no sense of history or authenticity. He was a Baptist. Theo would worship there today.

Rhetta turned and went toward the steps, half listening, half searching for Canada geese. But, upon reaching the wide steps, her gaze slipped from the sky, startled. In his underwear, Lyman Bearce stood inside the half open door. His great white beard fanned over his undershirt, and above Bearce's eyes glittered.

"Oh-fah-heavens-sake, Bearce. Get on your robe!"

Bearce's glare deepened. Then he said, "She's nuts, y'know."

Rhetta Bearce drew herself up full. "Is she?" She gave him a long cool direct look.

"She will be." Lyman smiled at her, rare treat. "By the way. Howe's moving that dinah. Be sometime this week. I got a spot fah it down by the sawlog mill."

Rhetta grimaced. *You think of this now.* But she said nothing, only turned to walk back along the drive toward the walkway. Upon reaching the back garden, she breathed deeply, taking in her resting autumn garden with hungry eyes. The air refreshing her nostrils, her whole being, she drew a second breath. The morning light was calming. This day, this Sunday, would be calm.

But, come evening, the wind would rise. The pines flanking the grounds would thrash and thunder.

The exchange of roofs was generally made on Saturday, sometimes on Sunday. This week it was Sunday evening. Elda Simon was out in the barn, caring for sick or injured wild animals. Daniel was already up in his room, with school books spread out. Balder had shown Benaiah and Nathan the varying hare, which Elda had been raising, and the two boys were together with it in the yard. In the kitchen Daniel's parents sat at the table, evening coffee in their hands. It was more usual for Chrischana to hurry off for she sensed it made him comfortable: Balder always had an excuse for not taking the time to talk... as in the past, when they began sharing the concerns of parenting. So Chrischana had been intent on dropping the boys and getting away, however—mysteriously—Balder had urged her to stay.

His long fingers, mechanic's fingers she always thought, reminded her of Peter's. They were fidgeting with a spoon. Now they were drumming on the checkered oil-cloth. The familiar furrow hardened between his eyes as he gazed down into his coffee.

He looked up. " 'Fraid theya's something you got know. Christy, Peter Prince is heah. I seen him working in the mill. I—didn't think you knew."

His direct blue gaze startled her. The kitchen light above shone on his yellow-white hair. She felt her jaw drop and quickly closed it.

He said softly, "We don't have t'talk.... but I thought you'd waunt to know."

He watched her gaze drift away, staring off into the darkened front room. "Peter...." She said it a second time, as though trying out his name, then murmured, "I guess it happened then. He came afta me."

She picked up her cup to swallow some coffee. She set the cup down, cocking her head a bit looking at it. As though she had never seen a cup of coffee before. Balder was waiting. Moments passed. She didn't think she should keep him like this, turning them both into statues, trying to make time stop. Make everything stop.

She stood and went to stare out the divided panes of the window. Benaiah and Nathan were out there in the dusk, but reflected light from the kitchen prevented her seeing them. She said, "That's a snowshoe rabbit, in't it?" Continuing to peer out, she put up her arm to shield the glare. "Haven't seen one since.... I 'memba catching one by accident up theya on the mountain as a kid. Hadn't been enough snow on that trap or he wouldn't'o got caught.... You know how they leap atop the snow, hardly sinkin'..."

"Christy...."

Make it easy on this man. Sit down'n talk t'him. He's not trying to get rid of me now. But she could not seem to make herself move.

He stood and went to her, gently turning her by the shoulders. "Okay, Christy?" The look in her eyes was forlorn. She seemed dazed and he wanted to take her in his arms, comfort this sweet wife of his youth.

But she was thinking, bizarrely, Maybe I ought to put a note on the camper... just in case: *killed by bear*. One of her ancestors had written it in his youth, on a handkerchief in his own blood.

She said, "I'm okay, Balder. We can talk now."

When they were seated again, she said, "It's strange. A part o'me is glad. If you met him you know theya's some worthwhile stuff theya. He is worth saving. If anybody can save'em. I can't. I think you guessed.... Peter didn't always treat me s'good.... Or, maybe Daniel told you?"

He shook his head. "Daniel says very li'l—speech-wise."

She nodded then settled back, letting her gaze wander over the horsehair plaster ceiling. There was an old water stain in the shape of Florida up there above the sink. Her gaze drifted back along the expanse, past a few cobwebs, past the grate in the corner where heat from the woodstove lifted to warm the upstairs. Chrischana let her gaze drop back to Balder.

She said, "It's strange to love someone like that. Peter. People would not understand this, but I waunt t'be true to love. And I... didn't do such a good job... first time." She hurried on. "I made up m'mind. I'd be faithful to love."

She looked at him, steadily. He nodded. He was hearing her, while leaving the allusion to himself untouched.

"It's only thing I found give meaning to life. But people think, She's got a death wish. Something's wrong with hah. Well, Balda, we're gonna die. Whether we *wish* it or not. It's not length'o time but how time's spent. Live long, they say. That's best. But it's not. It's what you live'n die *for*. I'd live'n die fah my kids. I'd even live and die fah Petey—if it'd save him. It won't."

Again Chrischana turned her exotic eyes away, toward the darkness of the front room. "It'd be lying to say theya's no fear. I'm awful sorry'n afraid sometimes. And I don't always feel like this... but, who knows? Maybe seeing finally that death is real... that his hands (so good with tools) could really destroy the woman he had to hold.... Maybe it would stop his bent toward destruction."

Balder recoiled inside, but gave no outward sign. Maybe if he waited her sense would reassert itself. If it had been theoretical... he might be nodding his head right along. But it wasn't a principal at stake. It was Chrischana.

"But maybe that would make it worse, too. Anyway, I caunt go that far and it wouldn't save him. I've got the boys t'think of. See," she said smiling, "my faith's not so great. I caunt trust what might become of them.... if Petey murdered me. Even now, with you s'good t'em. Something like that could change the spirit even of Daniel."

She glanced up toward Florida above the sink without seeing it and brought her gaze down again. "If it *did happen*? If theya wasn't a thing I could do to prevent it (like take my kids to Istanbul or someplace)? It would be all right. They would make it through—eventually. My faith's got be like that. But I won't put myself in harm's way or be negligent so long's I can protect 'em fom it."

She was looking at him with grave, beautiful and quiet, Native American eyes. Chrischana had reached, he thought, her full physical and spiritual maturity. He felt the strength of earth in her. That she had stature, dignity, calm. She reminded him of the mountains in morning where he drove along in silence; of the Meguntics glowing at their edges, the sun about to rise. He thought of it: She was Jasper Mary, among the thieves.

Something, not a sound or movement, made him look up from her toward the ceiling grate where a shadow hovered. Behind the crisscrosses of the grate, two eyes glimmered. Balder stared into the eyes of Daniel.

But now, distantly, they heard a passionate sound. All three listened with varying degrees of attention. And Chrischana's most acute. She was on her feet before the sound moved Balder. Still Daniel stared down, his gaze abstracted, yet on the lapsed conversation.

The sound came into the room as though a harbinger of things in the spirit realm. As though from a great distance and through dimensions misunderstood. The impression upon the man was of a war in a far off Asian land, or in heaven, and he thought he heard its words coming down on the wind. Now he realized that a wind had indeed risen outside the house, rattling the window panes.

"It's Nathan," he heard Chrischana saying. And she was going out the door.

Two boys played with a rabbit on the edge of the yard. Above them high on the mountain they heard a wind. It was a benign background to what they played. Light in the divided windows showed from the kitchen across the yard; in it they cuddled the hare that Mrs. Simon had been nursing. She found the hare stunned in a ravine, with both its eyes gouged out. Mystified, Elda could not guess how this happened, but the snowshoe rabbit was hers now to care for. A blind rabbit stands no chance in the wild.

Animals have an evocative effect upon Benaiah. With them he reverts to innocence, playing peaceably with Nathan. He becomes a younger Ben, tender and thoughtful, concerned with his charge. And, under this influence, Nathan is more settled, quieter, feeling the delicate softness of the hare's fur. He enjoys the rabbity twitching of its nose, the humor in its long ears.

Stroking the soft fur, Ben says, "Fiver needs these ears more than ever now he's got no eyes. Look how they turn this way'n that, listenin'."

Under Elda's care, the hare has become acclimated to humans. It seems not to mind the stroking or the soft rise and fall of their voices. "This rabbit can jump like anything," he said. "Ten, twelve feet if it wants, because it's really a hare."

Dark has fallen, deepening the woods that stand over them. The yellow lights of the house show and, when they glance in that direction, the boys see the shapes of Balder and Mother at the table. Their eyes adjust to the dark stealing upon them as the great shadow of earth falls in its turning from the sun. In a related manner the coat of the varying hare beneath their fingers is changing from dark to light—in reaction to lessening light as the season wastes. When snow falls in early December the white of the hare will be hidden in it. Tonight the process is visible in the molting of its coat.

"Fiver don't look bad with his eyes out." Nathan's voice rises a bit, as the wind of Jasper Mountain dips down. Eddying, it stirs up nearby leaves. "It just looks like they're closed a while." He spreads the rabbit's toes with his fingers. "Look how giant his feet are. Guess that's why he can jump good."

"She." Ben corrects him. "She was a mom, remember. They're called snowshoe rabbits cause their feet s'big. But guess what. When she goes into season, a buck'll come around and then there'll be baby rabbits. We'll have rabbits coming out our ears. They're famous reproductors."

"Huh?" Nathan was suspicious. "What's *that*?"

Ben begins explaining his superior knowledge. The hare moves off a bit, nibbling on sparse grass at the edge of the trees. The wind comes down the mountain, blowing and bending firs with its fresh breath. But now an extra breath moves over their heads, falling. A breath with wide wings. The wings cover the varying hare.

Nathan screams. Together they lunge toward the shadow, Ben falling on the great bird. He beats the predator, tossing amid a fury of talons and strong wings. Nathan falls back screaming—a torrent without thought: "Get'em, get'em, get'em, Ben! *Get'em, get'em, get'em.*"

Ben holds on, feeling the owl's mighty scapulas churning, but it will not release the hare.

"Pull-back-his-wing!" Nathan screams the phrase again and again, a singsong. And Ben, struggling, obeys, grasping the wing, jerking, straining his own young shoulders and fingers to keep hold, turning his face this way and that. The talons unclench. Scrambling the rabbit rolls away. With a shrug and waddle, the owl evades the boy's relaxed grasp. Screeching, it moves toward the woods but then turns again, daring them with circular eyes. Its face is split by a horned hissing mouth. The owl spreads its wings in a fierce rotating display. The white feathery feet are spread, its sharp talons splayed. Exhausted, Ben scrambles to his feet. The bird will spring with those talons.

Chrischana runs across the light-slashed yard, her braid flapping. "Get 'em, Mother get'em! Get'em, Balder," hollers Nathan on seeing Balder coming. "The owl wants Fiver for dinner, get'em!"

The owl turns, pushing off with mighty feathery feet. Beating, it reaches into the forest and after a moment of erratic flight is gone among the branches. Gone into the sounding wind on which it had but lately come.

One day before Halloween, Jeffrey Decatur, retired now from the diner named for his father (hauled away by its owner Bearce), finds himself walking quietly through the woods. He wears blaze orange and cradles an Ithaca 20 gauge shotgun, careful not to rustle the leaves in his path. Even before day was stirring, everything as yet indistinct and awaiting a surer form, Decatur got up, as though to prepare for today's labor. As though Monday would again be filled with soup, hamburger, tuna sandwiches, macaroni and cheese, pie. As though the eternal spot on the floor before the grill was waiting... as it had before, for almost the span of his life in Gottheim.

But Decatur donned hunting boots, an ancient pair of canvas trousers, thermal undershirt, flannel shirt and the orange jacket and hunting cap. On his way out he drove past two of the ponds in the valley where the Spirit of the Lord moved upon the face of waters. Already God was saying, Let there be Light. And Decatur saw that the light was good. He saw the little fir-choked island in the midst where Nataluk once threatened Dr. Lapham with captivity. It floated in mist-covered mystery as Decatur passed. God would be busy all week, commanding the appearance of dry land, gathering waters, telling plants and trees what to do, assuring the coming year's abundance of seed. Let there be light in the sky, divide the day from night, give them light on earth: The man Decatur's going to walk in this light.

Partridge supposed to be abundant this fall. Walking alone he wonders about this, for it has been dry. The diets of bird and squirrel overlap and even those rodents are hurting. Now he discovers that the ruffed grouse have spread out instead of grouping in their familiar coves. He flushes one on a new twitch trail and misses it—which he says to himself he ought'n'tove. It's as though the ghost of Father's saying, "Should've used #6 shot, Jeffy. Whad I always tell you'bout that?"

But he has only #8 with him. Aloud, he says as to the ghost, "Good theya ain't no wind this morning. Makes it hard to hear'em fly up."

And Father reminds him, "But it also keeps'em restless unda covah."

"That so?"

"Cuss, listen whad I tell you?"

Decatur chuckles, his glance slipping upward into the spruces. He dropped his gaze back down again, lest he miss something. " 'Memba that year we flushed... what was it? 30, 35 birds? We hit *one* bird that day, Fatha."

"Well, that was the day we learned how smot them birds can be, Jeffy. Wouldn't believe the eyes God give'em. Not like deer. Birds *see* the orange, y'know. They see way betta'n us. He give'em such eyes when he says, Let'em fly above Earth!"

"That's so, Fatha, but they stick to the understory. They don't quite make it t'open sky."

He flushes another one whirring out of the underbrush, straight ahead this time. He catches it with his #8 shot and it falls into the thicket. The faint acrid smell of his firearm wakes in his nostrils. He hurries to search among the leaves and conifer seedlings.

"That'away, Jeffy. It's heah somewhere. Those feathers makes it hard t'find."

Decatur finds the speckled lump among the duff and gingerly picks it up by a wing. The bird opens, unfolding, and he sees the tweed markings of its back, the white and brown stripes of its plump breast. The crested head flops down. Decatur is already thinking how to prepare it for the skillet, but Father stops him saying, "Don't choo think it's time t'say grace, Jeffy?"

Looking on the winged and feathered thing, thinking how its life has fled, Decatur draws a deep cleansing sigh. He gathers and holds the creature to him, respectfully. Looking up toward the firmament, beyond the boughs, he wants to see the partridge continue on its way from where its carcass fell. He thinks, *They must get past the branches after all.*

Won't evah living thing?

Decatur thinks, Bird hunting's worth it, now you showed me how again.

Like God who, once he had created, took his rest, Decatur will not work again.

Gloria left the Jasper Mountain Hotel and hurried along the walk beside to a wing of the building. It was a frosty November 3 a.m., a night as crystalline as topaz, as jasper or white quartz. After the warmth of Phillip's room and bed, the cold penetrated her thin blazer and skirt. She wanted only to get back to the Fay condo she shared with her brother Jimmy and wait for the sun to rise.

She wished for Balder, to speak with him and extinguish her loneliness. She wanted to forget that date with Phillip and subsequent sexual intercourse. Awful, clinical term! She had awakened after a brief sleep with him and then lain in bed, restive, miserable. It had taken 15 minutes to realize that she was perfectly free to get up, dress and leave his unit. Had he roused to see her departure, he would not have realized, until the next time he tried to see her again, that she had wholly abandoned him.

Turning a corner of the building, she came out to face the great heavens straight on. Even with the pinkish glow of resort lights competing, the stars above the mountains shone. Now came the dip in the walk for an intervening ravine. It was darker here, the pattern of stars broken by overhead branches. Away from the building she heard the roar of snow guns high above. Up there intrepid workers positioned and maintained the arteries, veins, and powerful fountains; a network slowly bringing the trails to life again. Certain trails were already open to skiers. For the first time in her life she had the opportunity to watch the silent giant take on its glorious rivers of white. The Goldings were transforming their slopes as they did every year.

Can men own mountains? She wondered it idly.

But tonight she was disturbed, and all this beauty hardly penetrated. She could make neither head nor tail of life. All was in a state of tumbling.

She unlocked the door of her parents' townhouse condominium. Upon entering she followed the pattern cast on the floors by lights in the parking lot, careful not to disturb James. Softly she went to her bedroom. He did not think much of the way she lived her life and the less attention she drew to it the better. It was not enough for him that she had given up Balder—a mechanic. If only he knew, she thought with irony, how alike their sexual mores were. Of course, it took more than that to satisfy James. You had to have position, a life that was worth something; prosperity, authority: It was God's benediction on you.

Beneath the skylights in her room, she cast herself backward on the bed and lay looking up at the stars.

Balder, what is all this—going on here below?

I live in this beautiful place, more beautiful than anyone has a right to—but I can't make sense of it. The days are crammed with this and that, but what does it mean while you're up there and I'm fumbling here below?

She turned on her side and looked at the phone, gleaming faintly with light thrown down from the skylights. I shouldn't be calling you at this hour. Not before dawn, anyway. Probably should not.... Does it provoke you when I call but won't come?

The phone jangled, startling her. She grabbed for it before he could ring again and wake Jimmy. Philip would be wanting some explanation, or simply wondering if she got in all right. She had been clutching the receiver to her blazer, but now raised it slowly to her ear. "Yes, I'm in, Phil," she whispered.

But there was silence on the other end of the line. Then the familiar Maine voice said, "It's me, Gloria. Balda."

She was silent. The line was alive not withering between them, but she felt sorry and shriveled inside. "I—I'm glad.... Balder... I was just... lying here wondering... if it was too early to call—you." It sounded bogus, completely lame. Her voice was tiny, incredulous of her own words.

"Sure?"

"Yes," she answered miserably.

His voice came gently. "What's wrong, Glory?"

"I... can't get it right, Balder."

"Get what right, Glory?"

"I don't know. *Anything.*" It was gibberish. She could think of no words to communicate her misery. She collapsed back on the bed, her eyes looking up at the stars. But his gentleness was encouraging, his mute understanding reviving her. Then she thought of something to give shape to the conversation. Still with a small voice, she said, "Um... why did you call me, Balder?"

"Numba one, I missed you." His voice was quiet. "And also to apologize. I misjudged you, Glory."

How can it be? I'm wrong from beginning to end.

Quietly he continued. "It's a sorry thing to admit, Glory. You got a whole lot more perseverance than I... gave y'credit fah. When we first met, y'made me s'happy. Just *glad* the whole time. I maybe thought all that spirit, that joy of yours meant... immaturity. That you couldn't stick at something, anathin. I wish I could think a li'l betta of what you do.... You work so hard, put everything into it. 'N I see now how important it is t'you. Misjudged you'n it's been bothering me. Couldn't sleep till I confessed." His voice was still soft, contrite.

She continued staring at the stars. Venus, is that you? "Oh... that's all right, Balder. Really. I admit I try. It *is* important to me. Most of the time. Not always," she added. She did not admit that sometimes she lost her sense of purpose entirely. But it always reasserted itself again.... Under what circumstances? IICE advised analysis: Could she contrive to bring about the desired balance between professional and emotional life—at will?

"Thank you for the recognition, Balder. I do appreciate it." This was so sweet. His concern, the call and confession.

"You betta, Glory?"

"Much. Much better."

There was silence again, and she said, "Thank you."

More silence. Oh, was the line withering? Why didn't he go on?

Then he said, "Well, that's all I wanted, Glory. G'night."

"—Goodnight...."

And he was gone, leaving her with a dial tone. Surprised, she lay there. Such loneliness in that dead tone. She felt bitter, cut off.

"Immaturity?!" She said aloud, not too loud. She went on her side, curling away from the stars. *Why*, Balder, *why*? Why is it necessary that I give up *everything*! Why why why! Do you require *all* that I am, everything that defines me, the things I *love*? Must I embrace what I *do not* like? What I have no caring or aptitude for?

She was no longer miserable, but Gloria Fay turned toward the wall.

November Waters

"So.... thinking of converting, Hermann?"

In a corner of Hermann Gottesman's *Kids Cafe*, Peter Prince, of medium height and broad-shouldered, stood looking down at the little book lying on the battered circular coffee table before the ratty couch. It was early morning and Prince was just off work. Gottesman was up and bending over the woodstove, huffing as he fed a couple sticks of wood onto the glowing coals.

The door squealed shut. "What?" The big man, straightening, turned. "Oh, the book of Samuel Johnson's prayers." His great forehead glistened, he smiled behind his wire rims. "Not me, Prince, although you might want to consider it. You have that Christian heritage in your background."

"Pummeled into my background." He stopped, his green eyes reluctant, then said, "Ever imagine that everything ever said about God is written down somewhere? I mean," he gestured toward the bookcases, "besides what's in the books in the world?" The room was still cold. Peter kept his jacket on.

"Like in the story of the recording angel?"

Prince nodded. "There's God, or somebody, actually reading the... the transcripts of all these conversations we have about the Higher Power. Maybe Allah, Buddha, Yahweh, Christ, but probably someone lower, like maybe dead people, angels, somebody. Or, maybe they're sitting listening somewhere. But, when you think God (and, hell, you can posit anything in any direction about whatever)—you make God in your own image. Maybe it was women who thought of Mary as the mother of God. That makes her God in their eyes. God has emotion, intellect and will. So he'd be interested in hearing what's said about him." Prince sat down on the cold couch, hoping for a cup of coffee. Hermann's place was always cold in the mornings now—before he had a chance to stoke the fire. And Prince always needed some drink …in his hand.

"I think you meant Muhammad, not Allah. Religions and religious figures are not alike. Not 'equal' by any means, as secularists like to believe or encourage belief about it," answered Gottesmann. He sat in the overstuffed chair at the end of the coffee table. "But going by your premise, I'd say God is more intellectual than emotional, but, having made emotion," he indicated quotes with his fat fingers, "he would have to understand and experience it himself, I … presume."

"But then, your parents and your environment would play a role in your deciding what God was like. He might be a real bastard. Or," Peter sneered, "a bitch."

Gottesman stared at him. "Well, we've already started mixing the imaginary with the true... which makes it all untrue. Is the Higher Power the least bit interested in such imaginings? An egoist? When we are thinking like that it's about us, not God. Your formative experience might contribute to your imagination, but once you're thinking and mature, you can't continue to blame someone else for your concept of God. The roots of these things may go deep, but they can become a form of sadomasochism... an abdication, refusing to refashion the image in the true. Or, I should say, *seek* to learn what is true."

"How's this for an abdication: Why should we believe in God? I mean, look at life. All the betrayal and pain, the way people treat one another, the shit. Maybe I abdicated because God did."

"So what we do to one another is God's fault? Ancient question. And we keep adding more. The way we live, the destruction of species for the sake of consumerism and convenience, the trashiness of our lifestyle, the killing fields and gas chambers, the escalation toward nuclear holocaust...." He shook his head. "A better question would be, Why should God believe in us? Bequeathing us free will (if it is, as I think so), was a tremendous act of faith. Of respect even."

"So you think I'm abdicating because I was beaten and slapped for skipping church to go to the playground, and now I can't stop mistreating Chrischana? My mother knew she was righteous all right, and she made sure I wouldn't forget it." He slouched down, staring fixedly. "I guess you can just thank God you were raised a Jew instead of a Christian."

"You know—it happens in any religion under the pressure of temperament. She acted under an erroneous image of God in child-rearing, inflicting some very unChristlike stuff on you. Bad, even sick, attitudes will cloak themselves in investments. But you don't see it in Christ himself— from what's in your Bible. Therefore can you assume such people are

115

deceived?"

Hermann said this and got up to fix coffee. From the kitchen section of the room at large, he said, "This is from a somewhat disinterested perspective—I didn't suffer like that from my parents. But I have an early acquaintance with great evil. If people are born evil (that's another question), are they definitely responsible for the evil they've done? Or are they making themselves into evil?"

"And God has definitely written it all down, what was done to me?"

"Well, we've talked about this before. It helps to understand how you got the way you are, but, if you're back on the recording angel, shouldn't you be thinking instead of your *own* account?" He set the coffee pot on top of the woodstove with a clank, came back to sit down heavily.

Peter eyed it dubiously. It would be another three hours before that coffee was hot.

Gottesman continued. "You gave the example of God as perceived male. A white, Anglo-Saxon Protestant male? Jesus fits only one of those categories, but we see Christians implying this paradigm and even insisting on it. Reading what his own disciples wrote about him, I can't see him countenancing this. And Moses, whom he quoted, wrote, "Let us make them in our image, male and female.""

Prince smiled. "You think because I call Chrischana little girl I don't respect her."

"No, I think that because you brutalized her." He let that stand by itself.

Prince just smiled and looked away.

"That is a smirk, Peter."

"Do I look female?"

"You're just playing games with the premise." He stood and took the pot to the kitchen stove, turning his massive back on Petey.

"Okay, Hermann," he called. "My mother was not God and neither am I. You want me to get over her 'mistake' in raising me. Well, it's not that easy."

"Have I said it was, implied it?" He waddled back to the low circular table and set mugs and milk beside the book of prayers. He said, "It's not for me to get over it."

"You could acknowledge the difficulty." He got out a cigarette and tamped it against the back of his hand, but did not light it.

Hermann raised one of his big hands, showing his palm in a gesture of acknowledgment. "Okay, Peter, I do. It will get *more* difficult, this process. In fact, it may get impossible."

"This is calculated to make me give up."

"No. You are not relieved of the responsibility to try."

"I am if I say t'hell with you."

Hermann crossed his fat arms and sat back against the dirty upholstery, staring down at the table. The sound of percolation, the smell of coffee lifted toward them. Apparently the fire was hot.

Peter Prince put the cigarette on the table and got up to walk around the room, his fingers jammed into the pockets of his jacket. His gaze wandered, then lighted on the bookshelves. He went to scan the contents. "Martin Buber," he said at last, touching the spine of one book. "What's he got t'say here?"

"That the bigot exchanges the I-thou of some relationship for the I-it. That we turn the subject of our bigotry into an object, something unworthy of our courtesy or attentiveness."

Prince took up his circuit of the room. A ping-pong table, battered pool table, kitchen table and chairs where teenagers could work on homework. Everything helter-skelter with cola cans, comic books, magazines. He came back to the couch and sat down. The chill was off the room. He felt warmth seeping into him and took off his jacket. The coffee would be very welcome. The night had been long but he was too restive to go back to his furnished apartment and bed.

"Okay," he said. "Let's get down to work. Ask me something, Hermann. I'm sorry."

"Tell me about Chrischana. What is she like?"

Peter yawned and stretched. He ran his fingers through his hair, pushing it out of his eyes, but it fell back immediately.

"Stubborn. Head-strong. She's the good one, always right. I'm always wrong. No matter what I say, she's the opposite, always got a better idea. My way of handling the boys is always wrong. I don't budget right, don't care enough, whatever. She's little miss good'n I'm the slob. Hermann, my escapes are warranted. There's got t'be *something* to kick back and relax with. Try to forget you don't measure up. The pressure never stops with her. There's always some way you could be better, think better. I want t'live without always thinking how I could be improved."

"Always is one of those impossible words. *Is* she by chance better than you? Somebody has to be better than you. Do you want to live with someone worse than yourself? If so why?"

There was silence while Peter thought about this. He could not help but smile at Hermann.

"You said you had good times. Rode cycles together, camped out in the desert, did things loving couples do."

"Yeah we did all that stuff. At first partied together all the time.

But she stopped doing that. I know—you're gonna say the partying did me in." He looked at Gottesman's steady gaze. "Okay—the drinking. Dammit, Hermann, you're not the most relaxing guy, either. Maybe you're like her. I can't be that good. Never could. In fact, most times it enrages me."

"That's where the Higher Power comes in, Prince. Recognize It as your help, a comforter. Someone who understands your weakness, with power to help when you're in the throes of anger or temptation. Face the *fact* of your particular flaws and faults and failings as part of your exercise on the planet. They may be a gift. Anyway, they can't be evaded, eluded, escaped from. You can't part with your intestines or any of your internal organs, and didn't make the twists and turns of your nature."

"Them why am I held responsible for them?"

"Because those are the rules."

Peter grimaced. "C'mon, Hermann. You're not one of those blind authoritarians who can think of no reasons but 'I said so.' " He tried the big man with a wry look.

But Gottesman replied, "I don't make the rules. I try to recognize them once I discover what they are. The help I get for obeying comes from somewhere else. Reason is limited in what it can do for us, Prince, but there *is* a kind of grace—the best word I can find. On the other side of some trial, I look back and see that something else, from somewhere else, brought me through. A friend, stranger, turn of events, change in the weather, a piece of pie, a book, a presence of peace.... The last of which by no means the least. The demands of Sinai were obedience to the words on the stone tables. Words impossible to observe entirely—given what we know about human nature. We live a while and learn: even when the will to attempt it is there, the execution is faulty. Simple acknowledgment of the need for help: 'Help me.' Afterward, you turn around and there's another acknowledgment: I was helped. Where'd it come from? But you know. It came from somewhere else. Somewhere outside your own nature or being. Grace."

"... But you're not converting."

"No. I am a Jew. I know who my Higher Power is. But your background is Christian. I don't need to depart from your stories to get my point across."

Peter Prince shook his head. "You're something else, Hermann." He looked away, heard the coffee still perking. "You brewing jet fuel back there or what?"

Hermann heaved his bulk up out of the overstuffed chair, went back to the gas stove, stuck a mitt on his big hand and took the pot. The smell of this brew had suffused the entire room, filling it with invigorating fragrance. Peter Prince could feel it revitalizing him on smell alone. If he drank it now, its strength might carry him away.

The rain began on a dim November morning, a Thursday, and poured all afternoon and evening. The people of Gottheim, of all Western Maine, heard rain sheeting across their roofs on into the night. It was the hard rain for which they had waited, filling their sunken aquifers with water enough to carry them into the following spring, seven months away. But now winter's rest is broken: Without this rain the mountainous land had gone to winter's bed in a covering of dry leaves, dark in the peculiar November dreariness which some hearts found bracing. The store of such folks lay in dreams kindled by the ominous coming of winter with its dissolving darkness, lighted windows, days ending in twilight so dense that only the distant sight of home might split it. In woodland echoed the thunder of hunters. Having risen in the dark, they gutted their fallen prey, counting its polished points with exhilaration. But now... that rain is hammering across the roof, is running in the brook bed empty until yesterday. Streaming downhill in rivulets and runnels, forcing new channels, weakening, widening; disturbing the old footholds of roots and rocks.

At midnight, one householder on a slight rise hears the crashing of conifer. The fallen tree gathers to itself down-spinning debris, choking the stream flow and forcing it sideways over new territory; making new ditches. Downstream the Arossagunticook takes on the overflow of its many tributaries, rising, filling its empty backwaters and hollows, creating islands and small new floods. Highways will be segmented as sections submerge. Roadbeds and remote notches will churn with new water. People in towns roundabout will be cut off from jobs, their relations and, in some instances, the comfort of their own homes. Some will be in danger of being swept away.

Having been soaked in a scamper from their car to the welcoming door, James Fay and his sister Gloria land in the Bean Corner Restaurant. Still shaken from the ride back down the flooding Copenhagen Road, Gloria Fay is a bit trembly and ready to be comforted. The road runs alongside the now raging Rabbit River, whose rocky sides have had more than they can safely hold. They have seen water spilling over the roadway in foaming brown eddies, frightening and forewarning them against continuing the journey into New Hampshire. Now, in entering the tiny dingy restaurant, they find the room crowded. The little place is chockablock with conversation, full of the hum of people caught up and thrown together. They sit down in the midst of the room at the one empty table.

Gloria shrugs her navy blue raincoat onto the chair back. James has already hung his London Fog near the door. He takes off his hornrims, picking up the table napkin to rub away condensation produced by the warmth of the room. Ever desiring to create a sense of presence or authority despite his small size, he wears a blue-black Brooks Brothers suit, burgundy tie, and custom-made shoes with lifts.

The door blows opened and in comes a man of medium build, wet hair hanging in his eyes. Seeing that there are but two empty chairs in the place, he approaches the pair to ask if they mind sharing the table with him. James Fay does not like the look of his brown leather jacket, nor the friendly smile in his green eyes. But Gloria smiles, indicating the chair diagonally across from her. "Make yourself comfortable. Some very weird weather we're having!"

James Fay frowns but says nothing as the wet man sits down beside him. His sister is always too ready to befriend the local blue collars.

"You wouldn't believe what it's like up that road," the man says, gesturing away from the highway in the direction of the notch.

"Oh yes we would!" Gloria says it smartly. "We were just up there, had to turn around and come back. It scared the stuffing out of me—seeing that white-water curving into the roadway. All I could think of was flash flood. What if a wall of water came suddenly down?"

"Someone up there did find out what if," answers the stranger. "A van was floating on its side with a woman standing in it, waving out the passenger window. It was trapped by a fallen tree or I wouldn't've been able to walk out'n yank her out of there. Be gone down the Rabbit by now. That's the name of that River isn't it? She had relatives, a sister or something just up the road. I left her off there and came down t'get something to eat, get warm." He takes up the menu.

James Fay says, "Doesn't seem very hospitable, making you come down here after you saved her life."

"Wasn't like that. They wanted me t'stay, but—didn't feel like it! I'm from away. That's what they call it here, right? If you're not from here there's only one other place you're from—away!" He smiles, scans the menu.

Gloria laughs. "Exactly! The story of my life!"

The waitress has come to take their orders and, hearing the last remark, is a bit stiff. Gloria smiles, gives her order and then makes a joke about asking for water. But the woman merely turns to go get the hot drinks and submit their order.

"See what cha mean!" says the man, smiling, flinging the hair from his eyes. He is buoyant, exhilarated from his recent feat on the Rabbit River. The rescue has sent his spirit soaring and forged a fresh bond with creation. His voice is rapid, a bit above the buzz of the room. The brother and sister quiz him for details and he obliges.

There are a few more words about the freakish weather and its wreckage, then talk fades and silence descends on the strange companions. At last food comes, distracting them. They eat, speaking little, then part on strands of talk and good wishes for the return home. The stranger standing, says, "Go back to Jericho, forget the trip to New Hampshire for that bike part."

"Right." Gloria smiles. "The weather calls the shots, sets the agenda!"

By the door he opens his wallet, pays and goes out into the weather. They watch through the streaming window as he hurries to his pickup.

The noise of people getting up to leave increases as Gloria leans over the table to be heard. "That was nice. Refreshing, don't you think?"

"Yes. You could tell he was glad to save that woman. Had a ... a quality that doesn't exist under regular circumstances. He climbed right out there and got into the struggle. Peril can have that effect...."

He would go on in this vein, inflating, but she can't help interjecting: "Oh why can't we live like that—always?!" Her tone becomes wistful. "So much sorrow—in our, our vagaries of feeling. You find yourself in the middle of some extravagance, acting out something you later regret. But it's done. Then you're filled with the old debris of it, choked."

The place is quieting. A child whines restively at the table across the narrow aisle, as its mother hushes it. Lingering over coffee, the brother and sister try to repair their rained out plans. The scheme to check out a resort on which the Goldings have cast their eye has been diverted by the flood.

"But the water will be gone next weekend," he reminds her. "We can start again then.... So, if you don't mind, I'll just go back and see if I can catch up with Theodora, find out what she's doing today. She told me last night but I don't remember." He looks around for a telephone. "Maybe I'll call her."

"I saw a phone out there." She gestures toward the outdoors, an eyebrow raised dubiously. "It's not enclosed."

They gaze out into the parking lot where gray sheets still fall in gusts. James signals for more coffee. "I guess we got our water," says Gloria. A glint passes into her eye. "Speaking of which, is Theo all set for Sunday?"

Jimmy smiles. "I think she's up for it. She agreed months ago. In fact she brought it up first. But later she was touchy on the subject. Then she gave it up altogether, but in the last couple weeks she's come around again."

Gloria raises an eyebrow. "Is it something she really wants—or is she just pleasing you?"

"Well, dear Gloria, I take exception to that word, just. People who belittle someone's actions on the basis of just. Just because they don't want to hurt someone's feelings.... Just because they want to please someone.... Are these insignificant insecure insincere little motives? Huh? Answer, speak up, defend your flimsy position if you dare."

Gloria flushes, debating whether the embarrassment is worth entangling herself in an argument on hypocrisy and pretense. She decides to let it drop, but she is peeved, seeing his point while remaining opposed. "Okay, I yield. For now. We'll credit her with a good motive. But— beware what they say about the road to hell. Dear James."

"But I happen to believe Theo really *wants* to be baptized. I admit to being doubtful at first, but she's really worked up a fervor. I'm entirely ready to claim that her desire springs from—well, desire. She was pretty brittle for a while but that's past. She's brightened up, smoothed out considerably."

Lucky her. Gloria brushes away crumbs on the cloth. "Well, I wish you both luck." *And I'll reserve judgment. That woman's got a long way to go.* "What I like about her is her lack of meanness. There's not a mean bone there." *All her other bones are cottage cheese.* "Don't see how you can go wrong. She adores, no worships you." *But be warned against reality setting in.*

Reality. Cloud nine is perfect until it slips to cloud eight, cloud seven. Six, five. It can drop to hell in no time. The vision of a god can dim fast in the clouds of life's real problems. Balder wants a commitment to grunt work. He wants me out there turning the soil with him, immersing myself in it up to my armpits. No thank you, Balder. I'll stay where the work is elevating. It's got to be something I *know* I can give myself to without rebellion. Without regret. Let those things stay in the storybooks where they belong. In fairy tales with princesses, knights and heroes, gods and goddesses. I'll be on the mountain, fresh air in my lungs. Ready to ski!

"Think what the rain's done to the mountain! All that perfect base they worked so hard to build!"

"Not to worry, Glory. Storm's an aberration, only a setback. There's plenty of time for them to get it built up again before Christmas. Before Thanksgiving!"

She sips her lukewarm coffee. "I miss those colorful crowds, don't you? The ghost town atmosphere is... I'm a bit bored. But you're all taken up with your house. Haven't got the roof on yet, though, have you? I haven't seen it since—can't remember! They were sheathing the walls."

"I'll get Theo to go. —Go out with us, sis. We'll see how it fares in this rain. They don't have the shingles on yet. It'll leak like a sieve. At least it's on a rise well away from the stream."

"Pretty exciting, this house, Jimmy."

"I could tell you. There's nothing like it. You've got to get started on one, Glory. It'll cheer you immensely."

She nodded. "I'm—considering it."

But the coffee is gone, the rain has slackened. They can see across to the intersection swimming under a pool of murky water. Cars on the highway slow to sail through, trailing wakes.

Cautiously, or recklessly, you drive into the pool, the body of your vehicle testing its depth as you go. Flooding, it inches higher, or, you back away... depending on the degree of your reckoning. You may find yourself committed, in the midst of a lake. Will water cover the floor mats? Will it lift you away? Your trepidation or regrets may be deep, but it's done.

After the flood, the water recedes, leaving debris of rocks and roots, dirt and gravel, or the wreckage of cars. The roads are choked with it—are washed away, barricaded, closed. You remember the flood for hours or years, depending on how well you judged the currents, their depth.

Or, you might have stayed safe and snug in your house or apartment, drinking cocoa, coffee or tea. If your house is secure, well-placed. If the foundation holds.

The pilgrim Chrischana thinks these thoughts, reading the flood today. She is perched high, alone in a camper on the top of Buck Hill, looking out through the distances, misty, obscure. Here she notes rivulets streaming beneath the staging supporting her little home. But her propane is lit, she's here to see to it. She might have chosen to go over the hills with her children to ride out the storm at *Simons Ledge*. She wanted instead to look out for her property. Being here is like being on the summit (instead of the shoulder it is) of some mountain, a summit wasting by rain. This is the place she has been given.

Theodora Prescott stands in the wings, on steps leading down into the baptistery. But for the little girl standing just below her, she is the sole penitent awaiting the call to immersion. Like herself, the little girl is modesty clad in swimsuit beneath a white cotton choir robe. The Rev. Dr. True, up from Portland, stands on the opposite landing above the great basin. He wears a white vestment. They are waiting for the choir and congregation to cease (singing *Shall We Gather at the River*?).

123

Theo looks down on the little girl. Her hair is the color of a mole's, and straight. At least, Theo imagines that it is the color of a mole. The small oval face and gray eyes are very grave, when she looks this way, as if aware what she is about... standing here above the water, awaiting the washing away of her sins.

Can we really wash our sins away so easily, wonders Theo. Of course this is only a symbolic ritual. It must be a matter of the penitent's intention. You can invest this act with meaning. Is the little girl doing this now? She's not fidgeting.... Does tend to twist the front of her robe. Her fingers are small girl's fingers, twisting and releasing a pucker. She smooths the pucker away.

Theo looks at the top of her head, at her white shoulders, as the girl steps down one step.

Is God doing anything at his end? Investing meaning, as she hopes she herself is doing? It must be so, or baptism wouldn't be in the Bible. John the Baptist wouldn't have bothered. Unconsciously, Theo begins twisting the front of her robe. But she catches herself, strikes at the pucker, grimaces.

The song ends, the organ closing triumphantly. From beyond the wings comes a hush, filled with the rustle of people closing hymnals, sitting. James, even Gloria, is sitting out there, watching. But, when it is her turn to step out and down, Theo will not look toward the congregation. In the hush she hears rain, still pattering distantly on the high roof. Roads out there are still flooded, some of them, parts of Gottheim are isolated. Here in the church they are sheltered, set somewhat apart from other towns till the waters lower.

The woman closes her eyes. A fluttering under her breastbone disturbs her, but the pastor is wading down into the basin now. He motions the little girl forward, and she advances into the water, her robe lifting, spreading out like petals of white. The little girl shivers. Now Dr. True is pronouncing words over her. Gently he takes her arm, covering her mouth and closing her nose with the thumb and forefinger of his great hand. He plunges the girl into the water, her gown and the mole-colored hair spreading. For a moment she is a wavery watery thing, as though made of water and no longer flesh. Gone in abstraction of grace. Then at once she is back again, a girl, flesh and struggling to stand.

The pastor is helping her out of the baptistery, into the hands of an elder who stands on the landing above.

The minister motions Theodora to come. And she obeys, stepping down into the water with a shock, feeling it take her breath. The hand of Dr. True is firm. He has come north to officiate over the two meager baptisms and to deliver the message. Theo looks briefly into his merry eyes. He seems to feel the awkwardness of the water, robes and onlookers; while being aware of the occasion, her commitment: the connection of this act to another and fuller existence. Rejoicing, he knows what she is about. For a moment Theo is glad this pastor is from away. It lends a peculiar pointedness to the ritual, inversely investing it with the spirit of locale.

She closes her eyes, feels his hand over her face, now abandoning herself to his keeping, allowing the sensation of backward falling into water, his firm arm beneath. She is under and weightless. No longer burdened by gravity, care or clothes. Theo relinquishes control, exchanging it for lightness of being.

Up the pastor brings Theo, guiding her toward the outstretched hand of the deacon. The weight of her wet rags is heavy, unbalancing. Staggering, shivering, she grasps the hand held out to her. If the clasp should fail now, she will fall backward into that carefree realm. But it is time to ascend from the baptistery and take on the weight of her new life. For as long as she wears the rags of her flesh, only rarely will Theo taste the freedom of these moments again.

She will put it so in years ahead, retrospectively. But there is only one thing she knows for certain now. God has released her from the turmoil of her guilty conscience over artificially low wages, and nonexistent benefits, at Gottheim Chair. There has been some rearranging during this flood. Some changes will come of it.

Jasper Mountain Breakdown

After the flood it became necessary to hike up and down the final section of the Buck Hill road until persistent request by a woodland owner brought town crew member Ferdinand Sessions out to repair it with the bucket loader. Curious, Ferddy drove up after his work was done to check out the ruins of the old Twitchell Farm. He duly reported on the campsite to town officials, with consequences to follow. In the meantime winter would come, but now its forethought, frost, was doing the work of hardening up the road, so Chrischana was able to negotiate it once more with the Bonneville.

Driving up the steep hill she turned the problem of approaching winter over in her mind. It was now deep November, the land stiffening, life pulling itself inward for rest. Plant tree rock soil duff bacteria: rigid, waiting, all hardening for the great endurance to come. Any day, soon, storm out of Canada would blast the Twitchells. Except for the great triple summit at their backs—southerly, and not in position to protect—they were open and exposed on Buck Hill. Yet, all her worth was in this place, and there was little money to spare for an apartment somewhere. Shelter: the great blessing of God.

Sometimes she felt that her manner of living had always betrayed her nature. Was it true for her to be so unprepared? It was not how she felt inside. Within, she felt provident, wise. It was that initial misstep... that flight into the West, the desert, and away from love and Balder.... It echoed still into the present. That one impulse had forever prevented her pulling effectually on her bootstraps. ...But she was Native, forever dependent on nature and God.

Somehow this encouraged her. Yuht. I like it. An odd kind of wisdom—doesn't need to be a curse. I can still do well with this—fruitful imperfection.

...But, whenever I come into their line of sight.... Like this morning when Sarah Roberts came into the tavern. Chrischana tried to think she exaggerated their notice of her, the town's elite. *She saw me at the dishwasher*. Seemed to forget the homeroom we had in common.

They had never been close, but it hurt to have one your equal in studies consider you a failure. Sarah's manner told her she had not fulfilled her potential. The owner of Farmingham Royal Tavern, Sarah had flown in, harried; the valued member of the Chamber of Commerce, chair of committees, trustee of town institutions. Her hands might rinse out a cup or stray glass after a gathering, but they were never red and cracked from washing a hundred plates and bowls.

So what, she thought as a clear-cut ascended into view above the hill. I *like* the challenge, the person I've become—even if I give myself trouble.

The Bonneville thudded along the dippy track until the camper came into sight. It looked tidier, different. She pulled up, staring and incredulous. Someone had skirted the staging support of the truck camper with plywood while she was at work this morning. In the crisp air she stepped away from the Bonneville and walked around the camper, taking in its new snugness. The plywood had been secured to 2x4 supports with Philips-head screws. There was even a hinged door, beneath the overhead berth, in which things could be stored.

"Caunt have you continuing to burden yourself with this, Balda."

That evening she said it to him, crisply, having dropped in after supper for the purpose. "You're doin'evah thing you should, right here at *Simon's Ledge*. No need to add time and expense to all this. I don't see how you even *had* time. Waunt you at work this morning?"

They were upstairs in the children's house, attached to the old settlers home. He had on gloves tucked into long sleeves and was stuffing the old lathed walls with fiberglass insulation. He glanced over his shoulder at her as he worked. She stood warming herself by the small glass kerosene heater that gave off heat and light. Its light came up around her jeans, throwing shadow and weird gleams over her features. Eerie shadows jutted along the bare walls whenever they moved.

"That's where I was. I plead innocent of all charges." He finished stapling one side and turned around. "Maybe it was Peter."

She stared at him, just as earlier in the day she had stared at the skirting. Chrischana frowned. The room became still, so still that he could hear Nathan downstairs in the kitchen of the settlers house, jabbering, clattering the dishes he washed with his brother, Benaiah. Daniel was in his room in the other part, studying. Mother was out in the barn, tending two wounded deer. She had been distracted lately, fearing death by doe-permit of her favorite, Posey. Posey had not been seen for two weeks.

Her shoulders drooping, Chrischana turned away from him, her brown braid trailing to her generous hips. The sagging shoulders signaled defeat to him, and weariness. Was he just projecting a sense of yearning there, too? She must long for a stable family atmosphere, a real home. He felt a rush of anger. Why couldn't Peter Prince contain himself? Why don't you keep a punching bag, learn to expel your aggression on the air? What are you using for brains—nuts and bolts?... But Balder was not subject to fits of violent rage, not after Vietnam, not ever. He could understand a... a holy frustration great enough for true anger—but not the gross loss of self-control toward those one is responsible for in love.

Her back to him, Chrischana did mourn the loss of what was stable, normal, and *clear*. Deeply she regretted the confusion cast by the bent of Peter's temperament and rage. By his laziness and lack of commitment to conquer his selfishness. In a shriveled voice she said, "It's all these glimpses into his goodness that disturb me, throw me off. They make it impossible fah me t'find my course." Her face crumpling, she turned to him. "The days, weeks, even months and maybe *years* we had of *fun*."

She glanced back in longing on their good times and shared eroticism. "He holds this promise out to me, then crushes it. Theya's so much confusion here! Is he stalking me? Is he caring f'me? All this pattern of crazy weather! He's like the weather. Don't like it?—wait a minute, it'll change. Balda, what's this man gont do?... See, that's the thing. What's this man gont do?"

The sounds below, Nathan's sounds, had shifted from the kitchen to the front room. The boys had finished the dishes and were roughhousing in the front parlor.

"One thing's fah certain," she said. "Substance abuse is a big factor. If he could avoid that, we'd be a lot closer home."

They delighted in the sprawling Simon house. Here, as no place before, they were happy, completely occupied in scampering along corridors, climbing any of three staircases, poking around the shed, hiding in cubbyholes or snooping through attics. They could do nothing more satisfying than to hurry along passages or through dark rooms trying to ambush one another. The game was always spontaneous, breathless, spooky, subtle and sublime. Its best feature was suspense. Is he squatting around the corner, ready to spring? Or is he clean out in the ell shed?

Breath bated, tense to his toes, Benaiah crept up the back stairs of the children's house. The staircase was stale-smelling, cold and dark; too dark to see the vapor of his breath. But nearing the top, along the wall, he saw a faint glow from the little end room. The grownups were up here, Balder was working. Yet, Nathan could come creeping up the stairs any moment.

Or? Maybe he was up here already. Nathan, you puppy. *You've had it if you're in any of these rooms.* Ben would test his skills of approach on the big people first. As he crept toward the glowing room, he heard their murmuring voices.

Then: Among shadows in the doorway opposite the lit room, he saw... *something*.... Dark and very still. Maybe it was an old stack of junk. Or maybe it was a bundle of Nathan.

Quiet, creeping, daring to move but an inch or two at a time, he slumped along the wall toward the glowing open door. Balder was speaking.

"Do you waunt me t'talk to him fah you? He don't seem to know about Daniel'n me. I'm sure he don't know I'm anywhere around you Twitchells. Maybe I betta talk t'him, anyway. He'll be my enemy if I don't'n he finds out elsewhere."

There was silence, and Ben forgot all about Nathan.

Mother said, "It's gone on long enough. The boys prob'ly ought know theya dad's here. One thing they miss, it's Peter. They ask when they'll see him again. Other night Nathan said he was scared Dad would forget what he looked like!" She stopped and Benaiah heard her walk about, restively. "Wish I knew if he's staying out o'the bottle...."

"I could find that out easy enough."

With caution Ben peered into the glowing room. The tall swaying shadows of big people who ruled their lives jutted into its corners and over its ceiling. Balder was kneeling to cut a strip of insulation. Mother stood looking down on him, her back turned. Benaiah stole across the hall into the cold and dark. A slash of light from the room opposite fell across to the window. By it he saw Nathan sitting in shadow against the wall, his knees up. Ben slid in beside him, quietly. No word was said, but he had seen the sheen of his brother's eyes.

In the dark they huddled together, listening and intent. The mist of remembrance settled on the older boy, his recollection of Dad.

He felt his little brother's shoulder lightly touching his arm, testing to see what Ben would allow. Benaiah gave a sign by not moving away. Then he felt Nathan lean into him. Just a little. They sat close together, listening to the conversation about their father.

Dad was somewhere near Gott'im. Somewhere very close. They would see Dad again, and he would not forget them. The adults, who ruled their lives and took them here and there and told them what to do, would see to it. They would remember Dad, and he would remember them, after all.

Outside and across from the little end room, light from Daniel's window gleamed. Deep in the intricacies of nucleic acids, he was completely absorbed in his studies. Daniel did not hear the intermittent pattering at his window. Then he heard it, called it sleet and became lost again. The sound ceased. He made another note and the sound returned, louder, like hail against the pane. Something familiar about it woke him from his work. Just so Cindabilla used to call for his attention. She never knocked at the door below but went around to see if his light was on.

He jumped up to look out, but the lamp's reflection blocked his view. He lifted the sash and looked down. Faintly, his eyes adjusting to the dark without, he saw the gleam of her uplifted face.

He hissed that he would be down. He let the window fall. He was out the door.

Hunched into their jackets they walked the frozen lane. She was laughing at him, her high thin laugh. "Thought I'd come back an addict, din'choo! Thought I'd come back pregnant! A pothead at the v'least. Admit it, Daniel."

No, I thought you'd die. That you wouldn't come back. He said, "We could've been killed hopping that freight or had our legs chopped off... and you know it. Things happen, Cindabilla. What *should* I think—afta Times Square?"

She was silent.

"I told you I only wanted t'see the Statue of Liberty, and I done that. I wanted to see the Empire State Building, World Trade—n' I done that. I saw Greenwich Village. I did not go theya t'get hooked on drugs! Daniel I got no money, but I can still be a tourist. All it takes is a thumb—and feet." She hopped three times, squeaking, "Feet feet feet!"

"It took three months to see Greenwich Village?"

"It was only two months, Daniel." They were out on the road now, heading downhill. She turned and began walking backwards facing him, her pale ponytail swinging. Her breath was all clouds. She wiped her nose on the back of her cuff. "The best part is—you won't b'lieve it!" Her face was lit with a Cindabilla grin. "I been—guess!—Florida! Palm trees! Beaches. 'N scraggly trees like papah birches. You nevah seen such houses—all spanking clean, pretty colors. The sea down theya's like bathwater. Alligators with skin like white pine. Orange juice is evah where. Fountains of it!"

She went on, talking about hitchhiking to Naples and Fort Myers

Beach. Of the kindness of strangers.

"Saw these sad white birds with round heads, looking at bulldozers bringing down trees. Just watching all bewildered as theya homes disappeared. Either that or because they stirred up insects f'them to eat."

On and on she went and Daniel let her, satisfied solely to see her, hear her squeaky voice again. He waited for her first vulgarity, relieved when he heard it. Happy again. They tripped down the frosty hill through clouds of breath. Around the curve, the lights of the distant village showed.

Cindabilla was back in Gott'im, safely, of her own accord. Accord. He thought of the dual meaning of the word. Accord was everywhere. He was ready for Thanksgiving now.

"So why'd you come back?"

Wickedly she grinned. "Pigs is in shot supply down theya. Nevah saw *one* whole time I was gone."

He stood by the back door of the Farmingham Royal Tavern at the end of breakfast shift, like a small mountain, apparently waiting for her. She had seen him through the window earlier sitting in his car. A massive man, he stood there now, huge as any Belgian draft horse or Clydesdale, great-legged.

"Chrischana Twitchell?" He backed off some as she opened the door. His voice was smaller than she had anticipated, higher and lighter.

She nodded, barely.

"My name is Hermann Gottesman, a friend of Peter Prince, a counselor, actually." He paused to let this settle. "May I talk with you?"

"...Yuht,... she said. "...Caunt think waya'd be a good place...." She looked around absently, mystified. ...Not here in the parking lot? His car?

He said, "Maybe we could walk around the Common, find a bench."

"Okay. Meet choo theya?" He didn't look like much for walking. They would *need* a bench. She looked over at his car, a silver sedan with bad shocks.

He nodded. "In a few minutes, then. Down by the gazebo?"

She finished up, got in the Bonneville and started out the parking lot ahead of Gottesman. His fat and bespeckled face in the rearview mirror made her recall that first impression of him, not slobby, quiet, intellectual, faintly ravaged. He had a high bald forehead, receding salt-and-pepper hair pulled back in a ponytail. He did not seem to have a neck under that beard.

Peter, you're blowing my mind.

He had been here at least two months, probably three, and she had not seen him once. It was either incredible cunning or remarkable self-restraint. Yes, he had found out her place and doings. He must have seen her. Wasn't that stalking? Yes.

At the moment, seeing this big man, she did not feel much threatened. She tried to recall the fun, love and intimacy of former days.... was there anything else on the side of stability... besides this (possible) demonstrated restraint?

What about that letter of thanks in *The Voter*, from someone who had been caught in the flood?... But that heroic act was something she knew Peter capable of without special effort. Caunt take it into account. After all, the woman was a stranger to him. He only has problems being kind to one woman. The one he lives with. The woman he's supposed to love.

He huffs, breath in clouds, waddling beside her on the diagonal path through the Common. Gottesman is needing that park bench. He sits down ponderously, relieved. In seating herself on the cold bench, she brushes him and it's like brushing against a monolith, no give to him. Briefly she wonders how this immensity perceives the physical world. What's it like having earth pushing so hard against the flat soles of his feet? Do his bones feel as though they'll collapse under this mountain of weight? Is there more friction with the atmosphere, are his internal organs deformed?

She thinks about Petey, waiting for Gottesman to speak. His gaze is on the old red brick block across the way. Above them great stiff branches of an old elm are lifted in a fountain of leafless limbs. He turns to her, massive arms the size of other men's thighs clasped crossed his abdomen.

"Ms. Twitchell, Peter has asked me to talk with you. Did you know he's in the area?"

"I knew it before I saw the skirting around the camper, Mr. Gottesman."

"Hermann."

' "N you call me Chrischana. How'd you come to know him?"

"I'm a substance abuse counselor in Jericho, where he lives. And I'm an alcoholic associated with Alcoholics Anonymous, where I first met him. I work by referral and meet people through that program, as well. Peter... is taking his Twelve Steps. You know about that? You are familiar with his temperament, dysfunction and lack of self-control—of course. He has confessed these things to me. He's been hard at it... the commitment. I don't think he's trying to put one over on me because he... forthrightly declares his ambivalence. His instability."

She thinks about this. "That's a good sign. He wouldn't do that before.... Just say he's sorry and then do it over again." *But he's a stranger... caunt know Petey yet.*

It is her turn to stare off across the Common. She murmurs, "It's been seven months since I saw him...—I had a horrifying letter fom him this past summer—"

He waits. When she persists in abstraction, he softly says, "Yes."

She sits still, silent.

"Chris—chana. Is there anything in your mind to... give you hope in your relationship with this man?"

There is a pause then she says, "Well, he sent you. Instead of coming himself. Couldn't've stood that." These words are said low, as though to herself. "But... I don't trust him. I *shouldn't* trust him. So I won't.... That word you use, hope. Hope for our relationship. What hope I have—if any—comes from myself. Not Peter Prince."

Hermann had not expected this answer. He thinks it a very good one.

"I know what *I* will do. Not what Petey'll do." She chews her lip, thoughtfully. "I'm concerned'bout what ah kids is exposed to. On the other hand, they love'n miss him."

A group of children, laughing, breaths wreathing, accompanied by a few adults, have come onto the lower end of the Common to gather around a young blue spruce. The pair watch as the group begins decorating the tree. Piping voices drift across the drab expanse. But for that glad group the whole day is drab and colorless. Hermann Gottesman glances back at Chrischana, but she keeps her gaze across the Common on the children.

"The truth, Hermann—I get along fine without'em. Life heah makes me—alive. He's nevah been interested, always made fun of me'n this place. He must love'n need me more'n I do him. But he don't know *how* to love. *I* know how to love.... is that right? Am I being fair?" She takes her gaze off the children, looking at him.

"Think about it," says the big man. "There is a certain amount of faithfulness in him—right now. He's not drinking. I know because I see him every day. You can't hide it on that basis. At the moment our fellowship replaces his reliance on the bottle, and he sees me because I understand what it takes to stay sober daily. So the effort is there. You are the catalyst. He knows it's what he needs to do, but I doubt he'd do it except for the hope (if you will) of Chrischana and his family. He's full of what it's like without you all.... Knows too that destruction is waiting for him. I think caring for you is a better motive than any he could have, even though it goes against current social thinking. We *should* depend on one another; it's right to be dependable. We need family, community.... But still I would not guide you."

"But that's why I came back here."

He had stopped short of saying that self-righteousness may be here but thought she sensed it anyway. He nods. "Yes your need was desperate, you were saving your family, your life. But can you also see what he has accomplished? It is hard to accept when the past has been so difficult. A prolonged pattern was established, but the question now is... has it been broken. Or broken enough to encourage you?"

She turns away toward the children again. "Why'd you come?"

"Because he wants to see you."

The course of the conversation should have prepared her for it.

"I'm sorry, Ms. Twitchell. It's a difficult part I'm playing but he was wise to approach you in this way as you've admitted, and I'm sorry for the intrusion." He looks off toward the library again.

And suddenly she is aware of his discomfort. She almost places her fingers on one of his big dimpled hands resting on his fat knee. "Please, I am grateful for this."

The man is an oddity. Later, when she has time to muse over this moment, she will think of his likeness to some old prophet: strange, and standing in the gap where repentance and a yearning for connectedness must merge. Maybe... maybe only by this strange man will the merging, or union, come. And, by some ... grace will the two be joined again. But only in peace can it happen. And it will be hard. Very hard.

But, today Christiana is unready. Sitting here beside this immovable mountain, she realizes that even her own feelings are unstable, changeable. Yesterday she may have thought, acted, only with longing. But today when it is asked of her she dreads the thought of seeing Petey again.

Firmly, deliberately, she says it. "I'll consider this. I will, Hermann. He did do something right by sending you, instead of coming himself. *That* would be the intrusion."

Sensing that something more is needed she hesitates. It's a difficult task—the actual reaching through this large man to Peter. Connecting with Peter by these words: "Tell him.... Said I'd consider it."

Again he thought it a very good answer. "How he reacts to that will be—telling. May I give you my number?"

She nods, barely.

He reaches inside his jacket and pulls out a small white card.

Dusk. From his pickup in the parking lot of the restaurant, Balder can look out on clouds pouring off the paper machines from within the mill just beyond town. The complex of great boxy mill buildings, pulp-log piles, conveyors and steam, is lit with the eerie orange glow of sodium vapor lamps. He sits idling outside Wilbur's Bar and Grille, a haunt of Adirondack Paper workers. Maybe he'll catch up with Peter Prince here. From this space he has a good view of the grille's back door. But, Prince might park on the street and go in the front door. Or, maybe he never comes here. Balder shakes his head. More likely Prince is out of the Guildford click. As he is himself.

There he is, pulling in in that leased pickup he drives. Balder climbs out, dashes across the parking lot before the other can reach the door. "Got eat, like evah one else, Prince?" He is almost jocular, the Balder Simon everyone thinks he knows.

"Nah," the other smiles, tossing the hair out of his eyes. "I come for the entertainment. Fun watching the little grill man drop buns on the floor and then brown 'em on the grill. That touch of grit really spices up the burgers."

Balder chuckles and follows him into the clatter and chatter of the bar. Together they walk through the grille and grab stools, the hot toasty smell of french fries just beyond the counter coming up at them from a basket set to drain. Sizzle and steam pour up as the grill man lays frozen patties down. Talk and cigarette smoke fill the air, waitresses go to and fro with trays, coffee cups, beers. Balder says, "Can I buy you a beer?"

"No. —Thanks, Simon."

"Something a li'l stronger, maybe?"

Prince shakes his head. "Think I'll just have what I do when I come in, the sizzler. Good steak."

His beard waggling up and down, Balder nods. "Let's get a booth, though. More relaxing—afta work."

The two men thread through the crowd, finding a booth near the telephone. Jukebox displays are fixed to the wall, above every table, featuring some very old tunes. Sometimes you'll here "Your Cheating Heart" while you eat.

Seating himself, Prince says, "I usually sit at the counter, there being only one of me."

"Not so much in the G'fid crowd."

"Nah. I work with'em, that's enough. You?"

"Same." Balder grins. "We could talk'bout that, but we waunt get out alive."

The waitress comes to take their orders. She walks away and comes back with coffee for Peter, a beer for Balder. A small brunette in her late forties, she's ready to kid. "I made this coffee special f'you. Brewed this here beer, too."

"S'pose you'd like us t'member that when it's time to leave the tip," replies Prince.

"Nope. When you make out your will."

The two men grin and watch her walk away. Balder's grin fades. A frown puckers his brow. He says, "Gut something important to tell you."

"Me?" Prince looks at him, aware of a drastic mood change. "Something personal?"

"Real. Do you know what I'm talking about?" His tone is stern.

"I have no idea."

Balder is giving him the creeps. Prince has never seen a look like this on his face. Simon's expression is transformed. As though he were another man. The black beard and white head always pose an amazing contrast, and now this fierce face. He looks like a pirate in an old B-movie, the kind they showed on TV after midnight when Prince was a teenager. "What the hell is this?"

"Petah, I don't know how to tell you except to tell you. I know Chrischana Twitchell."

"You do?"

"Her son Daniel is my son."

Peter Prince stares at Balder through the brown tendrils hanging in his eyes. A rush of rage, of disbelief, floods him. Of course! It's why she came back! He stands, searching for the waitress, goes to her fumbling in his wallet for money which he stuffs in her hand. He is through the crowd and out the door.

Out the window Balder sees him pass beneath a street light and out of sight. He ponders a moment. His food comes and he eats absently, thinking of Peter, of Daniel. And of ice fishing coming up in a little more than a month. Of buying sheetrock from Beecham's Lumber and Home. Before his meal is done, Prince is back, striding toward him down the aisle. He slides into the booth, running fingers through his wayward hair, curtly saying, "You really ran me up the jack ladder." It was a reference to the log conveyor in the wood room at Adirondack.

"Yuht, but no need t'go through th'debarking drum. You knew Daniel was another man's son. Now you know whose, that's all. He's been staying with me every other week. So've Nathan'n Benaiah."

Deflated, Prince sits back. Walking around outside he occupied himself trying to remember what, when, she had told him about Daniel's conception. Had she ever said a name? A place, even. From somewhere he had the idea that Daniel was tied up in her travels, not her hometown. Whether she lied or not, he should have known. Maybe unconsciously he did know it was Gottheim. Maybe that was why her talk of Gottheim irritated him.

Prince glances at Simon. In the recent sporadic spying on Chrischana he missed it all. He has missed so much in all his responses, his relations with her. His gaze drops back to the table. He glares at Balder's half-finished beer. His second beer. Still glaring, he looks up. "And Christy? Have you been makin'it with her?"

"No." It is all he is willing to say about that. Trying to convince him would only raise more suspicion. "She's got her own place, which you know.... But... I'll say this: she sees no man, Prince. Not that way."

"You know why she left."

"You? Do now. She wouldn't've left without that."

"Without my abuse. My hurting her."

Balder draws back, surprised. He has known men who bully and hurt their wives, girlfriends. Never heard one admit it straightforward like that.

"No more avoidance, evasions, Simon. Open confession. It's what they teach at AA. I'm an alcoholic and a wife-beater. I've got a lot to be responsible for and tell myself not to forget it. Because I do not know if I can restrain myself under pressure. Under the influence. Now let's talk about something else."

The waitress comes back and sets coffee down for Prince. Without speaking she goes away.

Prince draws the cup to himself, muttering. "Planned. This was planned."

Balder swallows his beer, eyes the other seriously. "Chrischana waunts to know if you're still drinking'n I volunteered to find out. And... I thought you should know'bout the boys."

"I sent Gottesmann to talk to her!"

"Know nothing bout that."

The urge to lash out seizes Prince, but he steals himself to consider: We both sent go-betweens. He swallows his coffee, wanting to ask about the boys, but his pride and pain prevent it. Instead, he asks, "How long'd you know—that I was—that it was me?"

"Couple months, maybe. I guessed you hurt her, but I kept quiet. Alert though. And we didn't know about AA."

"She knows now. If Gottesmann met her this morning like I asked. My counselor, Hermann. I wanted him to find out if she'd see me. Simon, I don't want her living up there this winter. They have to stay with me. Jesus, can you imagine! North wind'll pick their bones clean up on that hill. If they can get up that hill after the snow comes. The boys can't handle that, neither can she."

Balder frowns. "Betta be careful, Prince. She loves that place. Waunts to build a house up theya someday."

His jawline tightening, Peter bristles. It galls to hear Simon advising him on Chrischana and defending her joys to him. He brings his cup to his lips, looking away. But then he sets it down, hard, unwilling to swallow the indignity along with the brew. "Do you know how it feels for you to tell me that, dammit! Are you her—anything, now?!"

"Don't plan to be. Wait back a bit, Peter. We all got interests t'be discussed. We're all just talking heah, okay?"

"Stay out of advising me, Simon. I won't stand it. Have you got a wife, girlfriend? Can I give you advice?"

Balder falls silent, holding his beer, avoiding the other's stressed glance. At last he says, "Guess I'm all done." He stands, puts on his jacket and pulls out bills for the woman who served them. "I'm around. Come by the house, *Simons Ledge*. That li'l road above the pond outside Gott'im village. Mailbox out front has ah name on it."

Peter Prince does not look up. He mumbles. "Thanks, Simon."

He does not turn to watch Balder make his way past the booths toward the cash register.

The smell of gasoline mingling with that of roast turkey drifted into the front room. Balder was in the kitchen dismantling the carburetor of the snow machine. Elda Simon was hiding out in the barn.

"Dad's coming! Dad's coming! It's Thanksgiving! Dad's coming!" Nathan bounced up and down on the couch beside Benaiah. The TV was on and between commercials they wrestled and punched one another, alternately glancing at the screen; avidly they watched commercials, and always Nathan's mouth ran.

Daniel sat quietly in the Morris chair, absorbed in his thoughts, a textbook open on his lap. The flickering blue glow of the TV bathed the room until he leaned over and turned on the lamp. There was a chapter on the Middle East to look over for Monday's quiz. There was the Ayatollah and the Marine barracks blown up. The light showed bookcases at the edges of the dim room, showed the rag rugs and coffee table, the afghans and old quilts draping worn furniture; the glass cabinet where decades old whatnots were displayed. The sleek old walnut clock sat on the mantelpiece but he did not hear its ticking.

Daniel jigged his pencil up and down. He was thinking that Dad had always known they were not related. And he had never said a word about it... even when he was drunk. Nobody had said it to Daniel.... Mother said he was different now. He had changed back to more what he was at first—when Daniel and the boys were younger; when he was most of the time sober. Is it true? How does she know? Was it Balder found out?

He looked at the clock. Mother was coming, and Dad was on his way also. Their first meeting since April.

Just up from the pond under the street lamp she recognizes the pickup as the one they saw a couple of times that autumn on Buck Hill. She is glad now that they did not know who it was. Seeing him up ahead her armpits gush. Why am I doing this? It's not too late to turn around. Turn in the lane and go back. *Don't go looking into green eyes.* But her foot on the accelerator leads her, following Peter up the hill beneath Jasper Mountain.

Remember the first time you saw those eyes. On the playground in Phoenix. Talking with Sabrina while the toddlers, Daniel and Felix, were busy tasting sand. Daniel had just started walking. Juan Bacca and friends were there, Sabrina introduced her. Peter was one of two white guys. His Harley pleased her and so did the eyes. She would not have minded if the entire world, all the constituents of her life, could be in those eyes. God things change!

She turns and follows the pickup down the lane. Nerves. Tripping up and down, back-and-forth, thrilling her sickeningly as she shuts off the engine. She yanks the door handle to steady her shaking. She is really doing this, walking slowly toward him where he stands by the pickup. Light streams from tall windows, but he hangs back in shadows. Waiting for her.

If the boys heard the engines, car doors close, they'd be out here. Better that way. Let this meeting be mediated, dear God. But the boys do not come. She has to be firm, Quicken her pace, greet him.

"Hello, Petah. Peter." Her Maine voice, God.

"Christy...." He doesn't notice the accent. He stays by the pickup, waiting for her to come as close as she cares. Does she expect the glib contrition, played as usual after his violent episodes? Times when she stayed in the boys' room, bruised and aching the morning after? He pled then for forgiveness, believed himself absolved. A changed man.

She draws near, not too near. *Be remote from this.* "Nice night, Peter, stars'n all."

"Yes." He looks southward through the trees and up beyond their limbs. "It's like the trees are wearing lights." He looks back at her, wanting to say she is beautiful. But now it would offend her. She'll see it as facile. Words come too easily, a part of his charm. She sounded like Maine a minute ago, almost as she did when they met. Her life in Maine pleased him as exotica then. But it lost its look, became a form of frumpery to him. Now he remembers his merciless mockery, and how he tried to change her, make her into the image of someone to excite and arouse him. Weren't the beatings a part of that? Didn't it excite him to see her frightened and submissive, desperate to soothe. That horseshit drove her away, lost every bit of it for him. Now she must hate the lard of charm that covered the shit.

"Boys here?" He asks.

"Should be."

"Daniel knows?"

"I think maybe he always did."

This piece of insight begins a baptism of shame for him, triggering thoughts of how the boys must have seen him. How could he think they belong to him? Even Nathan and Benaiah. Like they were all motorcycle tools to be thrown in a fit when the obstinate part wouldn't yield.

"Christy... I—" He puts his hand on the door handle, yanking it open. "I think I'll come back—later."

She steps forward, putting her hand on the door. "Theya waiting, Petah." Her hand stays on the door. "Theya ecstatic t'see you. Well Nathan is. Daniel's looking forward to riding with you. Ben'll be bashful at first."

"It's not that." There is an outpouring of shame, and the desire to escape, a powerful thirst. His Higher Power is rejecting him. Peter will not tolerate this shame very long. Even now he feels the rage of it possessing him. *Rage*!

Rage against God's self-possessed purity!

Tricked out in an errant gleam from the windows of the house, his jawline tightens and seeing it Chrischana backs away.

"Goddamn it, Christy!" He yanks wide the door, scrambles in, guns the engine, slams the door.

Chrischana has already hurried to the house through its swatches of light. In the safety of its shadow, she turns to see him back, then swing around the Bonneville. Reckless. Leaving the protection of the house, she steps back into the lane to see his red taillights wane away. He turns right, heading up the hill. She can hear the screeching of his ascent, the gunning engine. Now diminishing. The faint squealing of his tires drifts down. But Peter is ascending on the lower parts of Jasper Mountain, climbing to a higher place.

Bounded with trees, the road curving—in a passion, his tires whistling, he remains alert for the gleam of any oncoming beam. The temptation is to curse God and plunge the pickup down some ravine. Let all this steel and speed and the trees of this mountain combine to pulp me! The ease with which he can mangle himself on these reckless reaches! The pangs of this evil demon!—God deliver me! He hears himself screaming it. "Deliver me! Goddamn it! Deliver me from evil!" Screaming like a maniac, he twists the wheel at every curve.

Suddenly at the turning of the wheel he finds himself on a new road.

There are houses up here, newly minted but vacant, not a light gleams out through the trees. He plows on till the road ends on a cul-de-sac. Peter's foot mashes the brake and he stops, gets out, still breathing and now kicking his passion. Working blindly around the circle of sand and gravel, stomping and kicking, eyes glancing toward stars, his mind is well enough to tell him something. And, staring at the almost circular wall of trees surrounding him he realizes that he has been shouting at God. Shouting for deliverance out of this rage. Purposely he slows his breathing and watches the passion of his rage weaken. *This is not the way to do it.* You can't choke God's help out of him. You've got to stop and whisper for it. Kneel down, make your voice small.

He glances about quickly, then goes in among the trees... to kneel; sheltered, hidden. The ground is hard and cold, studded with granite. But the discomfort to his knees rouses him.

"God...." He says it but finds his voice hesitating, false. "Jesus...." he whispers it, hesitant. "I know you're there. Help me." He stops, his mind working. It's not natural, right, but he tries it again, whispering and troubled. "Could you help me?"

Peter sighs deeply, leaning into the tree. The grip of passion falls from him. The feel of bark on his cheek is cool and smooth. He puts his arm around this tree, closing his eyes; sighing again, leaning on the tree. Cooling peace comes out of the beech tree into his spirit. Joining him, creating a comforting union. Gently this spirit moves, even so it is almost wholly still. A living stillness, hidden in the heart of everything good. And, in this moment, it comes into the heart of Peter Prince.

Christmas in Gottheim

It was late afternoon with snow gently falling as Asa Bartlett trudged along Front Street toward the clock tower in the Congregational Church. Sidewalks had not yet begun to collect these flakes. He liked the way they speckled the dim air; sparsely and sedately, as though December were thinking of snow, spilling flakes hopefully a bit at a time. Shouts of children, skating out on the pond, drifted in from alleyways and gaps in Gottheim's buildings as he passed the storefronts. He guessed the gentle snowfall invigorated the children, maybe getting them thinking of Christmas. Christmases come rare enough in childhood. *I've had a grip full of Christmases, I guess.* He tried to remember what it felt like to have only seven Christmases instead of nine times that number.

He had a 50-year-old image of Mother, calmly moving through the house as though alone, dressing the mirrors, the sideboard in the parlor, festooning the mantelpiece and hearth with ropes of pine. There were long fragrant boughs looped with cranberries patiently strung by his own fingers as he listened to *The Adventures of the Lone Ranger* on the radio. How he loved those old radio plays! Nothing like them now... except maybe the *Prairie Home Companion.* His mother would set up the Nativity with ceramic figures of Joseph, Mary, and a babe in a manger. Shepherds and stable animals. He had seen the significance of the manger early on because of his chores throwing down summer's hay for their own beasts in winter.

Fifty Christmases later he now felt the heft of them weighty upon him: He would be spending his first with Olive. They were married now. All her kids and two of his, and their children, uniting this year in a celebration wholly new. Asa didn't know if he could take it, and he wondered what the dynamics of it would mean. But Olive had said, "Oh, we'll all be togetha, eating, watching the kids open presents, reminiscing, singing carols—"

"Singing!"

"Singing carols round the piano." Olive had said this with a smile.

Asa came out on School Street looking toward the Common. Through falling snow he saw people setting up for the Living Nativity not far from the lighted spruce. Children would be dressed for their parts, including wise men bearing gifts. And there would be live animals, a cow, horse, goat, maybe sheep, to add that spice of the unpredictable. All the historic and mythic participants of the First Christmas Story would be in attendance upon the miraculous appearance of a single child delivered in agony. Asa hoped there would be no cold snap, nothing like zero with wind. Good*ness* don't let it rain!

He came up the walk to the tall white church and entered below the ticking tower clock. It struck the half-hour and he began to climb.

Everywhere, in the village and hamlets outlying, preparations for the season were ongoing. In each Christian house tradition would be preparing. When the day came, the child would be welcomed according to some beloved but trifling custom. In God's House and in each home. Israel Kimball, who was already an old man when Balder was still a child, looks down upon the village from his turret, high in an old mansion on Crazy Knoll. He was headmaster when Asa was in school at Gottheim Academy. To his somewhat dim eyes, the storefronts, churches, backs of houses and schools of Gottheim are tiny, the Christmas toys of the Giant whose hands are far larger than the hotel-in-planning, or the wood mill near the outlet of Ben Hutchins Pond. Israel Kimball is the son of the daughter of a Gottheim lumber baron, Oliver Mason. He was the giant who commissioned the building of this storied mansion now decayed. Oliver Mason became wealthy off the products, made by local workers, from the forests of Gottheim in the 19th century—but now he is earth in the churchyard behind the Congo Church on School Street. Oliver's children are earth, who once wore crinoline and flounces, and took singing lessons and owned stables and racehorses in the Fairgrounds outside the village. The Fairgrounds had been demolished and the runway put in. The Goldings and skiers land their planes there now. Israel Kimball thinks of these things, looking on the village through bleared and aged eyes. His thoughts on death and dirt notwithstanding, he looks on the snowfall and feels its gentleness and purity.

His frame is as frail and uncertain as his vague-seeming watery eyes. The way of his flesh, this tentative bag of bones, is what all come to if they live long enough. But, seeing the snow, he smiles. He too prepares for

Christmas, awaiting the Christ Child, anticipating the birth pangs of its mother. However, these preparations are not apparent—no one sees them. The old man merely prepares his heart, hoping to catch a glimpse. But it has been decades since he has seen a baby closer than half a hundred yards. Once, last summer, a mother walked her baby on the street below.

What's that? He turns from the speckled scene outside his window. That was a noise outside the tower room door. A knock comes, briskly, but he waits several minutes before shuffling, bent and stiff, toward the door. Slowly he negotiates a way around the worn table filled with the remains of lunch, morning papers, books stacked in teetery piles. His old turkey gobbler head and neck project between hunched shoulders as he leans into motion of opening the door. The knob rattling in his freckled claw of a hand, Israel opens the door tentatively.

Perfect timing. No one there. The supper tray sits on the little table of the landing outside the door. He should have put the dinner things on the tray for her, but he forgot. Are there any messages with supper? Not in evidence. Sometimes his niece Regina leaves a note for him about one thing or another, sometimes the odd letter, document or bit of news; perhaps some new joy or hardship in the town. In September it had been the lost children, in November news of extensive flooding and attendant dangers. Last spring he had seen someone sitting in her Bonneville looking out toward Mount Will. He finds less pressing news in *The Village Voter*. Israel Kimball knows what goes on in Gottheim, though he has not been out of the tower in decades. And he takes *The Sun*, *The Journal*, and the *Portland Press Herald*, learning what happens in Maine and the world.

He grasps the tray with long stiff hands, turning gingerly to make his slow way back into the warm room. The stairwell is chilly, but in winter he has a good fire in the little stove from morning till late night. In the cold of morning he can scarcely move, but his fear of creosote fire in the pipe makes it necessary to let the hot fire burn out. Regina keeps the junk box opposite the table on the landing supplied.

His hermitage is companionable enough. He reads the Bible, the Saints, the thoughts and histories of good men and women, the classics, medieval works and philosophies; keeping a diary, jotting down his own insight. There are bookcases under the window sills and piles of his notebooks scattered about the room. Regina brings up texts from the library and stores the old journals in the old study. He also gets air and exercise, climbing the stairwell. The door on the lower-level opens into a bath he had built long ago. She keeps it clean for him. In milder seasons, through open windows, he hears birdsong and observes their activities. His face is sometimes seen by passersby below. They may have the horrors seeing it, he knows. Usually he keeps it hidden behind the lace curtain.

The mansion itself is now a boarding house for students at the Gottheim Academy, which his ancestors helped found. Israel was once a scholar, then a teacher, then headmaster, there. In term now, eight or ten students make for Regina's living; and they are usually present only at night and sometimes on Sundays. Their days are handsomely structured with computer classes, hands-on science and biology, performance and fine arts, the rigors of math physics chemistry; with skiing hiking lacrosse and other sports; with travel and charitable works. The mansion below is usually quiet, but late at night sometimes he hears their manic music, remotely.

Israel's real concern is not reading or writing, nor even thinking. His real concern is praying. Sometimes Israel Kimball prays all day and night. He has hidden himself away like this for a very long time, ever since coming to terms with his own temperament. No—it was the conjunction of this with the loss of Ellie. His wife died more than 30 years ago. But he has always been quiet, shy, inept with people. Abrupt, even irascible. In their early decades, even Ellie did not understand his sense of separation. Yet, their last 10 years together were heavenly. These vanished like the once gracious forms of everything loved. All have vanished, but this house and its view. That will be gone one day, too.

Faith remains. And Christmas.

Israel sets his supper tray on the narrow table before the south window to eat his meal looking out through swirling snow. It's the view beyond the tracks with expanses of farmland reaching to mountains; a few straggling roofs of the Village. There the glow of street lamps is visible through snow. Anyone within and without Gottheim might be the subject of Israel Kimball's prayers—though he knows hardly anyone personally now. Like him, those he knew have aged. Some have gone to nursing homes in other towns and many are in graves along the river or behind the Congregational Church. All were rosy noisy babies once, but since have mutated beyond recognition. Like himself. But Israel does not need to know people personally in order to care and pray for them. He needs only hear about them from Regina's notes or read of them in the paper. If his prayers are feeble, he asks the Holy Ghost to blow on them. He prays continually for devotion. Even after many decades of worship he finds the prayers are always in need of help.

Israel Kimball's custom is to share the Christmas season in a familial spirit with the whole community. Birth notices, obituaries, wedding announcements, neighborhood and town columns, letters to the editor, articles, club bulletins, police reports: he learns from all. Very little escapes his notice. The prayers extend out past the notches and river valley, over mountains, into vast upcountry, down to the sea. They reach across borders, go down into Times Square, up to Alaska, and deep into the Arctic circle darkness. They run to California head-lands and, down the gullet of Central America, or into the stomach of the Southern Hemisphere. His prayers go deep into the ocean, see its creatures, cross fire and water to the continent eastward, and beyond the lonely islands of seas. Anywhere there is pain or abuse, the cry for healing, the hatred of what once was Lucifer. Israel Kimball's prayers are there. If there were need, they would take to the solar system of the next galaxy, but the stars do not need his little prayers. So far as he knows, the birth pangs of the Kingdom do not extend there. He leaves them to the devices of their stellar astounding mechanisms.

No one in little Gottheim knows what the hermit is doing up here in his tower attic. Even Regina little knows. They all have their suspicions and opinions—in which, he supposes, whatever it is doesn't amount to much. Everyone knows that Israel Kimball's life has been wasted the last thirty years. They perhaps surmise that he gave up the ghost long ago, only haunting his old body now and awaiting its withering, disintegration.

How right they are, he thinks. An old man, isolated, keeping up on what goes on in the House of God? He is the most provincial of provincials. Looking to become a stream of molecules, destined for a breakdown of the nucleic acids. He will leave it all behind for the babies, become a broken line of atoms and molecules, mulch for the children of the future. He was a baby once. But you'd never know it to look at him.

Looking out the steamy window of the camper, Chrischana rejoiced. "It's here. Boys! It's here! Get up! Balda's gut the evaporator! Get up!"

"It's here! Christmas's coming!" Nathan scrambled over Daniel with whom he shared the over-the-cab bunk. Snuggling close to mother, standing on tiptoe, he peered out. Balder had pulled out of sight, and the boy saw only the standing scorched trees, now coated with frost. Yet he catapulted back into his bunk to rout about for his clothes. Next, hopping about on one foot while trying to get into his jeans, he hustled Benaiah. "Maple syrup, maple syrup! Ben'ah, gonna make maple syrup!"

"Shut up, you grub," said his brother sleepily from his bunk beside Chrischana's knees. "We can't make it now."

"Right you ah, Ben," said his mother, prodding him to get up. His bed had to be converted into the table so that they could eat. "Tail end o'winta, almost March. "That's when sap stots flowing. "We're just gont'get the evaporator set up. Then, when time comes, we'll be ready." She lit a burner on the stove, took eggs from the tiny gas refrigerator, and began happily cracking them into the skillet.

The last day here would not be sad, now that she had this to look forward to. Maybe the tiny apartment in the village wouldn't be so bad if they could think about the evaporator sitting up here, waiting. Just two months, tops. Then they could climb up here, on snowshoes if need be, and start gathering, boiling the sap mother nature would send.

Balder was at the door, and Nathan reached around mother to open it. "Come in, Balder," he cried, as cold air fell into the camper.

"Don't know's I ought," said the man with a grin. He wore a black wool watch cap and looked, as Elda would think, like a sailor from the North Sea. "Don't think theya's enough room for me in theya, Nate." To Chrischana he said, "Think I'll stot down the trail with this. You can show me just waya when you get done in here."

"No y'don't, Balda." We waunt go down theya with the evaporator. It's the... joy of ushering it down—"

"Okay," he grinned. "But I'll wait outside. Not enough room in theya fah ants."

Ben looked out at the truck with its iron and steel treasure visible in the bed. "That thing got four-wheel drive?"

"Doaw: Don't need it. Once we get down, I'll go back out that ol' twitch trail down theya. Ground's like concrete'neath this dusting, anaway."

Chrischana shoveled the eggs, saying over her shoulder, "We'll hurry. Come on, boys."

Balder closed the door. While still in the bunk, Daniel turned to watch the man through the window. He was walking around the great burnt-out Twitchell Farm cellarhole. Daniel reached for his clothes. That was cool, the way Mother said, "usher it down," like it was the King Jesus riding on an ass. The peculiar phrasing and its context pleased him. Something like that could get you thinking. The placement of words could be pleasing.

Today they were going to go live down in Gottheim village. What will it be like in an apartment, Daniel wondered squirming into his jeans. He pulled on his sweatshirt and lay on his side to put on socks. Easier to get home from an evening's work at *The Voter*. Closer to Cindabilla's. He could walk to school if need be instead of taking the bus. The Gott'im Library and library at Hazel Newell will both be more accessible. Cool. Doing schoolwork there will be easier, research a breeze. He swung down, knocking into Benaiah. He looked under the table for his shoes.

Benaiah elbowed him hard. "You did that on purpose," he charged.

"Did not," said Daniel still stooping but elbowing back.

"Won't have it!" said Mother. She reached around Ben with plates of scrambled eggs and grilled toast, setting them on the table. There will be advantages to apartment living. Two-bedrooms, a living room, kitchen, bathroom with running water. Lights. Take a bath whenever you want! Peter might even visit there, but she did not count on it. Didn't hope for it either. She had not seen him since that Thanksgiving night when he took off from *Simons Ledge* without even seeing the boys. Maybe he was gone for good. Maybe he'd be back. She ought to know him better after all this time.... Running water. Room for the kids to fight.... But, if you had to keep quiet for the neighbors.... Practically only have to step outside to get to work. Life would be more expensive in Gottheim on top of the cost of the evaporator.... But there will be openings on the mountain, too. Maybe a chance and more money? Gut to have more.

"Balda's waiting," she said, sitting down next to Ben to eat her eggs. The savings that had come to Chrischana Twitchell from Balder had made it possible for her to purchase a small acreage from the original Twitchell Farm, plus secondhand evaporator and firebox to provide her first farm income. Made of cast iron topped with a hundred gallon stainless steel reservoir, the evaporator would reduce sap from Twitchell sugar maples. The same maples which surrounded them now as they descended the hill with great joy. The sap would pass where they were now passing with shouts, flowing through a network of carefully laid tubing. It would stream into a holding tank and then into the reservoir where it would heat, bubble and steam, sweetening the air about the family of workers who will tend it. Just so, their shouts now sweetened December's frigid air where they skipped and bounded beside the laden pickup as its driver slowly bumped down the steep grade. Twigs and briars plucked at their clothing as they passed, and their hands sometimes touched the cold sides of the truck. They could not have kept silent if all the sour tongues in town had called them foolish to think this old farm would yield a living again.

Twitchell Farm had never been a convenient place to dwell. There had never been power lines up here. And they would be lucky to build a sap house, let alone a homestead. But this joy did not care. It did not doubt, nor shake its head, warn itself of absurdity and failure. This joy shouted out, the Twitchells providing it tongue. One day those tongues would taste sweetness. A taste that would not come easily, required much work. It would be no glib accomplishment, but when it came: That would be true sweet.

Alone, late in the day, Chrischana. Chrischana came back to camp one last time. She had coils of tubing, spigots, spouts, and galvanized buckets for the few trees downhill from the evaporator; putting all in store in the camper. And she would take down to Gott'im the remainder of their meager possessions. Last night snow had been light, but enough to give them warning. Bumping in past the abandoned logging yard, she thought, Soon this hill will be locked tight in bitter winter, accessible only to snow shoes, snow machines, cross-country skis.

She might get back up here a few times. Maybe. It would be glorious, pure and clean and white. Maybe Peter would come around to share it. Maybe not. Peter was leaving her alone and she thought it a good sign. It showed restraint. Wasn't that a good omen for a relationship?

She pulled to a stop, yanked on the handle. Squealing, the big door protested the cold. The Bonneville might make it through winter, might not. What with rent, utilities, and plans for the future.... If the car could just get her past winter.

Walking beyond the cellarhole, she looked through stiff branches of the winter-sleeping trees to the view. Time to say goodbye to the somber sight, drear and lightly dusted with snow. The near mountains were charcoal colored, bristling with naked stems. Looking around she breathed in her deep gratitude, her sense of arrival and peace. Once an exile, she had come home. Through fire and storm to this place she loved. Chrischana had come back to God's House, to her home in Gottheim, Maine.

Adirondack Paper, in Guildford Maine, will ship 528 tons of coated paper today from #17 machine, but one of more than a dozen operating paper machines in the mill. The specialty paper will be used to make glossy magazines, filled with advertising. To be flipped through by people stuck in doctors' offices, in airplanes and laundromats, subways, beauty parlors—any place where boredom, that small kingdom in Time, must be kept at bay. The dumps and landfills of the nation are filled with the off-scourings of boredom. Insatiable boredom devours the forests whole. Boredom processes woodlands, cutting debarking chipping cooking bleaching, mixing with river water and chemicals; woodlands spraying across the wire, draining, being pressed dried wound-up coated polished slit and rewound. Boredom: spinning the woodlands of Québec, Maine, New Hampshire, and Vermont into tight rolls. Pressed, gleaming and spooled, the forests will be shipped in freight cars to wherever they print glossy magazines. Provision for the kingdom of boredom, thought Peter Prince idly when he trudged from his car to the mill. *You could live and die in a state of suspended animation among the living dead.*

Today, in the midst of the Christmas Season, Peter Prince is supposed to trouble-shoot the flow box of #17 machine. Electricians have already tagged out the breakers and, since the kingdom of boredom can't recognize the season, impatience blooms in management as millwrights test out the mechanisms at the wet end of the machine.

Is the problem in the plate adjustment, plate pivot, nozzle blade adjustment, or adjusting rods? The size of a football field, the building that houses #17 is shockingly silent as the men tinker. This is the stressed silence of managers hovering, white shirts, neckties, wingtips and pressed trousers, hovering. Anxious to let the grease goons know they are anxious. This ubiquitous presence of whiteness and neckties reminds the millwrights that $50,000 an hour is at stake. The machine will lose that amount in downtime, 1980s currency, if they don't come up with an answer. The function of this monstrous machine is to produce enough finished paper in one hour to reach from Guildford to Farmington, a distance of sixty miles.

In the midst of this back pressure of boredom, Peter Prince is strangely relieved. Remorse has vanished under it. For the first time in a month he thinks of something besides damnation. *There's emotional cowardice urging suicide. There's stark physical cowardice checking it.*

It seemed right that he feel the pangs of hell for the abuse heaped undeserved on his common-law wife. He should be annihilated. The demented members of his being should be smoke. He has wasted this careful creation on alcohol and rage. Now it is time to be wasted in return.

Yet at the moment he thinks only of perforated plates and flow elements, hot metal and hydraulics, of adjustments to make this machine yield its reams. Gross slice adjustment, slice roof adjustment, tube bank: get the white shirts out of your peripheral vision. His attention is focused on the mechanism of this plate adjustment, while the other mechanics put away their tools, stand around bull-shitting.

Now he is done, climbing down from the flow box.

After start up, everyone relaxes, the white shirts are back in their soundproof offices. Peter opens the tiny packet and pushes its yellow earplugs into his ears. The shout of this machine starting into its purpose is destruction to the delicate organic mechanisms of ears. In this building it's impossible to hear yourself scream. The force and roar of #17 goes through the soles of his feet into the cords of his body, feasting on Peter's enfeebled senses. Easily the machine absorbs him as he walks past its great length. When in proximity to #17, he becomes #17. On these premises the coated-paper machine tolerates no identity but its own.

Gradually, now that he has finished replacing the front plate adjustment, Peter Prince is beginning to think again. They could be his own but maybe they are really the thoughts of the paper machine he is drifting past... the massive *Fourdrinier* wire, loaded with paperstock draining as it moves toward the presses and dryers. His vacant glance shifts from his reflection through the glass at the great sheet winding endlessly up-and-down, over and under and out the dryer toward the calenders. Maddening, the great sheet makes its everlasting way through coaters and winders, and over gaps in the floor where broken paper can be shoved down out of sight into broke-chests below. Blades in the basement swiftly beat it once more into pulp.

Drifting past, the uproar beating through his frame, Peter Prince is thinking. That's the place for me. His hardhat towering, his eyes encased in plastic and ears packed with foam rubber.... Step into that gap and instantly pulped. One with the ruined forest. Down there the forest is in better shape than that clear-cut above Chrischana's place, with its dry and broken leavings. The paper stock below will be stained with Peter Prince. They could make paper out of his remains but he will be gone to his maker and then cast into hell.

Eloise Patadoe might have guessed. She is deep in Abenaki Notch, gathering spruce and balsam fir tips with which to make wreaths. Eloise got a late start this year owing to that gouache series on formations in Grafton Notch. Neighbors cared for the goats in her absence. She went south for the series and camped, carrying art supplies with her, enduring frost, rain and flood, but it was worth it. Now she is back home and longing to be part of the season, do her bit to make it colorful, lively, bright. To that end she will howl down the sun, howl up the moon, anything to be different. Eloise is sometimes consistently different even from herself. She rarely knows where she will be tomorrow, no matter how thoroughly she plans. In fact, the more she plans the more likely it is she will not be where she had supposed.

Twilight is falling and so is snow, clouding the air with its thick languor. Her eyes are adjusting to catch the loved dimness of dusk. All she has to do is stick to the trail, keep the burlap sack—heavy with prickliness and fragrance—from listing too far. Get those trail intersections right and there'll be no trouble reaching the Quarry Dog Road, no matter how snowy and dark. There's always a little light, right? She asks this of herself.

Can barely see it, but stuff's thickening. Big as saucers now and intricate. She imagines seeing into the structure of each plate passing her eye, winking. *If only I could get this in paint! The gradations of shadow and light throughout the microscopic intricacy. The feel of tiptoeing through the hallways of the snowflake.* The flakes, wet and soft on her face, cake her hair above her wool headband. To keep it from getting soggy, she gives her head a shake. Again, the sack lists on her back.

"Patadoe Patadoe Patadoe," she chides herself aloud. "When you gonna learn?"

Problem is, my schedule's too full. You can't go squeezing the big things into the least dribbles of time like you do. "Won't do won't do won't do." When alone, she sometimes says things in triplicate. Tonight is practice for the solstice celebration at the old Quaker meeting house. Meguntic Mountain Arts has rented it for the purpose. Every year Eloise coordinates the event. She laughs at herself for having hoped her wreaths would be ready in time to decorate the hall tonight. No way I get even one done at this rate.... Maybe if I gulp down some of that broccoli soup. Just one wreath'll make the evening. One small seasonal thing... with... maybe a sprig of cranberries! Some cones! Maybe another with braided ribbon....

Laden with the fragrant bundle, she jogs on through the snow. The intersection! Her path diverges right. Elated, she lifts her face to the feathery breath, howling like a bitch wolf. The sack shifts precariously, Eloise stumbling. Quickly she rights herself. "Hah!" She mutters. "Someday you won't be so agile. Can you imagine doing this at 45, 50? Someday you'll be old, girl, *old old old*."

She stops a moment, listening. There it is again, a coy-dog answering her howl. "Hah!" Eloise howls again.

But Eloise Patadoe *can* imagine herself old. Old and diseased, hurting. And she can imagine herself struggling to endure. She can imagine herself doing anything, especially when it first occurs to her. Out of this imagination have come some killer paintings. And some of the best schemes ever devised by woman. Life is *awesome*! "*Tsk tsk*. Must stop using that word. Heard *two* teenagers use it yesterday. It's becoming a commonplace and no longer your own. You're famous!—it's passed into the vernacular! It will live abused in infamy.... But, someday it'll be history. *Then* you can use it again. *Ahoooo*...." Watch it, El. When this howling thing catches on you will have to stop that, too. All becomes passé with use. In our perception: even belief in God. But it all comes back again. Who knows, maybe I'll be a practicing Catholic again one day.

From a greater distance comes the dim wild return. "Friends of the wild!" Hope I don't run into a moose in this dark. That'll break your kneecaps!... all the way to the top of your head. One more right onto the pale road. No problem after that, Gertie.

A few hundred yards on the Quarry Dog Road will bring her home. Not much in the way of human settlement there, though once farmers coaxed a subsistence living from the rugged country. Back there, in the willy-wacks, streams wandered away from bogs, beaver bogs in the narrow valley steep-sided with walls of rocks and trees. Few now are willing to study over how to get this ground to yield, sprout produce or forage for milk production. What we need is a cooperative. A funky place where you can unload your leaf motif butter and maple sugar, organic veggies, goats milk cheese. My neighbors—heck, the whole community—would benefit.... Something like that down in Farmington, elsewhere in the state, too.

Goats! "Oh poop!" Is it tonight I'm supposed to have Hetty up to the Common? But the flush of worry passes, leaving her jogging still, slower, puffing, weary. She remembers now, its next night. The show must go on with you aboard, Hetty. You will be a living Nativity.

She turns on the pale road, leaving the thickets behind. Walking backwards on the road, dimly she sees the imprint of her tracks. But it's coming down thick, quickly filling the pattern. She turns back, hurries on. Yes. She is relieved to have found the road.

Once, was it three winters ago? She did lose her way coming out of Abenaki Notch. Snowing like this but darker, colder. Eloise was a bit crazed with panic. How grateful, at last, to stumble unexpectedly out of the puckerbrush onto the Quarry Dog Road. She was shaky with fierce laughter, like a loon. She found it was only an hour, but had seemed like five.

That was a time of personal upheaval: the loss of male companionship. She was uncovering the course of her life in those days, and it frightened her. Having to adjust to the one thing she had been unable to imagine: She would be living her life alone. And trying to tell herself that she liked it, that Eloise could get out of the woods without manly support. For two years it frightened her, that wide loneliness. The radical schemes she considered in those days! taking on more domestic animals than could be properly cared for, even starting proceedings for foreign adoption. Thank God she learned enough about herself before the child could arrive. It would have meant an even larger curtailment and adjustment of her life... as living with a man had not been. But, in the end, she saved the child. Saved it for that couple who truly cared and had *time* to care.

Eloise Patadoe, would-be mother.

Well, is it really too late after all? Are you positive you can't adjust?

Patadoe Patadoe Patadoe. Get a grip. You will do all that you love (if you continue in health), but you will *not* be somebody's mother. Or lover.

They are waiting at the meeting hall. The solstice celebration is your baby. You and your fellow participants are grateful and glad, coming from miles around. We'll worship together what makes it all work. The Season comes into us and we embody it. The season with the longest night happens to be the brightest. The days are darkest and I'm alone, but still the light finds you, comes into your precarious existence. Go in joy, the joy found in faces of others in this community.

Even now she spies the yellow light of her own house. In winter she leaves the lamp burning for herself. Eloise Patadoe, artist, homesteader, coordinator of celebrations extraordinaire. Sometimes, and in this season particularly, she can be the saddest, loneliest, even the *emptiest* person she knows. But she has friends here in Quaker, and down there in Gottheim, Maine.

"Hermann, I figure our work's about done. Winter's here. Time to head south. Gonna miss you. You've accomplished a hell of a lot."

They sat across from one another in Wilbur's Bar and Grille shortly before Christmas. The place was strung with red tinsel garlands. Someone was feeding the jukebox to produce a string of moldering carols. Bing was here, Brenda Lee, the Carpenters, Dolly Parton, one after another. Except that Hermann had ordered another grilled sticky bun and more coffee, the two friends were just about done eating. Peter Prince got out a cigarette, tamped it on the table. "You mind?"

"Go ahead with your smoke." Hermann pushed down with his ham-dimpled hand, slicing off a forkful of the gooey bun. Tonight he would be lighting seven candles on the menorah, but now he chewed thoughtfully before suddenly asking, "Do you think Christians remember the birth pangs in that stable, Prince?"

Peter smiled. "I never do."

"Maybe the women think of it."

"Maybe."

"Is there significance in those pains—as part of the story, I mean?"

"You wouldn't be asking me." He smiled some, even to his wide set green eyes. "There's significance in everything else, the shepherds, wise men, the baby, the star. Everything both real and symbols for something. That what you're getting at?"

"Have you ever heard of birth with no pain without drugs? Without dilation, stretching, tearing—a doctor's scissors? A woman literally splits herself open to bring out that life." Again Hermann looked at him with serious brown eyes behind glasses.

"Is there anything worthwhile comes without pain, Prince? For instance, should people get married without going through labor first?"

Flicking his cigarette ash into the ashtray, Prince laughed. "Would they?"

"It would be dearer to them." He said nothing more in that almost treble voice of his. Just took another bite and watched Prince drag on his cigarette.

Peter Prince turned his head, exhaling a stream of blue smoke. He looked up at Gottesmann through locks of hair. "So what's your point?"

Hermann went on eating the bun. "You know."

"C'mon. Are you equating remorse with labor pains?" He smiled. "Have you talked with any women about this, Hermann?"

"I equate all kinds of pain with labor. I don't think women would mind so much the trope—mythic application of the term. It has a kind of heroic stature."

"I could remind you how commonplace birth is."

"Yes, it happens every moment: No one comes here without those pains. Isn't it one reason why each human, or any creature, is... costly. Consider this, Prince: You said I accomplished something. If your remorse is that something, it's mainly *your* accomplishment.... Should you be throwing away something that dear by walking away from here? You've been given another chance with your family. Few would have such chances after such misdeeds. Why not embrace the pain as a good thing... considering what it bought you?"

Prince drew on his cigarette, exhaled, thinking about the other's use of the word bought. "I'm not a romantic, Hermann."

"Romance is not a light, lying thing. There's no romance without pain. Are the people in your family worth this pain, this assault on your pride? Are they the kind of people whose good opinion is worth striving for? Don't let your fear of pain stop you from delivering this child."

He pushed his plate aside to concentrate on coffee.

Prince watched a family settle into the booth across the aisle. Brenda was belting out her *Jingle Bell Rock*. Peter said slowly, "Too bad you don't celebrate Christmas, Hermann. Maybe I could've spent it with you."

"It won't be Christmas, but you're welcome to come over."

Alvin and the chipmunks got off the juke box, arguing. Then Bing sang. Peter Prince said, "Sometimes I wonder about Judas. Announcing his betrayal, it says Jesus was troubled in spirit. Why was that? Was it selfish? Was he troubled for himself—that he was betrayed? Or for Judas harming his own self? Or maybe for the whole great ... play, or whatever, of existence that it could be so...—like this? That *we* could be so—like this?"

"I don't know, Prince, he's not my Messiah, but I recognize the questions, their types. They have the feel of answers disguised as questions."

Peter thought about this.

"Thanks. I may—or maybe not—be over on the 25th."

One of the longest nights of the year is in full moon, the slopes of Jasper Mountain cleared of the day's skiers, all gone below to the bistros, restaurants and pubs under the mountain and down in Gottheim village. As the week wears, crowds will swell in offhand celebration of God's mysterious birth. Two thousand years ago in the earthy world of struggle, far removed from the glitter-shine-allure of the resort, the baby plunged forth bloody wet tethered to its mother; a feeble unskilled thing, incapable of feeding bathing clothing itself against drafts in the sheltering rocks; unable even to turn over or lift its sorry head.

Tonight's celebrants include members of the Golding family and personal friends, guests. The brand new rapid-quad ski lift whisks them high above the hothouse vacation bustle toward a mountain staging area for holiday feasting. Gloria Fay, seated between her father and mother, looks back over her shoulder toward the lighted, diminishing complex below. Looking back on the wee lodges and living particles moving in the glow of the skating rink far below, her heart heaves tenderly. Night is fallen there, lit in the fair glow of all their accomplishments. She looks beyond them, even to the mountains having lost their glow and turned now to somber coals, lonely, vast and dim.

In the chair far ahead above their own, ride Jimmy and Theo, their skis dangling in silhouette. Beyond them ride the governor and her immediate family. The elder Fays, on either side of Gloria, have delayed their holiday trip to St. Lucia where they will spend Christmas with their oldest and the grands. Afterward, between the 25th and the 30th, they plan to attend a Bible conference for business executives. At the moment, Mom is murmuring over the silvery glow in the northeast where the moon hides, promising certain ascent. Dad is detailing for Gloria the fascinations of insect lives, something about hyper-metabolism expanding their sense of time. But, though attending peripherally to each, Gloria is aware of the surrounding stillness—vast, simple, yet shot with echoing chatter and glee coming to them from remoter members of the party. On the shadowed slope ahead, she sees glinting fire and the cheerful glow of parti-colored lights. Things will be roasting there for the delectation of all: glazed chickens, marinated beef, the pink flesh of Atlantic salmon. Higher still, the great dome of Jasper recedes, its snow mantle already catching silver from the promised moon.

"Just look at that happy glow up there, dear," Mom is saying. Still caught in her reverie, Gloria murmurs assent. "Now look," nudges Mom. "There, on the shoulder—the moving gems of the snow groomers. Oh, I just love seeing them ascend like that in tandem, don't you? Like angels moving on the mountains." At last Gloria turns to her mother in agreement. Mom's face is lit by Jasper's reflecting snows: a thin face, aging and fine-boned; gracious when seen above evening wear; pixieish now, being framed by an alpine cap. "It's good to see that smile," Mom says. "It's been... eclipsed... lately?"

But Gloria turns back toward the gleaming mountain. She does not want to talk with Mom about things. Does not want to bring up things insurmountable, the hash she is making of desire. The anger kindling at Balder. The fantasies she feeds on, concerning how they might, might not, live together. Even the mere fact of Balder would not be appreciated, so she says nothing... to anyone.

Balder, you are there, just beyond the white monolith.

Down and down and down among slopes and trees on the further side.... Getting ready to spend the holidays with your new family. The family that came between us and turned life away. How can you stand to live so messily, so all over the map? Embracing that squalor, which—I admit—I once found so interesting. From a distance. Is it so wrong to understand myself? To know that I'm good in certain situations and *so* out of my depth in others?

...I thought, believed, nothing was impossible to me.... That I would do whatever I set my mind to. I am tough, have dexterity in life, self-discipline for godsakes. I am goal-oriented. I attack!

No, she cannot bring herself to call squalor depth, to call french fries under the bed and the dirty clothes of five people a challenging way to live. Extended families and baby talk and diapers—deep? Deep all right. Deep doo-doo. And what if someone becomes really really ill, or has other problems you can't cope with?

... But he said he'd be in it with you. You wouldn't be doing it alone.

No. It's weak to think you can't do it alone. And I'm strong, have been since a child. My will is strong.

You could get your own family, on your terms! One child anyway. Harry is impressed with my education and communication skills—Jimmy said so. If I show interest, he'll consider me to head the ski school. Or, there's the New Hampshire Mountain, its wide-open. With a steady position I can have and raise my own child. Balder's child, too, if I decide. On my own terms, in a beautiful home of my own. God—where do these idiot thoughts come from?

The feast, fire and lights are fast approaching on their right. She sees smoke ascending in moonlight, smells its wafting aromas. The moon has risen, and she looks to it, quickly, then turns to take the ramp with her parents. Together they glide toward the straggling knots of people removing their skis, queuing up for drinks and charbroil on the platform. But Gloria hangs back suddenly, calling for them to go ahead: She just wants to take the view alone. (Before immersing herself in gaiety, babble, schmooze. Brother Jimmy will be pushing his pompous opinions. Theo will mindlessly mistake herself in every turn of the conversation. Dad will get into it with the anti-greens, and Mom will be looking at me all evening—is there anything wrong, dear?)

She watches her parents push toward the party, two black silhouettes against a gathering lit with lanterns. With painful suddenness all she wants is to go up to the snowy summit. Gloria glances toward the private lift with its tall poles and cables gleaming with reflected moonlight, standing silent, the chairs lined up beneath. Can't start it on my own. I could dare the climb, though. Up there the wind would nip her bones.

She might warm herself by climbing. Drag up the skis, glide down through the slopes, thickets, and hills on the other side. Right up to Balder's door, and declare. *I'm here to make babies, Balder. I'm ready!*

But the breath of Jasper comes down to her, holy and cold. Her mood falls to the fact of his wind whipping the snow high above. There is no snow on the lower southern slopes, she knows. The north side has snow because Harry Golding's snow guns put it here. The Golding's make their own conditions. He says: Let there be twenty feet of base, and twenty appear.

Looking toward the distant glimmering summit, she sighs. What are these thoughts? Am I up to any good? Could I love Balder if he *were* willing to come work for his girlfriend's father? If he suddenly got a business degree? He doesn't fit anything I imagine for him.... Maybe he doesn't fit because he *won't*.

... But he expects me to come after him, to change willy-nilly. Or maybe he wants me as I am, inadequate to the vocation. Willing to forsake all other options. Maybe he wants my imperfection to wrestle with itself in some alien environment.... Forcing me to embrace the life *he* chooses—or I can't have him at all. –Or is this another idiot thought?

$$\xi$$

Even so, up here, the summit shines like silver, like moon in a cloud. Below, Gloria the fay turns to face the great white disk, now well risen above the quiet Meguntics. There she sees the moonlight, queenly, calm. Dignity is in its appearance, say I, Jasper Mountain. I am Jasper Mountain, and I say Moon's appearance owes to the sun.

$$\xi$$

Christmas Eve, with snow falling over the northland where Gott'im's people gather within. Lamplighted windows glow distantly but any walker may approach easily enough. There are travelers, too, on streets and lanes leading to churches. Choirs stand to sing of Angels, of the nature and compassion of God, and of the Fear we are prone to.

Come closer. Windows are inviting, more so than doors for all their wreaths and decorations: A shut door may yield no light. Look within through the panes, walk around the house watching folks at the supper table or enjoying a seasonal TV show, taking sugar cookies soft and hot from the oven, or singing carols around the piano like they do at Olive Lovejoy Bartlett's house.

You could climb a tree beside the Simon house, peer into an upstairs window. In light beyond the falling snow, Daniel and Cindabilla are visible lounging around the radio with the bedroom door open to allay adult suspicions. The lamp on Daniel's desk casts a deeply yellow glow: He put a bug light in it for the occasion. If, by some means, the conversation within those windowpanes were audible, the tale of Cindabilla's family gatherings would be overheard. Christmas at the Sessions' house is hateful to her for its drunks damning one another and calling up abuse and accusation of wrong. But the aunts, uncles, cousins and grandparents would begin happily enough, descending into the nether regions only as the drink increases. Our eavesdropper without is soon made uncomfortable, turning away to descend the tree and steal around the corner toward the front window. These are tall windows, catching snow against divided lights. The crackling fire in a Franklin style woodstove with pipe up the chimney hearth glows appealingly. The mantelpiece is laden with evergreens and tiny lights among their needles. The hand of Balder Simon closes the stove door and adjusts the vent. Now the crunch of tires is heard in the snow blown wind. The stealthy watcher hurries away toward the edges of woodland, still within earshot of the dooryard.

A pickup stops short of the house in the falling snow and two people step down from either door. Waiting for the woman to come around, the man hesitates. She speaks kind words to him of which the watcher catches only their reassuring tone. Together they approach the door, now flung wide and streaming with light, and piping of a young voice.

"Dad! Dad's here!! It's Christmas Eve! You're here! I knew you'd look like that!"

The couple is taken inside. The door closes quickly on the falling snow and the watcher without.

Supper is served, glazed ham, piping baked potatoes, butternut squash with spices, salad greens with thin purple onion rings, a side of cranberry relish. For dessert there will be pumpkin pie with true whipped cream sprinkled with cinnamon. The Simons, Twitchells, and Peter Prince are here, along with one Sessions. Tentatively talking (tentative all but Nathan), they sit down. They wait. Chrischana gives the youngest a warning look as he reaches for a roll. Withdrawing his hand he looks expectantly at Balder.

"Word o'grace," says the bearded man with a subdued grin.

They bow their heads, Elda refraining a gaze wanting to slip toward the stranger Prince.

"Fatha! Thank you fah this food'n this Christmas gathering. Thanks specially f'your son, who came as a child t'be with us'n die with us. Help us dearly love him. In his name amen."

"Amen," says Elda unexpectedly. A blush passes on her thin white face.

Now, his hair sticking every which way, and with an eye on mother, Nathan reaches out his hand.

"It would be nice if you pass that t'Mrs. Simon."

Smiling Nathan hands over the plate.

Elda receives the rolls. "Thanks, Nate."

"Nice t'have your Dad heah, in't it?" Balder says this to the table in general. "Glad you made it, Prince."

"Good t'be here, thanks." He passes the bowl full of squash to Benaiah.

"Guess Chrischana had told you," says Balder, gesturing toward that end of the kitchen where a door stands open beside the refrigerator.

"Theya's a room up theya fah you t'stay in tonight. Save you having to come back in the morning. Got to get t'those presents under the tree early!"

Prince nodded noncommittally. Chrischana had told him of the offer. And he knew she would be going back to the little family's apartment down in the village. Jericho, where he lived, was a good thirty miles away.

"You *see* all those presents in there, Dad!" yells Nathan. "Ben'ah musta put a hundred presents under there for you. Wait'll you see what I gave you. Don't shake it or cover up the breathing holes, though."

"Nathan, you nerd," says Ben. He looks shyly at his father and Peter gives him a wink.

"Did you say you went to Florida, Cindabilla?" Chrischana wants to know. "You go to Disney World?"

The pale eyes of Cindabilla smile. "Couldn't get past the pockin'lot. Couldn't stand O'lando. Awful place, hot. Streets laid out in long straight lines, endless blocks. But Everglades is free. Just walk off the road, you're in! Wouldn't go fah, though. I like my leg too much."

Daniel smiles.

Chrischana turns toward Balder at the head of the table. "Thought Gloria'd be here. Din't choo invite her?"

"Cuss I did. Thought she might make it, too." There is no more to say.

Something stirs along the periphery of Prince's vision, and he glances toward the corner where the refrigerator abuts the wall. Two tiny mice sit nearby, nibbling crumbs. He shifts his gaze back to his children. "Hear you might go snowmobiling this winter." He says it to Daniel. He has noticed that his oldest boy drops his r's now, like any Mainer, and that he calls Balder father.

"You might give it a try, Dad," Daniel returns.

"Might." He is relieved to hear Daniel call him Dad. Maybe this can work out. He could get a Yamaha. Peter smiles, thinking how the guys at MMI in Phoenix would laugh. A hog-head on a rice-burner.

Talk swirls around the table, Nathan's happy warble punctuating. His Christmas present to Dad is under the table at his feet, eating crumbles of roll and baked potato. And there's going to be pumpkin pie!

Without, the snow continues falling, softly filling woodland and hollow. The lane leading to the house was once an old settlers' country road. Now it appears to dead-end at the family home. But, hidden and somewhat overgrown, it continues off through the backyard and woods, downhill where it winds back down toward the pond. On the USGS topographic map, the trail shows as a dotted line and is designated a Jeep trail. Balder uses this trail as a snow machine shortcut to the pond. Gloria noticed it on the topo map as she studied the Gottheim sector and saw the dot indicating the position of Balder's house, *Simons Ledge.*

On this Christmas eve, while others are home or at church, Gloria Fay tracks up the trail through snowfall and woods on slim cross-country skis. Soon she is sweating, puffing, unzipping her jacket and doffing her alpine cap. The snow, itself scarcely visible in the night, dims her sight. She searches for the Simon lights. Sometime later she stands resting on her poles at the top of the trail, looking toward the window-lit house. Laid out stem to stern like a many-angled ship, it seems anchored in a storm of white. Snow falls heavily into the dooryard. The windows send out yellow beams. Inside people sit at the table, tiny people, eating, presumably laughing and speaking to one another. Celebrating Christendom's big day.

Watching, Gloria realizes she is in the midst of deciding. Coming here has been a spontaneous act, decisive at the onset. She was accepting

Balder's glad invitation. Yet here she waits, still leaning on her poles, undecided. If she crosses, knocks at the kitchen door, she will be warmly welcomed. Should she enter the household, join the celebration... or turn around and ski back down to her car?

But there is too much here beneath the ledge on this side of the mountain. Too much standing in the way of how my life should look. Life should have a pleasing symmetrical aspect. It should be pleasant to bear—at least as much as one can manage. It should not be limited by strictures of duty. Life must be what one loves at the moment, and from moment to moment, always. That is the nature of life. Is it an unreasonable expectation? Is it unreasonable to expect fidelity in the face of obstacles, unpleasantness, straining and stress? These are pressures I should reasonably *flee*. If this kind of pressure is what God or somebody wants for us... isn't it right to rebel? Or would God even grant this joy—*life feeling will*—and then expect everyone to abdicate? To bend and bow and say, *yes sir*?

In her agony of ripe emotion she searches toward the snowy skies: emotion searing, heartfelt, proud.

She slumps exhausted on her poles, head down and waiting. *Why why why*!! Her tired mind cries out.

An earnest cry, it reaches upward through the snow, though her head and heart are down. Up surges the cry toward the dim heart of the blizzard. And beyond—toward the vast bright blizzard of elemental galaxies swirling through great gray regions of space and time. But one cry out of a tight little heart of one small creature longing for nothing more than to try her faculties and, above all, *to have fun*.

She leans on these poles, leans into this question, snow falling and soaking her sleek hair.

But only the snow comes, covering everything. Covering Gloria Fay where she slumps. Covering the nearby pile of leftover building scraps, castoffs from Balder's spurt of construction.

Comes a brief undefined noise, not close, to Gloria's ears. She does not look up. A sound, muted by falling snow, seems to come from the far end of the dwelling... in the direction of the barn. Now she hears and recognizes the shrieking of metal on metal. Still leaning on the ski poles she peers through her spilled hair.

A boy stands at the barn door in a swath of light, looking toward the dim snowy shadows of woodland beyond the far side of the barn. Gloria lifts her head to watch, straining toward those shadows. Now the patches of white, of snow against the barn, are looking bunched and fuller. This fullness moves toward the boy, and as it reaches the light, she sees the shape of a deer.

The white deer! She had thought she would never see it again.

The kitchen door opens, siphoning off her attention. There stands Mrs. Simon, Chrischana behind her. Chrischana. And Chrischana is calling through the snowfall. Her voice is muted, remote but distinct enough. "Benaiah! Come here, Benaiah!"

He comes toward her, pleading in his voice. Hearing his bemusement through the falling snow, Gloria's heart softens. She watches as Chrischana's middle son comes to his mother, his voice chastened and low but still pleading.

Then, with a shock she sees what she saw last summer, Elda Simon with that awful gun in her hands.

Mother and son enter the house, close the door, as Mrs. Simon steps away. She points the gun in the direction of the deer, but high. The deer has grown since Gloria saw it in summer. It now resembles a delicate long-legged dog. Alone. The larger reddish deer of summer, its mother, is nowhere to be seen.

The old woman sends out the weapon's invisible charge with a powerful bang. The deer leaps away, gone back into the storm.

Banished!

It's a bitter thought. Like *a scapegoat for somebody's sins!*

The little woman goes to the barn to turn off the light, tug the door closed. She seems to stand a long time, looking off through the snow where the deer disappeared. Is she sagging against the barn? But the light is gone, it's too dim to tell.

Exhausted, Gloria has had enough. Won't wait for that old woman to go. I can't stand this, stand here any longer.

The young woman turns on her skis, careless of whether Mrs. Simon might see or hear her.

She gives a push with her poles that sends her skimming back down the trail. Gloria Fay has had enough for one night. She needs to think again. It is time to go home and shut her windowless wreathed condominium door behind her.

God, I just want to go to bed.

The God's Cycle is set in the early mid-1980s

Guide to Characters

Asa Bartlett. Amateur historian, Congo Church clock-winder, millworker, married to Olive Lovejoy Bartlett.
Olive Lovejoy Bartlett. Caregiver, family woman, dowser, operates bed-and-breakfast, married to Asa Bartlett.
Lyman Bearce. Lumber baron, selectman, married to Rhetta Bearce.
Rhetta Bearce. Committee woman, married to Lyman Bearce.
Babette Buck. Dowel millworker, Ferddy Sessions' girlfriend.

Jeffy Decatur. Diner business owner-cook, bird hunter.

Gloria Fay. Graduate student, IICE facilitator, sister to James Fay, Balder Simon's love.
James Fay. Ski resort real estate salesman, brother of Gloria Fay, engaged to Theodora Prescott.

Harry Golding. Ski resort owner, maternal uncle of Amanda.
Julius Golding. Ski resort owner, maternal uncle of Amanda.
Amanda. Niece to the Goldings.

Jasper Mary. Historical and legendary healer, storyteller.

Israel Kimball. Town recluse, former academy headmaster, scholar.

Jim Nutting. The weekly *Village Voter* editor.

Eloise Potadoe. Artist, goatherd, homesteader.
Theodora Prescott. Mill owner, IICE participant, engaged to James Fay.
Peter Prince. Mechanic, common-law spouse of Chrischana Twitchell, father of Nathan, Benaiah, Daniel.

Robbie Robichaud. Logging contractor, father to Alvin and Ansell.
Alvin and Ansell Robichaud. Loggers, twins.

Celon Segar (pronounced Cigar by the locals). Tire dump owner.
Cindabilla Sessions. Niece to Ferddy Sessions, girlfriend of Daniel

Twitchell.

Ferddy (Ferdinand) Sessions. Town worker, Cindabilla's maternal uncle, boyfriend of Babette Buck.

Hannah Sessions. Farmer, domestic worker, mother of Ferdinand Sessions, grandmother of Cindabilla, sister-in-law of Nellie Sessions.

Melvinia Sessions. Diner server, domestic worker, distantly related to other Sessions.

Nellie Sessions. Dowelmill-worker, artifact collector, aunt to Cindabilla.

Balder Simon. Vietnam veteran, millwright, son of Elda, father of Daniel Twitchell, lover of Gloria Fay and Chrischana Twitchell.

Elda Simon. Animal rehabilitator, mother of Balder Simon.

Benaiah Twitchell. Adolescent son of Chrischana Twitchell and Peter Prince.

Chrischana Twitchell. Dishwasher, homesteader, common-law spouse of Peter Prince, mother of Daniel, Benaiah, Nathan.

Daniel Twitchell. Teenage son of Chrischana Twitchell and Balder Simon, friend of Cindabilla Sessions.

Nathan Twitchell. Youngest son of Chrischana Twitchell and Peter Prince.

Like this? Try the entire cycle.

THE GOD'S CYCLE